Bad Animals

ALSO BY SARAH BRAUNSTEIN

The Sweet Relief of Missing Children

Bad Animals

a novel

SARAH BRAUNSTEIN

W. W. NORTON & COMPANY
Independent Publishers Since 1923

Copyright © 2024 by Sarah Braunstein

W. S. Merwin, "Separation" from *The Second Four Books of Poems*. Copyright © 1963, 1993 by W. S. Merwin. Reprinted with the permission of The Permissions Company, LLC on behalf of Copper Canyon Press, coppercanyonpress.org. Used by permission of The Wylie Agency LLC.

For information about permission to reproduce selections from this book, write to Permissions, W. W. Norton & Company, Inc., 500 Fifth Avenue, New York, NY 10110

For information about special discounts for bulk purchases, please contact W. W. Norton Special Sales at specialsales@wwnorton.com or 800-233-4830

Manufacturing by Lake Book Manufacturing
Book design by Chris Welch
Production manager: Lauren Abbate

ISBN 978-1-324-05104-6

W. W. Norton & Company, Inc., 500 Fifth Avenue, New York, N.Y. 10110
www.wwnorton.com

W. W. Norton & Company Ltd., 15 Carlisle Street, London W1D 3BS

1 2 3 4 5 6 7 8 9 0

For AJT

I was on a farm. There was a cage. And I said, What's that cage for? And the answer was: That's where we put the bad animals.

—*Paige Cosgrove, age five, waking from a dream*

People speak sometimes about the "bestial" cruelty of man, but that is terribly unjust and offensive to beasts. No animal could ever be so cruel as a man, so artfully, so artistically cruel.

—*Fyodor Dostoevsky*

1

ON THE FINAL DAY of February, a Tuesday, Maeve Cosgrove got called to the office. "You're wanted in the office." Ominous phrasing, but only in retrospect—Maeve had no reason to assume trouble. None. She took the back stairs briskly, made a pretense of knocking on the half-open door, the daily, simple happiness of the library alive inside her for one last moment. Right away she saw that something wasn't right. Her boss, Gloria, wasn't at her desk where she belonged but on a chair to the side, underneath a poster of a garden buzzing with insects that said *Reading Is the Bee's Knees*. Gloria looked perplexed. Her spine was oddly erect. She sat with her hands in her lap, her feet pressed together, brown orthopedic clogs like two small loaves of bread.

Occupying Gloria's desk was a woman in her mid-sixties whom Maeve had never seen, who had pink skin and short white hair and wore a corporate blazer. She gestured to the chair facing the desk, and Maeve sat down.

"I'm C.J.," the woman said, blinking rapidly. "I work for the OFCS. Alphabet soup, I know. That's the Office of Family and Child Services. I've come to the library today with a concern."

Only one window, behind Maeve's back. Cold seeped through the casings—sleet on and off all day. The sky was low, the room dim, but the solar-powered cat on Gloria's desk waved its lucky paw.

Maeve said, "How can I help you?"

C.J. lifted a piece of paper from a manila folder and read aloud: "'The librarian Maeve Cosgrove has been watching me fool around with a boy in the next bathroom stall. Through the crack. Thought you should know. Signed, Libby Leanham.'"

Into the silence that followed Maeve said the only thing: "That's not true."

C.J. blinked. Turned her head to the side, meaning: Go on.

"That's crazy," was all Maeve could manage. "Nuts."

C.J. neither confirmed nor denied Maeve's assessment. In a level, professional voice, she told Maeve that she had met with the girl yesterday. The girl claimed that she, Libby, had been bringing a certain boy— "Let's just call him B., for confidentiality purposes"—into the bathroom in the upper-level mezzanine, the one furthest from the circulation desk, and had been engaging in acts with the boy, sexual acts, and that the librarian—"that is, Maeve" (C.J. looked away when she said her name)—had been in this bathroom too, and had been watching. Watching from the next stall. More than once, the girl said this happened.

Maeve, the girl had said.

Her.

"Me?"

"That's her report." C.J. held the paper on which Libby had written her statement, pinched between her thumb and index finger, outstretched, as if it might make more sense at a distance. Maeve wanted to grab it. It was typed, she saw. A freckle of ink in the right margin told her it had been printed on one of the library's printers.

"Jesus Christ," she said, her heart thudding.

"Obviously, we take things like this seriously."

"More than once!"

"It's our duty to inquire—"

"Jesus. It's outrageous. It's—"

No word meant what she wanted. Outrageous. Depraved. False! But the more she protested, the more her throat tightened—like an addict at an intervention, each recusal more defensive than the last. She heard a shrillness that seemed to implicate her, and then, without quite meaning to, she cried, "The bitch!"

"OK now, Maeve," C.J. said.

Maeve smacked her hand to her mouth, appalled. *Bitch* was not like her, not at all.

"We're on your side," Gloria said softly.

Maeve startled, somehow had forgotten she was there—"Gloria!"

"I know," Gloria said, "I *know*," and she rose from the chair and came to Maeve and embraced her, a quick hug around the shoulders. When she was sitting again Maeve saw sweat glowing on her upper lip, which she felt undermined the hug.

Gloria spoke in a tense voice. "I found the note in my box, Maeve. In the staff room. I was obligated to report it. Obviously, we know it's crazy."

But C.J. didn't say it was obvious. C.J.'s pen hovered above the notepad. She said, "Tell us everything you know about Libby. How about that?"

Everything she knew? There had only been—how could she explain—a mutual curiosity. An awareness. She couldn't explain. It was too innocent to deserve explanation, frankly.

Maeve said, "She's new to town. Only been here three or four months"—though of course C.J. knew that part. "She comes to the after-school program nearly every day. She reads a lot. I did notice that. Most kids don't read. And she and—that boy."

She paused.

"Yes?"

"They hang out. I've seen them, I don't know, snuggling, on the couch. But never anything"—she swallowed—"sexual."

Gloria said, "I think snuggling puts it too strongly. I told her just leaning into each other."

"Right," said Maeve. "Leaning."

"We'd put a stop to snuggling," Gloria said.

"Of course we would."

C.J. made no remark. Keeping her eyes on Maeve, she said, "Why would she say this about you, Maeve? You of all people? Have you any sense of why?"

Maeve did not.

"None?"

"I'm not a psychologist," but it came out more urgently than she'd intended.

C.J. tossed her pen down, smiling now. "We have that in common, you and me."

"What does the psychologist say?"

"I'm not at liberty to discuss." C.J. gazed at her patiently. Then she said, "Did you have a special relationship with her in any way? Or take a special interest?"

"Not any more interest than I take in any of them."

"Did she seem interested in you?"

"Not that I noticed."

"Me neither," Gloria added from off to the side. "For what it's worth."

"She does the ice cream program," Maeve said. "You earn coupons if you put your phone in a box. I talked to her a couple of times. About books."

Maeve blinked. Suddenly she saw it impersonally. She had done nothing wrong. The girl was nuts.

"Obviously she has an interest in me that I'm not aware of. Right? If she left a note like that? Obviously she's sick. If she believes what she wrote, she's delusional. I don't need a degree to know that. Or she's just trying to get attention. I have no idea why she picked me." She added, "I feel sorry for her," but feared it sounded bitter, condescending. Like a lie, which it was, at that moment.

"What about the bathroom?" C.J. asked. "You remember ever using that bathroom when she was using it? In the mezzanine?"

"Not that I can recall."

"No?"

"It's not something I'd remember."

"Of course she wouldn't," said Gloria.

C.J. said, "Unless it was happening a lot."

"Which it wasn't," Maeve said firmly. "I'm sure of that."

Gloria added, "We have a staff bathroom downstairs."

"Sure, sure," said C.J. "I'm not trying to insinuate anything. It's delicate. You understand."

The bitch, Maeve could not help thinking, despite herself. The bitch! Come on. What a prank to pull. What a mean thing.

There was a silence in which they heard the pattering of sleet on the windowpane, abrupt thrusts in the wind, like the shaking of a baby's rattle.

"I'll keep you both in the loop." C.J. put the paper back in her folder. "I realize this is upsetting."

"I love these kids," Maeve said, new heat in her eyes.

"We all know that," said Gloria.

Only then did Maeve remember they could ask the boy.

"Wait. Does the boy say it too? Have you asked him?"

C.J. lifted her chin, paused. "The boy doesn't speak. That's another piece."

"He can't?"

"He doesn't. I'm not at liberty to say more."

Gloria made an anguished face. "You know we're just doing our job, Maeve, right?"

Maeve hated that she'd said *bitch*, saw herself clearly. "Look," she said, to correct the impression, "you have to take her seriously. I know you have to. We're mandatory reporters."

C.J. said, "Exactly. A properly conducted investigation is never personal."

"I'm so sorry I said that."

C.J. blinked, cocked her head. "Said what?"

"That I called her that."

"Bitch?" C.J. spoke it nonchalantly.

Maeve, in her periphery, could sense Gloria's frown.

"Let me retract it," Maeve said. "Strike it from the record."

C.J. only looked at her, then made a mark on her pad, a dash, absently, because how can you strike a word, to what bureaucracy can a person appeal when a word has been spoken but the mouth wants it back? Maeve knew she was in the wrong, in any case.

Whose word did she believe in trusting? If a child, a minor, came forward to say what improper thing an adult was doing—a teacher or bus driver or doctor or priest or anyone, even those you least suspect, even the librarian—to whose account did she believe in listening most carefully? To whom did she give the benefit of the doubt? If you were innocent, you did not blame the child.

"Look. I understand you must take her seriously, that kids aren't taken seriously enough of the time. I know you must look at me." She heard the roughness in her voice that preceded crying. "I know that everything happens."

"Yes," C.J. said, perking up. "That's exactly right." She picked up the pen and drew an *X* over the squiggly line. She gave a faint, rueful chuckle. "There's absolutely nothing that doesn't happen. I've worked in this field for thirty years—I've seen things I would have sworn were impossible." Now she smiled as if they were old friends. "But you'll be fine, Maeve. This is due diligence. This is a very troubled kid telling stories. Try not to worry, alright? Try not to take it personally."

Gloria said, "Dear Maeve, she always takes things personally."

I *do*? But she didn't say it.

C.J. stood up to go. She told them what would happen next, the report she'd write after a few follow-up conversations, but Maeve was distracted by the woman's height, hadn't realized how tall she was, and watched as she stretched her legs, lean and bowed like a camel's, in their brown pants. Over her brown hiking boots she wore rubber cleats, for traction on ice, red netting studded with metal. A chill went through Maeve, seeing the cleats.

C.J. said, "Stay safe out there, you two."

"You too," said Gloria.

"You too!" said Maeve, sounding hysterical to herself.

And then it was over. Gloria said some reassuring things but the sweat on her lip made it hard for Maeve to believe them.

Maeve returned to her alcove. Saw the teenagers flopped in the space they called the Pen. Her head felt empty, her body a vapor.

The girl didn't come that afternoon; neither did the boy.

To make matters worse, Katrina wasn't working—Katrina would have settled her with a cup of tea, patted her back, and said, "Go ahead, cry if you like." Katrina, unsentimental but warm, would have told her that the empty, vaporous feeling was only shock, a perfectly normal thing to feel when faced with madness.

After closing, she found her Volvo sparkling under the streetlight in the staff lot, encased in ice like a foggy opal. She hacked at her windshield for a good ten minutes, stabbed with her scraper until the ice cracked and flew. February: this was the sadistic month the girl chose. Winter cracked her skin, scored her lungs—a whole life here didn't inoculate a body.

Raul came out the utility doors with a trash bag in each hand, wearing his orange beanie but no coat.

"You want me to scrape, Ms. Cosgrove?"

"All finished," she called.

"Go slow! It's an ice rink."

She drove home slowly, practically a crawl, shivering, her shoulders tight. The girl's words screamed in her head, shrill and blasting, like the improbably human noises some birds make.

2

WHEN SHE TOLD HER HUSBAND, he offered to give her a back rub. A blessing and a curse, Jack's equanimity. Today she was stricken by his calm.

"Did you hear what I *said*?"

He told her one of her shoulders was higher than the other.

"I don't want a back rub." She paced their living room, still in her heavy goose-down coat zipped to the chin. "Something awful has happened. I've been accused of a horrible thing."

"It'll blow over. Without question."

"It will? Will it?"

"The boy's retarded, you're saying? She was making out with a disabled person?"

Maeve stopped pacing. Faced him.

"He might just be slow."

"Slow how?"

"I don't know! He doesn't talk."

Jack considered this. "It's good the authorities are involved," he said. Then he unpacked his briefcase: his leather folder, his computer, an apple core and a teabag in a Ziploc baggie, so he could compost them at home.

When she began to cry he came to her, took her coat off. He touched the place on her face called the third eye, brought her to the couch, pressed his hands on her shoulder to level them, gently, a suggestion, not a command. He smelled of Neutrogena for Men, bristling menthol.

They had been married for twenty-five years and weren't fifty yet. He was an accountant. He wore faultless ties, colorful chinos, like the manager of a Banana Republic. They'd gone to the same high school but didn't know each other back then. Her senior year of college, home for Christmas break, she had seen him at a bar. She hadn't remembered his name.

"You're a professional," he said once she'd stopped crying. "Everyone knows it. And this is a sick child."

"Yes."

She waited for him to elaborate, but he said, "Can I be honest? I don't know why you're getting so upset, hon. No one will believe her. It seems pretty obvious. I feel bad for the kid."

She knew he was right. She perceived a distortion in her thinking. Why should she be angry at Jack? Still, they ate pasta with sauce from a jar. She didn't want to reward his casualness with homemade.

After dinner, she watered the plants in the greenhouse, their daughter's important plants, as Maeve promised she would do. Plants did not thrill Maeve as they did her daughter. Maeve could never remember their names. "They're mostly queer," Paige had said when she left for college. "Like all queer things, they're sensitive. Follow my guidance to the T, yeah, Mom?"

"To the T," Maeve agreed, not understanding how a plant could be queer but not asking, not right away. Paige had explained that a certain box—marked with blue popsicle sticks—was especially important, an unusual hybrid. "They're not supposed to be here. This box is entirely off the record, if anyone asks. It doesn't exist." She smiled at Maeve conspiratorially. "These guys at the lab—yes, *guys*—are deeply conservative. It's important to have a backup. Joe and I thought it made sense to plant some here. I told him you'd look after them."

"Got it," Maeve said, happy to be included. "You can count on me."

"That's what I told Joe. I said you could be counted on. They have a long latency period. Who knows when they'll grow, if they ever do."

Joe was a graduate student who had taken Paige under his wing at the lab. Maeve had been surprised when Paige announced this development only weeks into her freshman year, but Paige said they'd been writing to each other for a long time. She'd sent her first letter to the university when she was fifteen. Maeve shouldn't have been surprised; since middle school Paige had designed her own internships, followed professional blogs, cultivated a network of online friends. She had an osmotic capacity . . . soaked up information, like a person whose job it was to ask, who never wondered if it was OK that she was asking, the way Maeve wondered.

From toddlerhood, Paige questioned everything. Tugging her mother's arm, polite but urgent: "What is in the soil?" Maeve could not explain the soil to Paige's liking and drove her to the library to get a book, *The Story of Earth* by Violet P. Chesterton, renewed so many times eventually they bought Paige her own copy. She was a demanding and insistent child, but well mannered. Appreciative. The greenhouse had been a present on her sixteenth birthday, her interest in plants having grown into a passion—what you can only call a calling—and for her seventeenth they installed the supplemental heating system. Jack had received his big promotion by then, and since Paige was their only child, an extravagance like that was manageable. A far cry from the basement of Maeve's youth.

Sometimes Maeve worried about spoiling her, but Paige made so few demands, and none of the traditional ones. She wanted nothing except the greenhouse, seeds from a catalog. She wore the plainest clothes. Once she gave her Christmas money to the refugee support service—and didn't even tell her parents! She didn't even want credit for her kindness—they only found out because they got a tax document in the mail.

When Paige left for college, her chores had become Maeve's own. Maeve had not thought she would mind. But it required unexpected bravery, she discovered, to enter the greenhouse. She tended to the plants meticulously, per Paige's instructions, sometimes found herself singing to them, the songs she'd sung to Paige as a baby, the standards, "You Are My Sunshine," "A Bushel and a Peck," her voice wobbly and thin and not terrible, but singing only made her sadder. It was hard to explain. She felt bashed by loss in an embarrassing way.

Maybe this was akin to postpartum depression? She hadn't been depressed back then, just exhausted, heavy, watching the baby nurse and mewl with calm detachment.

So much gone. Decades, flashing in fast motion.

And now this accusation. Too much. Not fair.

A life can take a sudden and shuddering turn, is something the writer Harrison Riddles said in one of his novels. She didn't know Harrison yet, but his phrases sprang to mind. He was that kind of writer for her.

Sometimes the heart is stung by its own stinger.

Back in bed, she watched an old episode of *Murder, She Wrote*. Jack held her after they'd turned off the TV. A honey glow came from the night-light. He had just taken a shower and the air around his body was warm and soapy. She settled into it, sighing, and said, "Don't tell Paige about this bathroom thing."

"Of course I won't. It's your story to tell, honey."

"I'll never. It's shameful."

"Only if you'd done it."

Her stomach twisted. People will imagine me doing it, she didn't say.

They breathed together in the quiet. If she could see herself from a distance, all this might be much funnier. A mess but, in a certain light, funny too? In the fullness of time? Up close in the present, not funny.

"Why did she say it about me and not Katrina or Dee Dee or Nina? Or Raul?"

She felt her head rise and fall with his long breaths.

"You were there, I suppose."

"But we were all there."

She wanted to say the truth—what if I understood very well what was going on in the bathroom but was too shy to stop them? what if I thought about it sometimes when I was away from the library, here in our bed?—but did not. No. She felt better just riding his breath, allowing his body to regulate hers. If she admitted her odder thoughts, Jack could sometimes be . . . condescending put it too strongly. On paper he was faultless, but in his tone sometimes—only sometimes—she heard an edge of paternalism, a sort of bemused, self-satisfied patience, as though only an especially decent man could love this curious creature Maeve.

"This is a trap," he said after a while.

"What do you mean a *trap*?"

"You'll never know her motives."

"I guess I won't."

"My vote is for you to stop worrying. You have your own life to live."

Then he rubbed her back for a while, until she was too tired to talk or follow a thought—until she is gone, into a dream that will bring her to the dream in which the girl from the library comes to her door. Her own door. The crazy girl at the door to her own house, the girl in a hula skirt and lei, and here is dream-Maeve, hunting logic, saying, "Is it Halloween? It must be Halloween," because she cannot imagine why else the girl is here and dressed like that, cannot for the life of her, and Libby just laughs and laughs while Maeve goes in search of candy.

3

"I RANSACK PUBLIC LIBRARIES & find them full of sunk treasure," Virginia Woolf wrote in her diary. What does this make the librarian? Curator of treasure, treasure organizer, worker among drowned, almost-lost things . . . so that geniuses like Woolf might take what they need to build their own treasure. The service of the librarian to the ransacking genius: that's what Maeve saw when she read that passage.

"Say what you will about the British Empire," Katrina once told her, "but they sure as shit got their libraries right."

Maeve had mixed feelings about the British Empire but loved the library as deeply as anything else in the world. Her first contract was part-time. When a salaried position opened a year after that, Maeve wrote a personal letter, attached it to the standard application. *Dear Deborah*—who was then director—*Well, I'd better say it outright. I love the library with my heart and soul*—

Painfully clichéd, but it worked. That letter had been handwritten with a blue fountain pen, one of the few things she kept of her mother's. Back then Maeve took real pride in her handwriting, like a sample in a workbook when they still taught cursive, bulbous and swooped and somehow trustworthy.

She's not a voluble person but the library opens a valve. It's whatever we need it to be. A screen for projections, a field to be harvested. You will find what you need if you come with a question. God is a library, said lots of people, in different languages. *Happiness is a library*, said a sign over the water fountain.

Maeve was a layperson. No special school or advanced degree, though her colleagues over the years held degrees in library science or PhDs in other subjects, and she enjoyed the proximity to scholars, their awkwardness and precision. She herself was just a mom who'd wanted something to do when her kid went to kindergarten. "Just a mom," she'd say. Her humbleness, she understood, was its own form of narcissism, an overcorrection. She liked that no one expected much. She took pleasure in surprising her colleagues with her competence.

When Paige turned five, Maeve had decided she wanted a job rather than another child. Jack hid his disappointment kindly. It was only a matter of lucky timing that she'd landed at the library instead of filing papers in a law office, or hawking scarves at a boutique downtown—or doing what her friend Zoë did, which was read spy thrillers and romances to residents of a nursing home called Eagle Heights and grow fearful of her own death, and spend everything she earned on therapy.

In a certain way, there's no death at the library unless you go looking for it. Everything is hidden, tucked in its spot until called upon. A library meets you where you are. A library is not supposed to have politics or class consciousness or even ideas themselves. Its purpose is to house ideas. Librarians know where ideas belong, where to find them, on what shelf, in what volume, in what unique part of the World Wide Web. Knowing she can find what she needs to know comforts her more than any particular knowledge could.

When Deborah died (because of course death is everywhere), Gloria went up to director and freed a spot at the main desk. A few years after that, Maeve invented a title for herself: cultural coordinator. She didn't ask for a raise, so no one contested it. Also it sounded like something they needed, a title for a new era.

She called herself a jill-of-all-trades, ran the teen program and arranged social groups for new immigrants, whom she loved, believed in as a feature of a thriving democracy. Years back, when their city had been designated a refugee resettlement zone, she'd proposed the New Mainers group and been given a small fund— pitifully small, actually. But she was proud of this sort of thing.

She was good at drumming up small sums of money, pennies from liberals.

She invited local writers to give noontime readings in the sunny atrium, poets and scholars from the nearby colleges, journalists, members of the historical society. She covered shifts, trained new hires, could explain with ease and affection the particularities of the copier and printers, these machines like aging pets she'd see through to the bitter end. Because she blushed and shook when speaking in public, Katrina handled the public-facing work, the introductions at events, or one of the interns did, and this was how Maeve liked it. Once in a while she got a big-name novelist to give a reading or a talk, many of whom summered in Maine. Richard Russo and Richard Ford, Elizabeth Strout, Jonathan Lethem, one of Stephen King's sons . . . these were wild successes. Maeve had been satisfied, though she did not seek public recognition.

Her ambition was to get Harrison Riddles, her favorite writer, who was based in New York City but had a summer home on the Midcoast. Maeve had read everything he ever wrote. She found his novels beautiful and funny, wholehearted but not sentimental. Often they brought her to tears. They were the kind of books you finish and turn over to take in the author's face. You need to look at the person whose mind you just entered, or who entered yours. Who are you? How did you make this? Unarguably a good-looking man, though his most recent headshot wasn't the best Maeve had seen. He looked a bit shadowy, underslept, in a rumpled plaid shirt. She decided that she admired that, a writer who doesn't always make the most flattering choice, whose worry and fatigue isn't airbrushed out.

Of course in her letters she had not mentioned his face. They were professional, friendly but not familiar, for she wrote as a representative of the library, inviting him to visit as part of her new program. She told him why she loved the library. How it was the best job in the world. *I'm following my bliss*, she wrote, remembering Joseph Campbell, whom her college boyfriend Rich—her only boyfriend before Jack—read aloud in bed at night. Before he invited her to join him on his hero's journey, Rich had wanted her to understand the terms. She told Riddles she had lucked into the most blissful job in the world. The library soothed her, contained her. Not just Maeve—everyone. It was a place to think and learn and grow.

She loved how children came here to practice their quiet, serious selves. She loved the hushed, provisional air, silences broken by squeaky carts, stifled belches, the noise of people learning to conform. She loved the Dewey decimal system. Loved the signs everywhere you looked bearing maxims about the beauty of books, the great equalizing power of literature. Loved Kafka and Nancy Drew on magnets stuck to the staff fridge. Loved April, poetry month, not cruel at all.

She wrote it down like this, more or less, because she had read his essay in *Harper's* about the lost art of letter writing, the crisis of meaning produced by our absent narratives, how he loved a letter that was *a window into a life*. He loved texture, text, actual ink on actual paper. The essay concluded by saying he made it a policy to respond to any serious letter he received. He had acquired a P.O. box for this express purpose; this correspondence would not be mediated by agent or publisher.

She tried not to be too fancy and yet it was a pleasure, she found, to be a little fancy, to put on paper arrangements of words she would not speak aloud. She explained that over the years the librarians had become a family: Katrina and Nina and Lois and Dee Dee and Raul, and of course Gloria, who'd been there longest, whom she'd known from the start. Even if they didn't regularly socialize outside of work, they spent their days together, laboring in a place that felt—many of them said—holier than church, vital to the foundation of civic life, and this joined them in a special way, the way doctors are joined, or judges.

Katrina was her favorite. Maeve sometimes said to Katrina, "If I had my life to do over again . . ."

"You're only in your forties, Maeve! You're still young!"

Sweet girl. Darling girl.

Katrina had a master's in library science. She was brave and hip—at nineteen she'd been mugged while backpacking across Europe and had actually elbowed the mugger in the jaw. Later she'd been in a punk band and dated a woman.

"Don't be one of those people who confuse degrees with intelligence," Katrina told Maeve. "You can get the degree if it's so important to you. If you're so impressed by it! The master's only takes two years."

Oh no, Maeve had no use for such a thing. She needed nothing. The osmotic pressure of the books, the catalogs, the undisputed taxonomies . . . The library itself, she tried to explain, was her school.

Katrina was the most interesting person Maeve knew, and elbowing the mugger was the least of it. She was white and twenty-six and lived with her long-term boyfriend Willie, who was Black—a refugee from Sudan who had arrived a decade ago, as a teenager. Maeve met him first, when a social worker brought him to the library for the New Mainers. Katrina joined the staff a couple years later. When the New Mainers group got too big and moved to the new immigration center, Maeve noticed that Willie didn't go with them. She would see him reading magazines at the edge of the Pen, looking up occasionally, scanning the room. Soon, he and Katrina began leaving together, arm in arm, like an old couple out for an evening constitutional. Certain people expressed shock (the "backwoods side" of Katrina's family pitched a fit, she reported, and there was mention of a rupture in Willie's extended network), but for the library staff it was a beautiful story about the possibilities of the world, the inevitability of love. Maeve didn't get into all this detail in the letter to Harrison. But in her paragraph about the connection that libraries create, *deep cross-cultural friendships*, she was thinking of Katrina and Willie.

Maeve considered her sentences, thought about the kinds of things that would interest a person like him. And then realized, No, write about the things that interest *you*, Maeve, and the letters got easier to write.

Borges said paradise would be a library and Maeve agreed. She felt like a crew member, an officer, on a ship sailing toward a better world—more just and equitable and evidence-based. A sturdy ship. A good vessel. Virginia Woolf's library was a sunken place, but not Maeve Cosgrove's.

Wouldn't Harrison Riddles like to visit for an hour or two?

But he never wrote back.

4

THE DAY AFTER THE ACCUSATION—the first day of March. Libby hadn't returned but Katrina had, thank God, and Maeve pulled her into the staff lounge.

Katrina said, "Your hair looks cute like that. You should do that more."

Maeve had pinned it up to wash her face and didn't take down. She felt uneasy about the compliment; this was crisis hair.

"You should show your cheekbones off. . . You alright? Why are you looking at me like that?"

"Yesterday was a nightmare." She explained everything—C.J. at Gloria's desk, the accusation, which she found herself calling "an abomination"—and Katrina yelped and clapped her hand over her mouth. Gloria had sworn she'd not tell any of the staff, but the gesture felt staged.

"Did Gloria tell you already? I asked her not to say anything."

"What? No."

"Please don't tell anyone. I can't bear it."

"Relax, Maeve. No one will buy it."

"That's what Jack said too."

"Not a chance, I promise. You know what we're dealing with here, don't you?"

"What?" Maeve asked, grateful for the *we*. "What are we dealing with?"

A caustic whisper: "A *borderline*. It's in the DSM, a personality disorder. They crave attention. They invent weird situations. You remember my cousin Mandy?"

Maeve had a memory of the cousin, a story from a few years ago . . . a memory of indignant chatter among the librarians on Katrina's behalf. A raucous Fourth of July at the family camp on Sebago Lake, a druggie vibe, the cousin naked and upsetting a smaller child . . . She remembered the cousin requiring an actual padded room.

"Borderlines are emotionally violating," Katrina explained. "Their boundaries are *terrible*. They overpersonalize everything. My poor aunt and uncle." She shuddered. "I don't know about Libby. The tall one, right? Blond? With the resting bitchface?"

Resting bitchface! Maeve's heart surged. She nodded. She wanted Katrina to say it in front of Gloria and C.J.

"I'm no psychologist," Katrina whispered, "but she has all the hallmarks."

"What do you mean?"

"Lying, for one. Promiscuity. Inventing situations."

"What do I *do*?"

"Absolutely nothing. That's the trick. The compassionate thing is to totally disengage."

"I don't understand. She wants me to get in trouble? *Why?*"

Katrina laughed sagely: "A monkey picks nits. A cow chews cud. It's what they do." She had an appealing fierceness in her eyes, a seriousness of purpose.

"Borderline," said Maeve, tasting the word, appraising it.

"You always want to give people the benefit of the doubt."

"Is that so bad?"

"They sense when you're wounded. They're like scavengers that way."

"Wounded?"

"You know what I mean," Katrina said, though Maeve didn't, not exactly, and might have asked but the conversation ended there, for Nina poked her head in and said, "Raul can't find the vending machine key," and they both looked to Maeve, who knew where everything was, who got up and located the spare and went to the machine in the basement, where she found not Raul but a dour middle-aged man whose Twizzlers had gotten stuck, and she freed them.

———

Katrina's boyfriend Willie came in later that day, wearing Adidas athletic shorts in sky blue, aviator sunglasses. Katrina was out on an errand. He needed a book the community college library didn't have—about what Aristotle can teach screenwriters. His professor Chuck told him to read it.

"Screenwriting?" Maeve smiled. "You do look very LA today."

She saw this made him uncomfortable. He took off the sunglasses and slid them over the collar of his T-shirt. He was watchful and wary of attention. He'd been this way since he was a boy. Maeve remembered that first winter, the big blue coat given to him by the refugee resettlement agency, his face set back in his furry hood like an owl tucked in a tree. She knew what all the librarians knew about Willie, the bare outline: born in Sudan during a period of war, lived in a refugee camp in Kenya before he came to Maine, of indeterminate age but lucky to be young looking, a late bloomer, smaller than his peers, so they made him a seventh grader. A family of white people, Christians, had taken him in with some other boys. Now he was a community college student and had moved into Katrina's apartment.

She swiveled the computer monitor so the screen was visible to them both, entered the title and author. The book about screenwriting lived in the east mezzanine. He looked worried when she tried to give him directions, so she took him there.

"I used to do writing in college too," she told him as they made their way up the stairs. "I was an English major."

"There's no English at the community college."

"No *English*?"

"It's called humanities," he said. "I myself am a business major but they make you take one art. I didn't want to paint. That was the other class that was available."

"What's your screenplay about?"

He said it was more like a screenplay appreciation class. They wrote *about* screenplays.

"Chuck said I could read the *Poetics* or just read this book. He said it's like Cliffs Notes."

She was careful not to disapprove, said, "Well, it's fun to write. I loved it back then."

"You can write one for extra credit. It used to be mandatory but Chuck said he got tired of terrible screenplays."

She didn't have time to disapprove because they'd arrived; her index finger like a dowser tapped its spine—pop of pleasure, eternal pride, a book where the book is meant to be. This one was quite slim, which she could tell was a relief to him.

"Thank you, Ms. Cosgrove!"

"*Maeve*, please."

He nodded but didn't say it.

They looked at the cover of the book: *Storytelling Secrets from the Greatest Mind in Western Civilization*. You could not see Aristotle's eyes or face, only his beard, long and dense and concluding in rather dandy curls. In college Maeve had been confused about who'd been a real living Greek and who was a myth, had once embarrassed herself saying Aristotle when the answer was Achilles. She thought to say this to him, but instead she said, "You should do it. Try writing a screenplay, Willie. Why not?"

He made a dubious face.

"I'd love to read it if you do."

"I'm so busy." But then he said: "It has crossed my mind."

"I loved to write in college." He didn't ask what she wrote but she said, "Nothing good. A few short stories. Some pretty bad poetry. Oh, the poetry."

It was bad Plath. Mommy, mommy, all of it.

"Well, I need to make a living," he said, laughed.

"You will," she told him, had an impulse to say, *Don't sell yourself short, Willie*, something in that spirit, but he had not sought her mentorship. And what did a middle-aged white lady know about what Willie was or wasn't capable of?

Back at the front desk they found Katrina, lipstick reapplied, nose blotted. She must have reapplied her rose oil too, dabbed it on her pulse points; the air around her was infused warmly, sensuously. She threw her arms around Willie's neck. "I came for a book," he told her. And then, leaning close, a whisper, "And for you, baby."

Maeve, close enough to hear this, felt herself blush and turned away.

An old man in a wheelchair had dropped a stack of magazines and was bending awkwardly over the side of the chair to retrieve them. Maeve hurried to him, prepared to set them again on his bony lap. *Architectural Digests*, heavy.

"Here you go, sir."

He smelled of pipe spoke.

"I don't want to crush you . . ."

"Don't worry," he winked. "Nothing there anymore to crush."

On her lunch break, brewing a cup of tea in the staff room, Maeve could not stop thinking about the borderline girl who had entered this off-limits space to leave her note in Gloria's mailbox. The girl had seen the cozy chairs, the mailboxes, the whiteboard on which they left each other messages of encouragement, invitations to eat the brownies and leftover quiche. Maeve knew all of their handwriting—Katrina's postmodern slashes, Dee Dee's childlike bubbles, Nina who only used capitals. The girl had come in here and read the whiteboard. She had put the note in Gloria's box. But *why*? For what purpose? When Maeve carried not an ounce of ill will in her heart for the girl or for any other kid. Had only given her space, respect, let her make her own decisions. Wasn't that what every kid wanted? Why had the girl punished her for it?

The *girl*, Maeve prefers. But it's Libby. Libby. Libby. She lets it plays in her mind like a song she's learning. She needs to get it down. Make it dull. Desensitization. That worked during a spell in her twenties when she'd been terrified to fly, when she followed her brother's advice and read pilots' diaries and sat in the airport parking lot sweating and watching planes take off. You can get used to anything. Teach your body to relax. So she says the name until there is no girl anymore, no person, just a chorus of loud and harmless bugs.

5

Libby libby libby Libby Libby Libby Libby Libby Libby Libby
Libby Libby Libby Libby Libby Libby Libby Libby Libby Libby Libby
Libby Libby Libby Libby Libby Libby Libby Libby Libby Libby Libby
Libby Libby Libby Libby Libby Libby Libby Libby Libby Libby Libby
Libby Libby Libby Libby Libby Libby Libby Libby Libby Libby Libby
Libby Libby Libby Libby Libby Libby Libby Libby Libby Libby Libby
Libby Libby Libby Libby Libby Libby Libby Libby Libby Libby Libby
Libby Libby Libby Libby Libby Libby Libby Libby Libby Libby Libby
Libby Libby Libby Libby Libby Libby Libby Libby Libby Libby Libby
Libby Libby Libby Libby Libby Libby Libby Libby Libby Libby Libby
Libby Libby Libby Libby Libby Libby Libby Libby Libby Libby Libby
Libby Libby Libby Libby Libby Libby Libby Libby Libby Libby Libby
Libby Libby Libby Libby Libby Libby Libby Libby Libby Libby
Libby Libby Libby Libby Libby Libby Libby Libby Libby Libby
Libby Libby Libby Libby Libby Libby Libby Libby Libby Libby Libby
Libby Libby Libby Libby Libby Libby Libby Libby Libby Libby Libby
Libby Libby Libby Libby Libby Libby Libby Libby Libby Libby Libby
Libby Libby Libby Libby Libby Libby Libby Libby Libby Libby Libby
Libby Libby Libby Libby Libby Libby Libby Libby Libby Libby Libby
Libby Libby Libby Libby Libby Libby Libby Libby Libby Libby Libby
Libby Libby Libby Libby Libby Libby Libby Libby Libby Libby Libby
Libby Libby Libby Libby Libby Libby Libby Libby Libby Libby Libby
Libby Libby Libby Libby Libby Libby Libby Libby Libby Libby Libby
Libby Libby Libby Libby Libby Libby Libby Libby Libby Libby Libby
Libby Libby Libby Libby Libby Libby Libby Libby Libby Libby
Libby Libby Libby Libby Libby Libby Libby Libby Libby Libby Libby

6

THE RHYTHMS OF THE DAYS are a comfort, Maeve explained to Harrison Riddles in one of her letters. If you are a person who people-watches, who imagines what others feel, sees metaphors in tableau, you can do no better than being a librarian.

Mornings were old people, bused in from assisted living at 9 a.m., who paged through magazines or newspapers or wore giant black headphones and sat staring into the middle distance. Few read proper books, even in the largest print. It was imperative to Maeve that old people didn't see you look disgusted in their proximity. She found an unexpected strength when chiding an intern on his expression of revulsion. "Be kind," she told the kid. "Everyone is fighting a hard battle!"

She didn't attribute this wisdom to its source and later felt ashamed of her plagiarizing, as it were, and so wrote the dictum on an index card in magic marker, taped it to the welcome board, citing Plato (circa 400 BC). By noon the elders got collected and returned to assisted living. Later in the day, when school got out, teenagers whose motility and odors Maeve found reassuring claimed this space. The teenagers were kinetic, exhausted. They whispered and passed notes and made lewd comics. Or sank into chairs and stared at their phones, beat at their screens with their thumbs, necks bent dangerously. When they napped they collapsed severely on the carpet, their bodies giving off guarded, anxious energy, like soldiers on a break. They were supposed to put their electronic devices in a box behind the counter and do their homework—if they did this for a certain number of days in a row they got a coupon for a free ice cream—Maeve had secured the grant that made that possible—but most did not give up their devices.

Yes, it was a holding pen of sorts, but Maeve tried to make it more than that. Librarians are like social workers in a certain way, she wrote to Harrison, which didn't mean she interfered or advocated. The social work she did was to be quiet, to leave them alone, to offer a safe space in which nothing was asked except that they be calm, or at least quiet. She put pretzels and granola bars in the lounge and subscribed to teen magazines, and made sure the brochure rack was full of literature about STIs, sexual violence, GED certification, citizenship, voting.

She didn't know most of their names. They were a mass, came and went, the program not requiring any formal check-in. Always a few stood out. These days, everyone knew Donna because she was in a wheelchair, Darius who was so tall and funny. Everyone knew Jordan with red hair and the boy called Billy who, if he didn't take his medication, shouted profanity. Several of the girls wore hijabs. Maeve was ashamed that she found it difficult to tell them apart. Najmo she knew from the birthmark. Otherwise, a mass, shape-shifting, here and gone, kids for a spell and then grown up, and sometimes they'd come back with a baby to show the librarians, or a husband. Things like that had begun to happen—she'd been a librarian for fifteen years.

Last October, Libby Leanham had moved to their town and became one of those kids. Sometimes it took Maeve a while to notice some-one new, for people floated in and out daily, but Maeve spotted Libby right away. It was Libby's style she noticed first, her clothes. Not something Maeve usually paid attention to.

Real style can't be bought. Her brother Deacon taught her long ago: real style transcends money, class, color, is innate, cannot be learned. Very few people have it, he told her. Maeve was sure he'd say Libby did. She wore ordinary clothes in a way that felt differ-ent, strange. Big black wool pants cinched at the waist with a piece of blue rope, a T-shirt that said *Cancel Prom*, jagged at the hem like a scarecrow's, farmer's overalls. She carried a beaten green army backpack. She was skinny, tall, especially straight. Sharp-boned and purposeful, like a girl from a comic book. Her skin was vibrantly pale, blue veins vivid in her wrists and temples. She was always eating or reading something, her face busy—calculating, gnawing, sucking, staring—never empty or resting. This intensity felt like a kind of style too. She was indifferent to the gaze of others, like someone being photographed who truly does not care.

She came nearly every day, always put her phone in the box.

Maeve's program had not been particularly popular, the youth preferring their devices to sweets. Several obese children happily relinquished their phones and Maeve worried she was failing them, but when Libby came and put her phone in the box and began to read actual books, Maeve felt better.

There was a boy who followed Libby around. Light brown skin, shaggy black hair. He might have been Italian, or Puerto Rican. Maeve didn't know. Didn't ask. He was handsome but did not have style. His name, for confidentiality purposes, was B.

Maeve's one conversation with Libby happened on a day when Libby was sucking on a lime green lollipop. She'd been coming to the library for a month or so at this point. That day she was wearing a giant white sweater, Maeve remembered, and black leggings and tall rubber boots that had been entirely covered in silver duct tape. She nodded at Maeve when she dropped her phone in the box.

The greenness of the sucker—neon, unnatural, did not belong in a healthy body. It made Maeve think of radiation, Fukushima only a year before, that horrible clip she'd seen on the news before she could turn away, children swept to sea.

"Hello," said Maeve.

Her gaze was unusually steady for a young person.

"I've noticed you read a lot," Maeve said.

Libby shrugged, like So what?

Maeve said, "I wish that wasn't such a rare thing."

"Yeah, well. I wasted my time on the last book. Where the guys go up the river and find all the heads?"

"Joseph Conrad."

"No, not him." She shrugged the backpack off her shoulder, retrieved a glossy mass-market paperback by someone named P. C. EVERETT, waterlogged.

"I found it at a bus stop. It's set on another planet. They're not human heads."

"You should read *Heart of Darkness*."

"Oh, I did." She spoke flatly, almost glaring. "The ending cracked me up."

"The horror?"

"Right." Now her face softened; the suggestion of a smile. "But later when the wife says, 'What were his last words?' and he says, 'Uh, they were . . . *your name*.' That made me laugh out loud."

Again the puppy-boy, B., found the girl, tugged on her arm, paying no attention to Maeve.

"Not now," Libby said, shaking him off, and he slunk away.

"I need my coupon," she told Maeve. She meant for the ice cream. "I'm due."

The records showed it.

Libby got her coupon and left and came back in ten minutes with an ice cream cone. It looked like pistachio. She gave it to the boy. Maeve thought this might be the beginning of more conversations about books, that perhaps they'd connect in this manner, but things didn't go that way.

She watched them, slantwise, over the next several weeks. The boy followed her around. Nina knew from a social worker friend that the girl was in the foster system. There was light gossip among library staff. Maeve heard but did not seek it out. That was her approach to gossip—Listen, don't stoke.

Gossip: That Libby had spent years in foster care. She was sixteen now and trying to emancipate herself from the system, had recently moved from a depressed former mill town in the central part of the state, came down here for the social services. Evidently the girl had lit a bench on fire, or a playground, and had been sent to an institution. What kind of institution? No one said. Her eyes were steady, shone with knowing, as if she had been at a school for supernatural seeing. *Libby* was her official name. That felt sad to Maeve, a nickname instead of a proper name, a kind of deprivation.

Unlike most of the kids, Libby read books. No telling what. She deposited her phone and hunkered down with Oscar Wilde and Dickens and Harlequins, or hip science fiction novels with metallic covers. Emerson. *Mrs. Dalloway.* The biography of Janice Dickinson, the world's first supermodel. Her face alert with suspicion, as if she could not possibly get what she needed from this thing in her hands but would try her hardest, would try if it gave her a migraine. Sometimes she sat on the bike rack and smoked cigarettes until Raul the building manager said, "Hey lady, no smoking thirty feet from the building," and then she perched on the fire hydrant like a crane, glaring at the clouds.

The boy, Maeve heard, didn't have parents. He lived with an uncle. Katrina told Maeve he was developmentally disabled. Sometimes after napping on the couch he bolted upright and Maeve saw the addled vigilance of someone compensating for a deficit. The messy hair was not on purpose. He wore oversized T-shirts, long shorts— off-brand, out of style. Clothes someone else bought him. Handsome, but had none of what the girl had, none of her magnetism. He gave off a prepubescent vibe, a latency-period aura, though he already shaved his chin.

Maeve had wondered at first, idly . . . perhaps they're related? Cousins? Familiarity in their dynamic, a kind of candor. Their thing did not appear romantic. He behaved like a little brother, wanted simply to be in her presence. She was casually mean to him, short-tempered, eye-rolling, but once in a while she'd bring him ice cream

or a lollipop. Once in a while she'd sling an arm over his shoulder
and they'd rest on one of the public couches, a familial, throwaway
tenderness between them, sunlight streaming onto their faces. He
clearly loved this, yielded instantly to her touch when she came for
him. In her presence his eyes turned sweet, his face placid. Sometimes they went for a walk outside together.

Maeve decided that the girl's candor was her way of showing
respect for the inferior boy. She didn't pretend he wasn't what he
was. It would feel good to be under the arm of a girl like that, Maeve
decided. It would feel the way it feels to be about to fall asleep and a
hand is resting on your upper back. Someone wakeful and trusted is
telling you to rest. OK, the hand says. You can let down your guard.

Then Libby started bringing him somewhere. One day she took
his hand and led him away. Maeve saw them disappear into the
stairwell. She imagined they went to get a juice or a snack from
the basement machine. In ten minutes they came back, neither
eating nor drinking. It happened again a few days later. This time
Maeve followed. They took the stairwell to the mezzanine. She saw
them moving through the stacks, then slipping together into the
women's bathroom in the PAs. She stood there, in the hall, waited.
Heard nothing.

A public bathroom. Two stalls, one sink. No lock on the door.

She should have opened the door, she knew that. Knocked at
least. She should have called out, Alright, kids, come on out now. No
boys in the girls' room! She might have used the firm, unflappable
voice she'd found when Paige had been small, which she found easily
enough when other teenagers got out of hand: That's *enough*. But she
couldn't find it now, or wouldn't.

She didn't. It was too embarrassing to be the person who scolded
the girl. She just could not. She pretended she didn't see. She
returned to her desk, where she organized her paper clips by color.
She squeezed the rubber band ball, lined up her stamps, rubbed hand

sanitizer into her damp palms until they were cool and dry again. Ten minutes later they came down, intact, tucked in, but flushed.

Libby took him into the bathroom another time. Again Maeve trailed, saw them go in, and failed to intercede. Another time. Soon it was a regular occurrence. Through December. January. Letting it go on was wrong, she knew that, probably illegal. She forced herself not to notice, because it's not illegal not to notice. She looked down when they passed her. She thought, Don't be so straight, Maeve. They'll be doing it elsewhere if not in the library, that's for sure. By the dumpster. In the alley behind the Chinese restaurant. In the cold. With other eyes on them, other presences lurking. She was helping them stay inside, in a safe place. Couldn't that be considered harm reduction? Like the needle exchange? Everyone is allowed their first-love experience, or sex, or whatever this was. The more it went on, the more it seemed wrong—the more it seemed, frankly, cruel—to break in, to deny these two whatever pleasure or comfort or reprieve they were finding.

It must also be reiterated that all this made Maeve terribly shy. That she did not want for them to know that she knew.

Maeve's own bedtime thoughts, Libby and B., were not grotesque, not pornographic. Their furtive coupling, as she drifted off, was tender, gripping and nuzzling, fully clothed. They warmed her. These two lost kids who'd found each other. These were not real people but representations. Not even on paper. Only in her mind.

Maeve didn't use that bathroom. Not typically. There was a staff bathroom, as they'd told C.J., though Dee's digestive plights meant this single toilet was often occupied. Sometimes if Maeve was shelving up in the mezzanine it was easier to pee in that bathroom, which was how it had happened that one day, in the middle of February, passing by and feeling the weight of her bladder, she went in.

Two stalls, both empty.

In her mind they used the left, and so she chose for herself the right. She locked the stall door behind her. Recently the walls had been painted a glossy red—only one bit of graffiti marred the paint job, a cactus etched above the toilet paper dispenser. Or a penis? A penis with thorns. Right at eye level, for the young ones to see. She would ask Gloria to ask Raul to paint over it promptly.

She thought about them when she peed. Libby and B., a secret couple. She was close to them here—not them, only the idea of them. She did not want to be close to the actual *them*. Did not!

The choice was not hers. Because then came the creaking of the door, and the sweet abstraction took actual human form, two bodies, four feet. The speed with they threw themselves into the stall next to hers, the suddenness, the alignment of their presence with Maeve's imagination, made her feel she had dreamed them into being. But it was really them. Next to her, behind the partition, Libby and B.

Next to her.

They made no sounds except the sounds you can't help, kissing, respiration, friction, a huffing helpless clamor, silence so effortful it screams. His moans could not be restrained, like an infant who can't not burp. Surely Maeve's feet were visible. Surely Libby knew Maeve was in there. Surely she was fucking with Maeve.

Maeve left, fast. Didn't tell. Was too shy to tell. It was an accident, her being there. She hurried out, swore she would never use that bathroom again.

Fifteen minutes later, they came down again. Libby sent the boy back to the couch with a flick of her wrist, then strode to the alcove, to the counter above Maeve's desk, dropped down on an elbow, and said, "You have a copy of *Crime and Punishment* in this place?"

Maeve met her gaze. Her eyebrows were white-blond, slim, like two bioluminescent fish. Up close, the girl was so young. Maeve was overcome by a tremendous sense of propriety. *She* was the adult here. Whatever game the kid was playing, Maeve would not fall for it.

She performed obliviousness, kept herself heroically neutral. She told Libby where to find the book. She spoke coolly, the librarian she had cultivated over these years, clipped, professional, never saying more than truly necessary. She wrote the call numbers on a scrap of paper with a steady hand.

"Have you read it?" the girl asked, taking a step backward.

"Yes, I have."

"Does it have a good ending?"

Maeve remembered.

But before she could speak Libby said, "Don't tell me. I want to be surprised."

Two weeks later, on the last day of February, Maeve was called into Gloria's office. Part of her wanted to tell them the whole truth right then, but she found she could not. It would be too embarrassing to say it. It would reveal a lapse in judgment. A failure to intercede. They were mandatory reporters, after all. Yes, but—she wanted to say, could not say—what was there to report? Nothing much, right? Kids. A couple canoodling kids!

She had been trying so ardently to be cool, to give them space, autonomy, and the girl had called her out.

The bitch!

The bitchface!

The boy played no role. Did not produce his own version. Only much later would Maeve wonder, Did the boy want what happened in the stall? How impaired was he? Maeve had a Seven Sisters education, sure, but that was ages ago. She'd forgotten which wave of feminism they were in, had been raised on Take Back the Night, raised to fear the desires of men, to believe a boy cannot be hurt by a secret sexual encounter, so she didn't worry for the boy. In any case, she knew for certain—knew against her will—how much he liked it.

7

THE OFFICIAL RESOLUTION came much faster than Maeve expected. Two days before the end of March, C.J. returned to the library. Now it was a sunny day, cold and cloudless. C.J. wore the same blazer, same boots but without cleats. Maeve panicked when she saw her, fearing bad news, something even more complicated and sinister unfolding, but the social worker said the news was good. She would have just called, but she happened to get a message from the library—it was her turn for the new vampire book, so she came in person.

Again they sat in the office, Gloria off to the side, and C.J. said, "Clearly these are baseless claims. See, Maeve? You didn't have to worry." There would be no charges. Was no evidence. Absolutely nothing but the word of a foster kid, a girl known to lie. "Known, let's say, to tell unvalidated stories about those in positions of authority."

"What do you mean? She's done this before?"

"I'm not at liberty to say more."

"What's unvalidated? She made up a story about someone else?"

"We're careful about what we share. We respect the rights of the accused."

"She's only curious," Gloria said.

C.J. said, "Yes, well, would she like me to tell *her* name to the next person Libby accuses?"

"No," Maeve said.

Maeve was going to throw up. No she wasn't. She was. Finally she excused herself, ran upstairs to the mezzanine—far away, for privacy—acid-dissolved Life cereal burning her esophagus, bloating bits floating in toilet water. She crouched in the left stall, tears and snot coating her face, feeling she had been freed from something, had expelled a poison, clasping the rim of the toilet like a life preserver.

Libby hadn't come back since the accusation. Not unusual on its face—kids stopped coming all the time, found other programs or after-school jobs and abruptly stopped attending—but her absence had felt so strange. She had said such a terrible thing. She had lit a fuse but not returned to see the damage. Why would you do that? And where had she gone? Were Libby and B. together somewhere? Maeve put them in a booth at IHOP. In the red spell of a Target bathroom. In a car, a lovers' lane at night.

After she vomited and cleaned the toilet, Maeve washed her face and hands and arms with foamy antibacterial soap, knowing it would dry out her skin. She returned to Gloria's office, where C.J. and Gloria were deep in laughter. They stopped when they saw her.

"Sorry about that," said Maeve.

"You OK?" Gloria asked.

"Relieved."

"Of course you are," said C.J. "Anyone would be."

"Anyone," Gloria echoed, but wore a look of concern.

C.J., visibly more relaxed now, as though she'd had a drink, murmured, "The girl has some issues."

"Naturally she does."

"She has been taken—though this is *not* to be repeated—I am only offering this to reassure Maeve—she's been taken back to the hospital, a special program for girls like her."

"Well, that's a relief," Gloria said.

Girls like her? What did that mean? Borderline girls? Girls who took advantage of people? Who invented situations? Maeve wanted to ask. Could not. Suddenly C.J. was standing, was above, like a teacher releasing them from detention.

"I'm off now. I have a date with a book in my bathtub."

Just like that, she was gone. Libby too, being treated for something that was not Maeve's fault. That's all Maeve needed to know.

C.J. hadn't said anything about the boy, and Maeve didn't ask. She didn't care.

"If I never see that woman again, it will be too soon," Maeve said in the weird silence that followed C.J.'s exit. "Or that girl. Never is too soon."

"Oh, Maeve."

"Don't ever tell anyone."

"You've got to relax."

"I know you're not a gossip," Maeve said.

"Goodness. You really are taking this hard. Look, I understand. I'd probably feel the same way myself. But it's over now, sweetie. Let it go. Get a manicure or a massage. Treat yourself to a spa day."

"I told you," Jack said. "Do you feel better?"

"I threw up."

"I mean now."

"Yes. I do."

"Now you can really let it go."

She did not appreciate this phrasing. In fact she did *not* feel better. She felt uneasy. New questions occurred to her. What if the girl had been looking for someone to intervene? For supervision? Why hadn't Maeve considered that?

That night at dinner, she asked Jack what he thought. "Maybe she was reaching out. Needing something. Maybe I misunderstood it. Maybe she was trying to communicate . . ."

Jack dipped a saltine into his soup. He was wearing a salmon-colored button-down with a bright white T-shirt under it.

He said, "I think you might be exaggerating."

He ate the cracker and dipped another.

"Exaggerating what?"

"Your role in it. Your part."

He made her thoughtfulness feel like narcissism, like pathology. "She named *me*, Jack. It's not solipsism. She used *my* name. I'd love to see how you'd react."

He thought about this. "You're kind," he said finally. "That's a good thing. But too kind, sometimes." He ate his soup neatly, taking measured bites, thinking. Then he said, "I don't know. I mean, you have a lot of empathy."

It was a new buzzword, *empathy*. Even Jack was saying it. He looked at her warmly, then away, traced a cracker along the edge of his bowl. "I'm an accountant, honey, what do I know?"

Finally she told him: "I suspected it, Jack. I saw them snuggling on the couch. I saw them going off together, to the bathroom. I could at least have checked in. I could have knocked, right?"

He appeared perfectly unmoved. "I see a group of teenagers anywhere, I assume they're secretly screwing. Or not-so-secretly."

She loved him for saying that, and kissed him, and after dinner took him to the couch in the den, the good leather one, which was not usually where they did it.

It was over and done.

Later that night they were in bed, watching an episode of *Murder, She Wrote* from 1988, or she was watching and he was reviewing documents on a clipboard. She loved J. B. Fletcher, the character Angela Lansbury made famous. Her stoic, self-respecting clarity. The convoluted plots, bloodless murders, terrible hair. How J.B.—Jessica—gets to the bottom of everything. No detail slipped by her, nothing ever. TV was getting too good, Maeve felt, too hard to fall asleep to, but the nostalgia channel did the trick. Jack's favorite was *Quantum Leap*, or *Columbo*.

Then she remembered, just as she was settling in: "Oh shit. The plants."

"Do it tomorrow." Jack yawned and set his clipboard on the bedside table, on top of a book about Jackie Robinson he'd been reading for several weeks.

"She insisted it's very precise."

"A few hours can't matter."

"They're sensitive," she said, and thought but didn't say: queer.

She kept watching the show. Someone discovered the body, an orderly heap on the side of the road, and by then Jack was asleep, his jaw splayed open, showing off his well-flossed teeth, and Maeve pressed pause and got up. Because the task in the greenhouse made her sad, she did it with especial diligence, did it as if it did not make her sad. She went downstairs and put on Paige's old slicker and went out into the night. The special plants she was responsible for occupied several rows along the west wall. They appeared—after so long—to be close to sprouting. Thick stalks had popped up. Hard, dark pink buds the size of walnuts. She gave them water, and a dose of whatever was in the jar, powdered vitamins she'd mixed with the water, per Paige's instructions.

Back in bed, she resumed the show, raising the volume above Jack's snores. Soon the murderer makes his meticulous confession. He is fat, bald, an archaeologist whose wife betrays him by stealing a priceless relic while he sleeps, a priceless thing for a price, which is an *abomination*—that's the word he uses, it pierces Maeve—and in retaliation the archaeologist kills her, his own wife. It doesn't make sense. There are too many characters. But Jessica, writer, detective, understands everything.

J. B. Fletcher, a Mainer like Maeve. Jessica took to writing late in life, after her beloved husband's death. Her first book, *The Corpse Danced at Midnight*, had been secretly taken to the publisher by her nephew, Grady. She wrote it for her own pleasure, Jessica said. It would have lived in a drawer if she'd had her way. Maeve liked her for that. Jessica was not a sellout. If people enjoyed what she wrote, great. Otherwise, she'd be happy puttering in the garden and teaching high school English. Of course Grady took the manuscript against her will, without her consent. That part Maeve could not get behind.

At eight the next morning the phone rang and Jack went to his office. When he came back, he said he had to go on a business trip the following week. Maybe longer than usual. On Monday. To Ohio this time.

"You want to come? You should come, honey. Play *Eloise* again?"

She sat up, stretched, considered the prospect.

Jack did the complicated taxes of a major American appliance maker. Often he traveled to manufacturing complexes where he audited the finances. Earlier in their marriage she had gone along on these trips, swimming in the hotel pools, watching TV and reading novels, eating mini yogurts she'd hustled upstairs from the breakfast bar, hoarding the unbruised fruit. Those had been sweet days, nothing on the horizon, no ambition but to rest and eat and cuddle with him when he returned from long days in a branch office, and maybe get pregnant. But the thought of it now made her lonesome.

"They need me at the library."

"They can't survive a few days?"

"No," she said, briskly. "As a matter of fact they can't."

He nodded but didn't look convinced. He went downstairs to make the coffee. She closed her eyes and pretended she was in a hotel room.

When he came back he said, "I don't want to leave you here, stewing in your juices."

"My juices? Jesus, Jack."

"Promise me you won't stew."

"I won't."

"You won't *what*?"

"I won't promise you."

"It's over now. It's official. Don't let this loom too large."

"I won't let it loom," she agreed.

He got back in bed with her; they drank their coffee leaning against the headboard, shoulders touching. He rubbed his jaw, a performance of thinking, as if the idea was occurring to him right at that moment.

"Maybe talking to someone would help. Or one of those groups at the Y. They have a huge catalog of activities."

They'd been here before, after Paige left for Uganda last summer.

"Maybe I'm bored," she said, huffily. "Right? Maybe I need a hobby? Is that your advice?"

"I think you have a hobby," he said. "I think we're talking about your hobby."

"What do you mean?"

Libby, Libby, Libby was her hobby. That's what he was saying.

She didn't kiss him back when he kissed her goodbye.

At work that day, Maeve was sour.

"You OK?" Dee asked.

Maeve said, "Husbands," lightly, waving a hand, and Dee, who enjoyed other people's problems, nodded and came closer, but Maeve found she could not say what her husband had done wrong. *Had* he done something wrong? If she said, He treats me like a child, Dee would purr, "Oh Maeve," and reach to hug her, which would also make her feel like a child.

She felt suddenly sorry for Libby. To be talked about. To be watched. All these authorities, these adults, always looking, noting your faults!

Though if you set a playground on fire, maybe eyes are what you want.

The danger of the girl's situation, her precarity, revealed itself to Maeve gradually. What if Libby had been asking for help? She did not have a mother. She'd had none of the privileges and care Paige had received as a matter of course. She had glommed onto Maeve. Glommed on by accusing her. Maeve had a sick feeling, as if *she* had been the one to put the girl in whatever special hospital she'd gone to, as if her own failure to responsibly intervene had caused Libby's madness. She feared that she, Maeve, was still in trouble. She had said *bitch*. That couldn't be taken away.

All week she felt weird. On edge. She saw a tall girl with blond hair but it wasn't the girl. She kept thinking it was Libby all day, startling herself. Eventually this blond girl, nothing like Libby, seemed to notice Maeve's glances.

She took a few drives that week—twice on her lunch break and a few times after work. Slow, lazy drives around different parts of town. The CVS on Cumberland, on Tafton. The McDonald's on St. Luke. This wasn't something to tell Katrina, nor her brother, and Jack was getting on her nerves, somehow above the human fray, and so she spoke aloud, to herself, "What are you doing, Maeve?" as she drove between the 7-Elevens and the drugstores of the city. She answered her own question.

"I'm looking out for a troubled girl."

That was the whole of the answer right then. If she saw Libby, Maeve was not even certain she would stop. She wanted only to know where she was, to keep an eye on her, in a manner of speaking. She had been caught off guard but would not be again.

It was still cold but the sky had begun to change—a warm white that foretold spring. The light was getting longer, things opening in the greenhouse and in the ground. Harrison Riddles said in one of his books that spring was like a coin in a threadbare pocket, about to fall. Maeve waited for it to happen.

Any moment Libby would get out of the hospital and walk in. Maeve couldn't get that thought from her mind. Cranky elders, restless kids. Darius broke a lamp with his yo-yo. They kicked someone out for stealing a chocolate bun from another kid's backpack. A tension in the air, a collective bad mood. It snowed on Wednesday, a spring squall as if out of spite, and a senior citizen who'd come for many years, Barbara LeMay, beloved for her joyfulness, died on Thursday. A full moon, Nina explained, and described the arrangement of the planets, conniving astral forces.

On Friday, Maeve saw Katrina and Willie standing on the sidewalk that ran along the west side of the building, involved in an intense conversation. At one point he took her face in his hands, as if to kiss her, but only pressed his forehead to hers. Were they having a fight? Or making up?

Paige did not call, and did not answer when Maeve called.

Every night her husband's snores went tut-*tut*, tut-*tut*, tut-*tut*. She fell asleep to their iambs through the waxen plugs in her ears.

She missed her old thoughts. She missed the story she'd told herself about two young people who feel most alive when they put themselves in a small space, mash their faces together, hold on to each other for dear life. There was an empty space and she wondered what would fill it.

8

ON MONDAY MORNING, Maeve drove Jack to the airport, kissed him a sweet goodbye, swore she wouldn't stew in her juices, and went to work. She was at her desk only twenty minutes, not even done with her coffee, when she got called into the office. Just like on the day of the accusation: "You're wanted in the office."

Maeve's heart beat faster. Her throat tightened.

She found Gloria sitting at her desk, frowning deeply, a funereal expression, somber but composed. She wore her amber necklace, whose largest middle bead she touched when she spoke. "What I have to say is deeply upsetting."

Maeve was laid off. Gloria did it. Gloria said it:

"We have to let you go. It breaks my heart. Our heart. The collective heart of the institution."

She crossed her arms over each other, gripped her own shoulders, as if to demonstrate the embrace she wished to give Maeve.

Maeve's face grew hot, tingled, flamed allergically.

"This is crazy," she heard herself say.

Her cheeks, her forehead, neck, as if she'd applied astringent toner.

"I know. I do. I'm so sorry, Maeve."

"Is it because of the accusation?"

"Of course not. Absolutely not. That was dropped."

"It's because of her, though."

"Why would you say that?"

"Everyone will think it."

Gloria reminded Maeve that no one knew about the accusation—she had told no one.

"You told Katrina."

"I most certainly did not! Why do you say that?"

She realized she had no idea if that was true.

"If Katrina knows, it's not from me. I promise you, Maeve."

The cat on her desk, the lucky cat, waved its paw.

Gloria sighed, promised that Maeve was only a casualty in the budget fight.

"But why not *Lois*? She always says she doesn't need the job, it's just to keep her from going senile. She herself says that. Don't I have seniority?"

"To be honest, Lois works for minimum wage."

"Oh. I didn't mean—I love Lois, it's only—"

"I get it. You don't need to explain."

"I *love* Lois."

"They felt their hands were tied."

"Who felt?"

"The board."

"All their hands?"

"You knew this was a possibility. All those meetings, Maeve. All the talk of layoffs . . ."

"I hadn't thought it would be me!"

She said it before she could think better of it. Her devotion to the place had bred denial. It was her now: Maeve. Maeve who was getting fired, who had been in denial. The shame of her denial. And then the woozy implication of any surprise: What else am I not seeing? What else have I failed to squarely apprehend?

As a means of reassurance, many figures were pulled out. The decision could be quantified. Seniority was a complex thing, went by educational grade—Katrina had an advanced degree. The board decided to cut Maeve's position entirely: there was going to be no cultural coordinator as such.

"As such?"

"The rest of us will share the burden," Gloria said gently.

"It was never a burden!"

"Oh Maeve."

Gloria tapped the tissue box toward her. Maeve was not crying but her armpits were wet. She had the strong urge but couldn't wipe her armpits in the office, had enough dignity to hold back. She smelled the synthetic lilac of her deodorant.

Is that all there is to it? Are you absolutely sure? but Gloria was biting the side of her mouth so that it contorted, became ugly, and Maeve's instinct told her to be quiet, to fear what might come out of that twisted mouth.

No use fighting. For a moment Maeve saw it all impersonally. Someone was going and it was her, this time. She had not thought it would ever be her and now it was.

Both women dabbed their eyes.

"How do you want to handle this, Maeve? Shall I call the staff together?"

"No," Maeve said. "Just let me leave quietly."

Katrina wasn't working today. Maeve realized she would never work with Katrina again. There were a handful of teenagers, slumped in the reading room. The girl was gone, not among them.

It was three o'clock in the afternoon. She returned to her desk to gather her things. Not many things. A photograph of Paige at her high school graduation, standing before her greenhouse in the giant red robe, her hair in a loose pile on her head, clasped by something meant to hold papers together. A papier-mâché bird Paige had made in third grade for the parade of animals, a robin with fragile yellow feet, which had perched for so long in the same spot on Maeve's desk that its feet had fused to the Formica. Only one foot came away when she lifted the bird. One yellow foot stayed behind. Dismemberment.

9

A FEW YEARS BEFORE, Maeve had read a haunting book of nonfiction called *The Adversary* about a Frenchman with a second life. He had been fired from his job but admitted this to no one, not a soul, not even his wife. For years he drove off in the morning as if going to work but instead sat in a park all day, or a restaurant—for years did this until he could no longer bear it and, seized by some culminating madness, murdered his wife and children in their sleep, and then himself.

Once you read a book like that, it's in you, like something the liver can't process. It comes back to you when you've lost your own job. It came back to Maeve, to her liver and everywhere else. She imagined those first few mornings when the fired Frenchman drove off, performing normalcy, valiant and deranged, filled with a kind of grief he is convinced cannot be expelled or made visible without admitting something terrible—without becoming something terrible. A truth about himself, like a cavity in a tooth, begins to ache, threatens to reveal itself. She considered trying this strategy for a day or two, saying she was going to work but just sitting in a diner all day. For a couple of days. Coffee and crullers like a normal person, and then coming home and saying to her husband—Oh it was a good day, oh fine, nothing special.

Maybe she would?

On that last day after being fired, she left the library by the back door. She searched her bag for her car keys, rummaging in her giant tote, her hand shaking, terribly afraid she'd left the keys on her desk—her former desk—and would have to go back—unbearable, she could not—but then she located the Volvo's clever key fob, flicked it open like a switchblade, held it hidden in the bag.

Raul was standing at the edge of the parking lot, in his orange beanie, breaking down cardboard for the recycling dumpster. "See ya, Ms. Cosgrove," he called, as always, and she wanted to cry, I'm out! I'm done! It's over! But she said, "Take care, Raul," and jammed her key into the ignition, waved once more, still in the disguise of her old self.

Of course she had to tell her husband and called him immediately upon returning home. He picked up the phone. He was in a shuttle moving from the airport to the hotel. She heard a recorded voice from a loudspeaker, the slamming of doors.

"I've been fired," she told him, and wept.

"What?"

"Fired!"

"One more time?"

She couldn't.

She was sitting on the living room couch, still in her jacket and scarf. She had tracked in mud. Mud on the glossy blond floor, on the Angela Adams rug with the thick blue circles. Like cyanobacteria, Paige had said when Maeve brought that rug home.

She saw the mud on her favorite rug and still didn't take her shoes off.

Suddenly it got quiet on the line. He was off the shuttle. He couldn't believe it.

"Oh honey. Oh my poor thing."

He felt helpless in Ohio. He wanted her to call someone: one of her friends. Call Katrina, honey!

It was humiliating, somehow, she could not. Katrina would call her, she told him.

He had to go. He was meeting Doug. There was a car waiting for him—he was watching it pull to the curb now . . .

"You're going to be just fine, Maeve. Just fine."

"I know."

"A change of course. It doesn't have to be a bad thing. I'll call you later. We'll talk it through. We'll make it work."

"Say hi to Doug for me."

She hung up. Stood in the middle of the living room. Her heart beat in her ears. Her armpits. In all the lymphy, protective places.

She could phone Deacon in New York City. Or Zoë, her old friend from Paige's elementary school days, whose own beloved daughter was attending the local community college. Or Paige herself, wisest of them all! But it was not sound to call your daughter in tears. She knew that. She knew how hard it had been on Deacon, to have had to wipe their mother's tears, to navigate her grief and madness.

Dread muted her. She felt perplexingly as if she were a character in a book or a play, someone whose life has been violently, grotesquely rearranged.

She cleaned the rug. She made faces in the mirror, did jumping jacks, squeezed two oranges. Like a movie montage, that frazzled lady longing to restore order—but she couldn't sustain it and collapsed on the couch with her pink hand weights at her feet.

She opened a bottle of wine. Drank a bit. Not too much.

Her mother used to say: "Nothing left to do but moan about it!"

The first few nights were hard. Her husband was gone. Temporarily gone, sure, but the monkey brain doesn't know he's on a business trip. The bed is empty, a plain and present fact, and she has been sacked from a job she deeply loved, accused of something awful. Her husband who holds her at night is gone. In Maeve's world, in the first world, this is pretty fucking rotten. In any world!

One night she couldn't sleep. Idiotically, laughing as she did it, with a weird earnest thrust of straightforward pain, she googled: things to do when you lose your dream job.

The internet told her it was time to determine her true destiny, that the Chinese symbol for crisis is the same for opportunity. People often tattooed it on their skin. It was recommended that she start exercising. That she connect with a therapist or life coach: these days you could hire one online, a real person, talk to them through the camera on the computer, easy as pie.

Sleek interface. Expensive as real therapy. Fantastic reviews:

My understanding of myself has blossomed.

I was codependent with Satan! Now I see myself as I truly am: precious and free.

I am truly a different person. I walk with confidence now.

People got happier and made more money, the site said; there was data, reviewed by a third party, to back up the claim. People got thinner and stronger. Funnier too—less data here, but video testimonials full of charm.

Libby, Libby.

On an impulse she ordered a steak burrito from Carmen's. Then grew nauseous thinking about it, regretted the order, called to cancel but the girl on the line said, "Lady, the driver's out. These things take a minute to make."

When the burrito arrived she ate a bite and dropped it into the trash can. Again she felt like an actress, someone on-screen, where people are always tossing perfectly good food. She remembered Jennifer Aniston on *Friends*, dumping a slice of blueberry pie, a protest against a man who injured her.

She drank a glass and a half of wine, getting buzzed enough to go online and try a therapy sample. She clicked a series of buttons and supplied a description, per the instructions, no more than ninety characters—*45-y.o. woman, Maine, married, librarian, one daughter age 19. Enjoys books, family.* She removed *librarian*. Then added it back, preceded by the word *former*, and then went back to the original and clicked submit. Then she took a so-called personality test—Coffee or Tea? Salt or Pepper? Baseball or Football? Cat or Dog?—and in the next moment there was a person on her computer screen, a face looking at her face, a real human, a Black woman, blinking and nodding and wearing red-rimmed glasses like the old talk show host Sally Jessy Rafael.

Face-to-face with Maeve, in the middle of the night, an actual woman with whom Maeve had been paired with on the basis of—well, something, surely. But how sophisticated could the algorithm be? Maeve had said practically nothing about herself. Or did the site see all her internet searches? Had she unwittingly checked some box that granted them full access? If so, the woman sitting before her could know a great deal.

Maybe she was forty. Fifty? Older or younger than Maeve? Hard to tell. Her hair was close-cropped. Her starchy white blouse called to mind a lab coat. Behind her: a screen on which a mountaintop was projected, snowcapped hills, a blue river woven into the earth like a child's stitching.

In the lower right corner was a little picture of herself, Maeve in her living room, and even in miniature she saw how ragged she was, her hair lank, eyes smudgy, her smelly robe torn at the shoulder.

Surely the life coach had seen worse, Maeve decided. And she couldn't smell the robe.

"I like your glasses," Maeve said.

The woman smiled. "Thank you."

The first hour was free. If she crept a moment over fifty-nine minutes and fifty-nine seconds, a charge would be sent to her credit card company. Faster than a blink.

"I'm not sure I can afford your services," Maeve said at the start. "I'll be up front with you. I just want to try, only an hour."

"Trying is good. But not afford? I suppose I wonder what we mean by 'afford.' I believe we must cultivate an abundance mentality."

"I've lost my job."

The coach nodded.

"I was fired," Maeve said. Her head was already throbbing—the hangover arriving before the pleasure of the drink wore off, before the detachment subsided, which didn't seem fair.

"Fired," the coach said. "I see. Go on."

"Laid off, technically. I didn't do anything wrong." She allowed herself some petulance.

"Better to ask: What did you do right?"

"Where are you?" Maeve said. "Can I ask?"

"I am with you."

"Geographically, I mean."

"I'm a person without a country." She offered a cool smile. "I am a blank screen."

"I see."

"I am here for you. I will tell you whatever you want, whenever you want, but I suggest you wait. Yes? This is my method. I am a person interested in your welfare. For this hour, only that. This is the policy, for the good of all involved. Does that sound right?"

It sounded right. Sure. Right enough. Why not?

The life coach had a series of questions. She would take a history, she said. For the baseline.

"Baseline?"

"I need to see the dimension of your universe."

Smaller by the minute, Maeve thought.

"Start at the beginning, yes?"

And so Maeve described her childhood in southern Maine. The house her mother inherited from her own mother, a tilted Cape off the main road in the gulley behind a low-rent strip mall. Her father who ran off with a dental hygienist after the mother got fat, after the baby weight—from her, from Maeve—did not fall away. The mother got bigger. Madder. The mother was a yeller, operatic. And the father, the coach asked, what was he like? Maeve barely remembered him. There was a brother. Deacon. Thank God. Five years older—he pulled her through. She spoke about them like characters in a book, the only way she could describe her life to a veritable stranger. The solid brother. The dear husband. The brilliant girl. Quickly, too, so the coach could give her assessment, so she would have time for the return of insight, but the coach kept slowing her down, asking her to restate things, peering deeply at the camera so that she did feel, Maeve couldn't deny, as though they were in the same room—just as the website had promised—at ease and unafraid to talk, though that might have been an effect of the wine, which she kept drinking, not hiding it. The life coach made no mention of the wine. Maeve kept talking. Because why not? She would get something back. Insight. Guidance. Why not? Why be so stingy with herself? What was she protecting?

At the end of the hour Maeve said, "Well, do you have any advice? I have to go soon, I'm afraid."

The clock said fifty-two.

The coach seemed surprised.

"Do you want advice, is that what you're looking for?"

She said she supposed she was, yes. The coach nodded. Closed her eyes, her forehead pinched, as if solving a calculation.

She's eating the clock, Maeve thought. Don't fall for it.

But then the coach opened her eyes. Such kind eyes. The cynical part of Maeve was supplanted by another part, a child part, stunned and submissive in the face of another person's complete attention. The coach said, "We need more time to see the full picture. I see that you are suffering. I recognize that you're in pain. I see that you've lived for others for a long time. You've traded service for protection, perhaps. You're deeply sad."

"I am?"

It had been fifty-five minutes.

"You might be carrying some sadness that is not really yours."

"Not mine?"

"Only a hunch."

Whose is it? But she didn't ask. Saw the clock and said: "I share my credit card with my husband. I can't talk more."

"You do not want him to know?"

"It's not the kind of thing we do."

"He will hit?"

"Oh no! Not like that."

"Does he care about your happiness?"

"Very much."

"He will think your happiness is not worth the expense?"

"He will think I am silly."

"Why is your happiness silly?"

"He will think I am—"

The word she would not say, was *sick*. Sick like her mother, or turning in that direction. Sick not for needing therapy but for seeking it online, not from a regular doctor but from a website. Her credit card would be charged a flat hourly rate. The rate was not insignificant. This had been explained to her at the start. Otherwise, there would be no record of their interaction, so she said, "I have to go. But thank you. I've enjoyed this."

The coach bowed solemnly, like a yoga teacher at the conclusion of class, and then the screen went black and Maeve was asked to rate her experience from one to five on the basis of likability/helpfulness/use of time. She gave the woman fives.

10

IT TOOK THREE DAYS for someone from the library to call her, to check in. *Three days.* Later on, after everything, when she finally tells her brother the whole story, he'll say, Of course you lost your mind. If I got fired and no one called for three days, I'd be homicidal too.

On Wednesday, finally, the phone rang. Dee Dee. She said how sorry she was. How different it would be without her.

"We hope you come visit."

"Visit?"

"You're always welcome."

"Of course I'm welcome," Maeve said. She heard the effort of restraining tears. "I can't imagine not using the library. I don't need to be told to visit."

"It's not personal," Dee said quickly. "That's what Gloria's telling everyone."

"She is?"

"And that the culture is crumbling. That it's out of her hands. Everyone knows it sucks. It totally sucks. You're so nice, Maeve, and so smart and competent and all, everyone's sure you'll land on your feet. But they feel really bad."

She didn't want "bad"—she wanted pissed, angry. Seething!

"I wonder if there'll be more layoffs."

"Gloria says no. She told us not to worry. It was very reassuring." She coughed, an awkward beat. "But listen, everyone misses you. They told me that. It's going to be so much harder without you."

Maeve hung up feeling worse. Also confused that she hadn't heard from Katrina yet. Why didn't she call to commiserate and reassure?

Maeve had the worrying sense that they'd elected Dee the representative, the one to handle the unpleasant task of checking in with Maeve—that she was calling on their behalf. *Everyone misses you. They told me that.*

It was unacceptable to be treated like that after fifteen years.

She resisted the impulse for two hours, then gave in and drove to the library. It took ten minutes to get there. She arrived half an hour before closing.

Dee Dee lifted a hand and said, "Oh good! Maeve!"

Dee said that Katrina was out sick. Third day in a row. Maeve felt a measure of relief at that. So she hadn't called to check in on Maeve because she was felled by something.

Again she found herself with Gloria in her office, the cat's paw metronoming. Gloria, in the cranberry corduroy dress she'd worn for so many years, gazed at Maeve. Maeve saw it was an error to come this late in the day—Gloria only wanted to get home, to finish the tasks that would permit her to leave. She made a tender face but her eyes no longer watered.

Still Maeve handled herself well. She said everything she meant to say. She said it didn't make sense, that the library was her "heart and soul"—those old words, tried and true—and she said that she could not help but feel that this inflammatory thing played some role in her dismissal—

"After all my years here, after giving so much to this place . . ."

Gloria said, "My hands are tied." Maeve heard the first flicker of irritation in her voice. "I wish it weren't so."

The room seemed to sway. They loved Maeve, of course, she was the quiet spirit of the place, and it was a mark of a decaying culture that our libraries are so hideously underfunded, challenged at every turn.

Then Gloria looked away. She had a hard time saying the full truth.

"What do you mean, 'the full truth'?"

Gloria said that indeed they had noticed some changes in

their devoted employee. She tried to say it. "You've seemed more . . . inward. That's all."

Inward?

"Look. I'll be frank. You really shouldn't let it upset you so much. I mean, no one accused me of something like that. But I think I'd try to let it roll off my back a bit. You know what I mean?"

Rage begins the way snow does. A change in the light. A melancholy dusting.

She swallowed. She thanked Gloria for her candor.

She put *inward* in a box and would not take it out for a long time.

And yes she went back the day after that—which she understood could be construed as overkill—but only to assert normalcy. She didn't want the last exchange with Gloria to be a pleading one, wanted for them to see exactly how much she could accept this. Her intention was not to beg but to reassure her colleagues that she intended to remain friends, that she wasn't bitter. But Katrina was not there that day either, and seeing the others, Maeve suddenly felt unsure what she was doing. She found herself saying, "I think I left a scarf here, a special one, one my daughter gave me," and made a great show of searching for it.

She left a message for Katrina on her voicemail. "You must be really sick. Poor thing. Let's catch up when you can? You've heard my bad news. It doesn't feel real! Please call when you can. But get well first, of course."

Possibly a part of her wants to see if the girl is back. Not that she would go to the girl. Not that she would speak to her.

Possibly there is some sense that the girl would go to Maeve, speak to Maeve.

These are not Maeve's thoughts—they are underneath her thoughts. Frogs in the mud.

It had boggled her mind, when Paige said that frogs live frozen in the mud all winter long. Paige found it funny that Maeve was surprised. Did her mother really think all the frogs died every winter? *All the frogs?* And yes, Maeve realized she had, and was embarrassed by her ignorance but also proud to have a daughter who was only seven and already alerting Maeve to aspects of the universe she had fundamentally misunderstood.

She had a terrible fear that she would go back to the library the next day too.

"Stop going there, Maeve," Jack said when she called him to say good night.

"I'll stop,"

"Have you told your brother? Why haven't you called him?"

"It's gross. I don't want to say it."

"Gross? You sound like a kid. Gross. Icky."

"It is!"

"I didn't mean that bathroom thing, anyway. I'm talking about being laid off. Tell Deacon you were laid off. It's no one's fault. It's not gross to be laid off. It's a part of life." Then he said: "Listen, I have an idea. I'm afraid I need to go to Florida again. Next week, after I'm done in Ohio." He gave a long, multitonal sigh. "Nothing too serious, but they want to go inside again. Branson's optimistic."

"Oh shit! Oh no, Jack. I'm sorry."

He explained the nature of this particular injury, a stumble on the lip of the patio, and the treatment plan. His sister needed his help, grew resentful if Jack didn't pull his weight. She had handled the last accident, only eight weeks ago.

"Kelly-Anne knows we have a Tampa office," Jack said. "She knows I can work from there. And she knows you can come, now that you don't have to go to work. The rehab place is twenty minutes from the condo. Florida would be nice, wouldn't it? You could fly down Saturday."

She said maybe. She said she was tired.

"I might insist you come."

"Insist?"

"Strongly suggest."

"*Insist*, he says."

"I didn't mean it."

"I knew a girl in college from Tampa. She called it Tampon."

He did his disapproving laugh, a chuckle that had quotation marks around it.

"Get a good night's sleep, Maeve. Maybe you'll feel differently in the morning."

The library pulled on her.

No wonder Jack is worried. Why is she acting like a jilted lover circling her beloved's house, watching for lights, for shadows?

11

MAEVE DREAMED THAT HER VAGINA fell out. Jesus! She woke up slick with sweat, queasy, the image of that organ on the floor beneath her feet—round and wet and coated with wiry hairs. She would have thought it was a dirty tomato except someone in the dreamworld, a girl's voice, was saying, "Oh shit. Your vagina just fell out."

These words stayed alive in her head when she woke. She clasped a hand over her crotch. A vagina like a stewed tomato. A girl's voice: Oh shit.

"Jack!" she cried out, but of course Jack was in Ohio. She picked up the phone to call him but stopped herself. She wouldn't tell him. It would be a mark against her, a dream like that. He'd insist she get on a plane. She sat up, took a few breaths.

Time to call her brother—she'd put it off long enough. He could be counted on to be awake. Deacon rose early to exercise before he slayed it on Wall Street—that's what he used to say when people asked what he did, "I slay it on Wall Street," cheekily, as if showing them the character he played at work. He stopped saying this but the slaying had not ceased, for he lived in a high-rise full of metal and glass, with a TV that rose from a special cabinet when you pushed a button, and an espresso machine fitted into the wall, and a view from the living room that was obscene. Awe and vertigo on the balcony, a trembling edge above the city—even looking at that balcony, even the curtain being open, induced cold dread. But Deacon stood out there every morning, shirtless no matter the season, and stretched his arms like an action hero.

Today he answered the phone like this: "Christ, Maeve. It's six in the morning."

"I woke you. I'm sorry!"

"No, no, I've been up for an hour."

"Then why did you say that? Like I woke you?"

"Are you crying?"

Her face was wet, she realized.

"I don't know. I had a bad dream." She feared he'd laugh. "Why'd you yell at me?"

"I'm sorry. Teddy and I had a fight." He moaned. "I'm in a sour mood."

If she had any will to tell him her bad news, it was gone now. His sour moods could last for days, and he could be sniping.

"Don't cry, Maeve. Honey. You're OK. Take a breath. You're safe. That's good, you're good."

Instead she told him about her dream, the tomato thing on the floor. He didn't laugh or make a joke about the mystery of vaginas, and she thanked him for that.

"Distract me, will you? I need to be distracted."

He took a long inhalation. "Well, I'm standing on my balcony. It's raining here. The sky is dark. Reddish. Did you hear about this storm? Al Roker's waxing rhapsodic. The light's weird—like dusk. Everyone's headlights are on. You OK, Bug?"

This, the oldest nickname, lowered her blood pressure.

"What did you and Teddy fight about?"

"Bathtubs," he sighed. "Also tulips."

"Those seem like nice things."

"Not when the tulips aren't tulips. He has a new shrink. A Jungian. She's diagnosed him with archetype deficiency disorder."

"Oh poor Teddy." Then she laughed. "It just felt so real, Deacon. Not a normal dream."

She heard his coffee grinder. When it stopped he said: "I have dreams all the time about my penis. Beheading. ISIS comes for it at night. Does that make you feel better?"

After they hung up she went to the window. Strange light here too, dusky, gauzy pink. Pink glass in Paige's greenhouse. Even the grass looked pink. The unreality of it lifted her spirits. She took a shower. Shampooed and blow-dried her hair. She did everything impeccably that morning: made the bed, breakfast, washed the dishes, called her mother-in-law, left a message on her voicemail, said she was sending love to her and love to her dear hip, and then prepared an order of flowers to arrive at her room in Tampa the next day.

.She felt calmer, clearer.

That's when it occurred to her, the next step. What to do. It was exactly right, perfectly simple, a way to assert normalcy, to reset, to peacefully declare a new standing: she would check out a book.

She called Jack. He didn't answer, so she left a message in an industrious voice about how much she had accomplished that morning, how much more like herself she felt. She told him she wanted to stay here this weekend, to really enjoy the solitude and read a novel before beginning a job search on Monday.

"I've turned a corner," she insisted to his voicemail. "And you know how much I hate it there. It's not personal, it's only Florida."

A rainy weekend tucked inside with a novel—what a lovely thing. She meant it too. Maybe one of books from the SHELF OF SHAME. Dee Dee's cheeky idea: the shelf of all the great books you feel you *should* have read. They had made a sign and found an open endcap near the research desk. It worked, too—those books began to fly. *Moby-Dick* and *Bleak House* and Faulkner and several long Russians novels. Women too, Dee Dee insisted, Sontag, Simone de Beauvoir, Woolf. Toni Morrison, of course. They added her after a patron asked about the whiteness. That patron had not been particularly polite, but the tension passed soon enough, for there were so many books to add, and no one, Dee Dee insisted, planned to police that shelf. Zora Neale Hurston. Ralph Ellison. Chester Himes. The shame got bigger all the time.

12

WELCOME ALL, SAID A SLAB of granite on the door. Redbrick face, crisp white trim on the windows. The flagstone path urged a straight, brisk march to the door, but Maeve took it slowly. The air smelled of mulch. Raul had recently turned the earth and it glimmered as if with tiny bits of glass, as if with diamonds. Then the wheeze of the automatic door, the bright musk of this and every library filled her nose.

The girl wasn't cross-legged in front of the ficus tree or in the New Release alcove, the two spots she favored.

Only a few teenagers in the Pen. No boy.

But there was Katrina, arms slung with magazines.

Oh Katrina. Dear Katrina, back after being sick, looking pale and tired but otherwise perfectly herself—plum lipstick, black eyeliner. Perfect face, holey tights. Maeve loved these competing signals, the punk rock indifference, curated just a little. Katrina! She almost called out her name. Her beautiful friend, her righteous comrade, practically family. Katrina saw Maeve, and for a moment—or was she imagining it?—Maeve saw concern on her face. Worry? But then the dimpled smile.

"Oh Maeve!" she cried, rising. "I was going to call you."

They embraced. That rose perfume oil, her unexpectedly antique scent. Katrina squeezed her, said, "Maeve, Maeve," and they clutched each other.

"I should have called," Katrina said when they stepped apart. "I'm really sorry I haven't called yet."

Maeve's throat felt knit together. She forgave her instantly, said, "I wasn't really ready for talking anyway."

Katrina had something to tell Maeve. She suggested they should go to the reading room off fiction, often empty this time of day. They walked there together. On posters throughout the building movie stars in unexpected spectacles held books and made beseeching faces: READ! Even in the library one had to scream about reading.

They sat in plush chairs in the empty room. On the north wall, where Maeve had hung her years ago, Marilyn Monroe in her striped bathing suit read *Ulysses*.

"First of all, I'm sorry," Katrina said. "I'm so, so sorry. It sucks. It fucking sucks."

Fucking sucks was good.

"I'm in shock," Katrina said, cupping her own face in her hands.

"Me too," said Maeve. "Oh my God."

"We all are."

"I'm trying to stay calm," Maeve said, swallowing. She felt shy. She wanted her friend's help. To mount a complaint. She didn't want to just accept it. "I'm using this as an opportunity to reassess . . ."

"You're smart, Maeve. We knew you'd take it well."

"I don't know how well I'm taking it. I want to fight it."

"Sure you do. It's bullshit."

"Right? It is!"

"The whole system. Our priorities as a society. It enrages me." Katrina paused, frowned. "Listen, Maeve. I have to tell you something. I think you deserve to know."

"To know what?"

Katrina looked around, confirmed they were alone. "It's like a cosmic joke, the timing. I want you to know before it goes public. No one knows yet. I'm glad to tell you in person."

"Oh no. Oh God. Is this about the girl?"

"Girl?" She frowned. "No, it's about Harrison Riddles."

Maeve gasped.

"It's good news." Katrina gripped the armrests and gritted her teeth, like a person on a ride at the fair. "He called. He's coming."

"*What?*"

"He wants to do the storytelling thing with the kids."

"He called?"

"On the phone. I know, Maeve. The irony is not lost on me."

Maeve did not know what to say.

Her brainchild. She had written the supplicatory letters.

"He asked to speak to you. A cosmic joke, I know. His actual words were, 'May I speak to Maeve Cosgrove, the coordinator of culture?'"

"He said that?"

"Right? I thought that was funny. I told him I was handling cultural events now. He was on his cell, on the road, coming through town as he spoke, and so we met for dinner that night. I would have called you—"

"You had *dinner* with him?"

Katrina swallowed, looked uncomfortable. "Just a quick burrito at El Rayo."

"Oh."

"His kids were asleep in the car. I would have invited you if I'd had a minute's notice. It was you who made it happen. I know that. Everyone will know."

"Oh," Maeve said again, feeling very stupid.

Katrina's eyes welled up.

Couldn't Katrina have at least invited her to get a burrito with them?

"They can't fire me now. We have to fight it! Do you think—is it possible—"

"I asked Gloria if it can be reversed."

"You did?"

"Of course I did! You should have heard me in her office when I found out. It sounds like her hands are tied."

"I want to make an appeal to the board."

Katrina sighed deeply. Then she said, "Everyone will know you're responsible for Harrison. We'll all know it, we will," as if this were enough, them knowing. "It won't be the same here. Everyone's really sad. We took you for granted, like everyone does with the best people. But you'll find something else. I'll help you find something else."

"You will?"

"It feels awful, but you'll find something great."

What had Maeve been trying to prove by showing up? She wished she were back home, felt banished from her own life, like a child kicked out of her own club. She looked at her lap. And by the time she could get her face in order, could fashion a response, the room was occupied, a woman nursing a baby under a scarf, a father and his young daughter setting up a game of chess.

She needed to change the subject or she would cry. She cleared her throat and said, "How's Willie?"

Katrina's indignation did not abate. "You want to know something? He got a *B* on his Ethnography of War paper. What do you think about that?"

Maeve didn't know what this was meant to draw from her. Paige would've flagellated herself, would rather sleep in the yard all winter than receive a mark below 98.6. "Body temperature at minimum"— that's what Paige used to say about grades.

"He survives a genocide and gets a *B* in the Ethnography of War? You don't see the irony?"

Maeve shook her head. "That does seem—putting it that way"— what could you call it?—"perverse."

"Perverse." Katrina whispered the word to herself, nodding. Then she lowered her eyes, took a breath, and brought her eyes back to Maeve. "He only has two more semesters. We're going to get married when he graduates. Don't tell anyone yet—you're the first to know."

"Married! Katrina! Oh how wonderful!"

Married! Married! Confetti in her eyes. So much had happened in just a few days! They embraced again.

Katrina looked at her watch. She had to go.

"Be in touch, Maeve. Stay strong."

Between Maeve and the door stood two teenage girls. They aimed their laser eyes in her direction. Neither girl was Libby, but they had something feral about them, sly, in Libby's ballpark. The girls whispered to each other. They were the same height. Both had bright blond hair and stubby ponytails. Both wore white jean jackets: one jacket was perfectly clean, the other full of safety pins and magic marker squiggles. The girl with the clean jacket had a face riddled with acne, and the one with the pin-covered jacket had an excellent complexion—their linked arms gave the impression they'd planned it that way, top to bottom. Creepy girls, Maeve thought, and held her breath when she passed them.

13

SIXTEEN MONTHS BEFORE, Maeve had written her first letter. A fan letter, though she wouldn't use that term, and began with an announcement to that effect: she would not call herself a fan, resented its sporty affiliations—she was only an appreciative reader and, as a librarian, a custodian of his books. Her handwriting had not lost its loveliness, though it got quirkier through the years, took some shortcuts. She used her mother's pen. If she wrote a serious letter, he'd write back. If *she* were serious—is what she told herself—a person whose mind should be taken seriously, whose ideas deserved underlining—then a return letter would appear in her mailbox.

Riddles wrote sprawling books of social realism that tended to win big awards. Warmer than Roth, cooler than Irving, easier than Pynchon. All the librarians admired his work. Since he had a summer house in Maine, he was considered a "local" and a shelf near the entrance was devoted to his volumes, though he'd never visited the library. Barely fifty and already he had four best-selling novels under his belt, and a memoir that became an off-Broadway play. He looked like an actor too, had a face that retained its integrity when blown up. In the movie version of his first novel, starring John Cusack, he'd had a cameo as a carnie who gets beat up. He had recently written and illustrated his first children's book, *The Story of Moi*, about a boy from working-class New Jersey who learns to embrace his Francophile pretensions, inspired by his brother who died young. It was the children's book that had given Maeve the idea for the kids' program. Why not give the children the most exciting visitors? She wanted kids to feel important, wanted them to write about their lives to be inspired by a great storyteller to put their own words on paper, whether they came from down the street or across the world. She had suggested a title: The Journey Project.

He didn't reply. She realized he was inundated; any kind of serious letter could be missed. She wrote another one after that. Another and another. Four total. In one she talked about what his fiction meant to her, hoping she didn't sound obsequious. You are a humanist, it seems to me. One of the last humanists. Beyond borders, geography, language. He made the world available to her, and—she tried to explain—he renewed her compassion for the dispossessed. Her favorite was *The School for Seeing,* in which a young girl from an unnamed Islamic country overcomes a hundred degradations to create a school for lost children. A touchstone novel, Maeve returned to it again and again. She loved Aina, its plucky protagonist, too much to say. She simply did not have enough ink in her pen.

Were her letters serious? They were at least abundant in detail, each several pages, her script assuming a fatigued, rightward slant toward the end. In the third letter she tried to show him the kids she hoped he'd meet for the storytelling project. Right here in Maine, kids from all over the world! She recalled their stories, things she'd overheard . . . an Iraqi boy who'd lived in a motel room with his family of seven, a Somalian girl born in a refugee camp who won the spelling bee, all the little girls over the years in their bedazzled hijabs. She thought he'd appreciate that phrase, *bedazzled hijabs.* She worked as much charm as she could into her prose. She actually thought about it that way—*prose,* a word she hadn't used since college. She wrote about Willie, the big blue coat he'd been given when he arrived, but of course hadn't used the children's names, nothing actually identifiable. She wrote about other kids too, but she knew the New Mainers were the most interesting, their stories the most dramatic, and she had wanted Harrison to like her letters. For the children's sake, of course, so that he'd visit, but also for her own. She wanted to move the man who moves everybody. And had she? He called the library! He asked for her!

———

She began to write another letter in her head. Dear Mr. Riddles: I write with the bad news that I've been SACKED. I am the one who invented the program. And by a stroke of magic you agreed to come! An honor of my life! Now my position has been cut. I feel heartsick, sideswiped, hoodwinked, sucker-punched. Fifteen years at the library. So much of our programming I am responsible for. I am simply filling you in, since you know how deeply I care about this place. I'm not asking you to do anything except to be aware that the person who wrote you all those letters doggedly seeking your presence, who has been sustained by your words—well, she won't be there. *I* won't be there. Part of me, out of pain, wishes you wouldn't come at all, I am so aggrieved. I can admit that. But you must come, for the kids, who will be so happy.

She spoke this letter to herself for several days. Eventually she wrote it down, more or less. She wrote: *The board's hands were tied. All those hands, tied up. I keep picturing that!*

She used a paper clip to hold the pages. She put the letter in an envelope and, furious and exhilarated, mailed it to his P.O. box in New York City. She remembered something an older girl told her in grade school: if you receive a letter with an upside-down stamp, it means whoever sent it is in love with you. The stamp Maeve used was an American flag—generic, Forever. She'd considered putting it on upside down. No. That would be too much. But she'd needed to alert him, to send some kind of signal, so she placed it sideways, at a tilt, a shiver running through her.

14

WHEN THEY WERE CHILDREN, Deacon tried to teach Maeve not to be afraid of the horror movies on channel 9, to delight in their kitschy glory, but her fear grew worse the longer she watched. Eight, nine years old. Saturday nights when their mother thought she was asleep Maeve would slip down to the basement, sit close to him on the couch under their dead grandmother's afghan. Deacon talked her through them, predicted plot points, which she appreciated but which did not make her less afraid.

It was somewhere in this period of horror movies—before their mother confiscated the antenna—that Maeve, walking alone, ran into her Uncle Cedric on the way home from school. Cedric was so bedraggled and skinny, she didn't recognize him at first. He lived in California as far as they knew, came rarely. They had not been expecting him. She was a mile from home, had taken the long way to avoid other kids, when a maroon sedan slowed down next to her.

"How you doing, sweetie? You want a ride?"

She kept walking, her head down.

"Hello? You even going to say hello? Let me give you a lift. I know where you're going."

His laugh had a crackle in it, like someone recovering from laryngitis. Sweat stuck her shirt to her back. She felt her heart. She felt the key on a lanyard inside her shirt. She did not look at the driver. She would not.

"Maeve! It's me."

She stopped walking. The car stopped rolling.

"Your Uncle Cedric. Hey!"

Oh! It was.

"You're so skinny, Uncle Cedric!"

"I'm coming off the flu."

"Where's your van? I didn't know you were in Maine."

His hair was grayer, buzzed close. A crumble of blood at the corner of his lip. Blood! He smiled. "Only here for a day. The van's in a junkyard outside Bakersfield. God bless her. This is my friend's car. How you doing, sweetie? You got taller. How are you?"

"I'm good."

A smell was coming from the car, not good. Smoke, sweat, BO.

"You know what? I'm happy you ignored me for so long. Don't trust men in cars as a rule. But I'm me. Do me a favor? Don't tell Molly you saw me. I'm here on business she won't approve of."

"What business? What do you mean?"

"You sound just like her, how you said that."

Uncle Cedric had taught her gin rummy and let her ride on his shoulders when she'd been tiny. He didn't visit them a lot, but when he did things were better. Molly yelled less; Deacon rode his bike. Cedric brought bananas and made sure Maeve's shoes weren't too small.

"I had the flu. I'm slowly putting the pounds back on." His face got serious, emphasizing its skeletal quality. "Things OK at home?"

She said that they were.

He said, "Can I buy you an ice cream cone?"

"I have to go. I'm meeting my friend."

"Who's that?"

She made up a name: Nancy.

"Nancy, huh? How's your brother?"

"He's getting all A's."

"A warrior, that Deacon. Hang in there, alright honey? I'll come back soon and buy you a cone."

"OK."

"Two cones. You and your brother," he said. "Troopers."

That was all. He drove off. She didn't tell anyone, not even Deacon. She was spooked by how skinny he was. It was embarrassing to her that people could change so drastically, that her family members seemed so prone to this.

A year or so later Cedric returned. He came to the house restored, jovial, twenty pounds heavier, and gave her a painted coconut shell from a recent trip to Puerto Rico. Now he drove a gold sedan with a bumper sticker for a failed Democrat. He'd gone on a bender, he explained to them, but he'd been in rehab. And rehab *took root*. His hair was longer. He'd even quit smoking. It had been six months. He said he was hopeful—now he had pride to combat the cravings. He gave Molly a bundle of cash and said he would be sending more. He never mentioned the day he'd seen Maeve walking home. She was relieved he didn't bring it up. He brought them bananas and new shoes and frozen meat and several gallons of ice cream. He stayed three days, then drove off again and—well, that was it for her Uncle Cedric. A few months later he died in a car crash, in Nevada, where it turned out he'd invested all his money in soft-core videos. Spankings.

They were a little off, her people. All Maeve had was Deacon. Thank God for Deacon!

The horror movies kept her close to him, even if she got nightmares. Maeve couldn't remember if she dreamed certain things or saw them in the movies or just made them up. The closeness was worth bad dreams. Maeve found that the famous, archetypical monsters weren't as bad as ordinary people who had some deranged part or secret side, like the doctor who opened his lab coat to reveal a second mouth, salivating, between his nipples, or the regular mom with the eyeball drill in her purse. One night their mother heard Maeve screaming and rushed down with a knife, her face slick with Vaseline, prepared to meet an intruder. Her rage, her clicking jaw, the face in the TV light, gluey as a burn victim's—

the siblings agreed Molly was more terrifying than anything in any movie.

"Deacon, for shame. Showing this filth to your sister. She's only eight! What do you want her to become? You want to give her a complex?"

"I'm nine," Maeve said.

Molly yanked the antenna off the TV. This was before cable. The screen went to slush. She locked the antenna in her safe with their birth certificates. Her wedding ring was in there too, and the opal necklace their father had given her before he took off with his dental hygienist, Lucinda. She didn't give the antenna back.

Don't you think you're overreacting, Mom?

Such a question could lead to another flare, wasn't worth it.

It's just as well, Maeve told her brother. She admitted she'd been getting bad dreams.

Without the antenna, they turned to books. Deacon read about getting rich, visionaries of industry. Maeve discovered V. C. Andrews, delicious Gothic horror novels whose protagonists are abused but don't turn out borderline.

Cedric's death underscored how alone they were. All through her childhood Maeve worried what would happen when Deacon left for college. The anticipation turned out much worse than the reality, because by then Molly couldn't do the stairs on account of her back, had no choice but to leave Maeve alone in the basement to read books. High school was easier than she expected. Her grades improved. She worked after school in the storeroom of the Snip 'n Save, in the quiet background. Deacon called every night from his dorm at Columbia, to keep their mother calm, to make sure she was taking her medicine. Even from New York City, he was looking out for them, protecting Maeve.

Why hadn't Maeve told Deacon about the accusation or losing her job? She didn't want his disappointment or pity, or to be another crazy person in the family. A lie of omission. She thought of the Frenchman who went mad in *The Adversary*. How long was it safe to keep a thing inside?

One more night. In the morning she'd call. Tell him what happened no matter what mood she found him in, tell him everything. He'd be angry if she kept it from him, and rightly so. And so when the phone rang right at seven the next morning she felt a weird alignment, as though she'd sent a signal and he'd received it, out there on his balcony. She woke immediately, lunged for the phone, ready to spill everything—Oh Deacon, you won't believe it—

But it was Katrina. The screen said: Katrina.

Katrina!

Her friend who would not abandon her, like a daughter.

"I need to see you," Katrina said, out of breath, as though she'd stopped jogging only a moment before. "There are things I couldn't say at the library. Can you meet me? This morning? At the Grind House?"

15

EIGHT A.M., BUT THE STRANGE pink light retained the mood of night.

A couple of seagulls picked at a croissant on the sidewalk in front of the café. In the eighties this building had housed a nightclub. The café remained matte black in homage, decorated with faded band posters. One whole wall was covered with ticket stubs, one atop another, resembling a lizard's scales.

Katrina hadn't arrived yet. A willowy barista swept the floor. "Hiya," sang the barista. She wore big ugly glasses and ugly acid-washed jeans, but a beautiful old-fashioned blouse, with lace trim and pearl buttons.

"I like your shirt," Maeve said, and the girl said, "Two bucks, Goodwill." Maeve gave a thumbs-up.

She felt she was getting more attentive to style. She bought a small coffee and a giant blueberry muffin to share with Katrina, and then chose the most private table, near the plate-glass window. A potted plant provided a barrier between the next table, where a man with soup-can headphones beat on a laptop. They could talk in peace here.

She was revved up even before her coffee. Katrina would not let this injustice stand. Possibly they'd mount a petition. File a law-suit? The phrase *hatch a plan* sprang to mind. Surely they'd write letters. Surely—the thought arrived with righteous clarity—they'd ask Harrison Riddles to do something. Maeve had been the one to get him there. You don't lay off a person capable of such a coup. And, really, who axes the *cultural coordinator* in this day and age? A letter began to form in her head. A general repairing of the world was underway, they could say, a long march to justice that the Obama presidency showed was working, really gaining steam. Wasn't a library's cultural coordinator a part of that? On a local level? This was one approach they could take. Opportunities opening up, a new world coming online, the library a nexus of sharing and assimilation . . . shouldn't it be a political disaster to terminate her position?

Katrina's dinged-up hatchback came into view. Maeve watched as she expertly parallel parked at the far end of the block. To her surprise, Willie got out too. They walked toward the café hand in hand, even in the drizzle taking their time. Katrina wore a short black jersey dress and black leggings and pink ballet flats, Willie jeans and a T-shirt that said HOPSCOTCH DELUXE. That was a band they liked, Maeve remembered. Sometimes he and Katrina traveled to Boston to see them play.

He wanted to help too, she realized. Of course. A New Mainer speaking on behalf of the cultural coordinator.

They waved at her when they entered, then looked at the bakery case and counted bills but only bought coffee. At last they settled across from her, close together. Behind them through the plate glass the sky morphed from pink to green, and Maeve grew nervous, as if at a job interview, the irony of which pierced her, and she said, "Can you believe this?" not sure whether she meant the layoff or Riddles, meaning both.

Katrina thought she meant the weather. "It's supposed to rain, like, forever," she sighed.

Willie bobbed his head. "We need it. The ground does."

A barista shouted, "Double mocha skim no whip!"

Maeve pushed the muffin in its saucer across the table. They'd been waiting for an invitation—both lunged for it, broke off big pieces.

Katrina said, "You going to be OK, Maeve, with all this rain? I know you get blue. If you want to come over, play some Monopoly. We're always around."

Maeve had never been to their home. She'd love that, she told them.

"Or Clue?" Willie said, chewing. "That's my preference."

"We just got Clue. He's completely obsessed."

"Obsessed," he agreed. "I've been playing Clue in my dreams."

Maeve felt strange.

"My vagina fell out in my dreams."

She startled herself a bit. It wasn't like her, but somehow the moment called for openness. Katrina laughed, then Willie joined in.

"*Can* it fall out?" Willie asked. "Is that possible?"

"No, Willie!" Katrina slapped his arm playfully.

Maeve's face grew warm. "It was a weird dream. I don't know why I said that. Everything's a degree or two off."

"Once I dreamed that I found a windup crank on my butt, like on a music box," Katrina told them. "And I thought, *That's* why I'm so tired. I've been forgetting to wind myself."

They all laughed though the knobs in Maeve's shoulders tightened.

Finally Katrina said, "Listen, Maeve. There's more than what I told you at the library. About Riddles. Willie, do you want to explain?"

They both looked at him. Willie brushed the back of his hand across his mouth. He took a breath and said it plainly, came right out with it: "Harrison Riddles is going to write a novel about me."

Maeve didn't hear right.

Katrina said, "He wants to use Willie as the basis for a book."

"Me-but-not-me."

"He thinks Willie's story is amazing and staggering and heartbreaking, all that. Which it is. And he wants to write a book. A book all about Willie, his story."

"A book?" It was all Maeve could say, so she said it again.

"A novel," Willie clarified.

"Based on Willie."

"At first I thought he was wrong," Willie said. "Mistaken. I am one of so many, I told him. He has no idea how many. It felt outrageous that he'd want me, of so many."

"But only one Willie. Harrison thinks it needs to be told. And I agree. And so does Willie."

"You do?"

"I do," Willie said, firmly. "I'm ready to tell it."

Maeve, bewildered, said, "You mean about Sudan?"

He nodded. "Also the places along the way. Maine too."

Katrina said, "It's all they've been talking about for the last week. They've been spending time together."

"We went hiking," Willie said, smiling slightly.

"Three times."

"Twice," he corrected. Then, matter-of-factly: "Two hikes and a walk on the beach. We have been talking."

"They took us out to dinner last week," Katrina said. "Harrison and his wife. Theodora. *Dora*. They took us to Asagios, Maeve. They swore me to secrecy. Oh, look at your face. You look so confused. I couldn't talk about it in the library . . . *no one* can know, not yet. I wasn't actually sick! I'm sorry, I am. I've been dying to tell you."

Asagios was the nicest place in town. The wallpaper was purple velvet. The cheese plate cost more than Maeve's shoes—that was something Maeve and Jack liked to say.

"My story is a common story," Willie said. "So many like me all over the world. Why me? I asked Harry."

"Harry?"

"This surprises you?" Now a hint of slyness, a shy smile. "It's a surprise, that I could have a friendship with him?"

"No! Well—of course not. It's just—"

"You have to remember, Harry was her white whale," Katrina said gently. "She's been trying to get him to come forever. And now you two are, like, best buds."

The café was filling up, the bell on the door jangling. The barista shouted, "Morning Glory! Toasted!"

"That's right," Maeve said. "I'm surprised. I'm stunned! And happy!" Her heart raced. She felt but resisted the impulse to put her hand over Willie's.

The espresso machine roared. When it stopped, Willie said, "Anyway I said to Harry, why my life? I got a *B* on my Ethnography of War paper. I'm one of many many many. And you know what he said?"

She shook her head.

"He said, I like you. You're not just a story. You're a person. I like some people and don't like other people. I don't automatically like someone just because they survived a war. Just because they're a victim of genocide. I don't think all victims are heroes, as the media says."

Maeve felt herself nodding, dumb with astonishment.

Katrina added, "It was weirdly beautiful."

"No one talks to me like that."

"They don't?"

"Certain people are nice to me because of what happened. By many I am liked. It's automatic. They want to be, you know, politically correct."

"They want to touch his hair sometimes," Katrina said.

Willie's face was calm, his voice smooth, bemused: "People here ask about my tribe. People say, 'You need to use sunscreen?' Harry likes me. But he promised if he didn't he'd tell me. I respect that. I like his directness."

Harry, they were calling him! And Willie so voluble! He'd always been a quiet, thoughtful presence on the periphery. Maeve liked him, she did. Wouldn't, of course, have said if she didn't, but even after he and Katrina got together he didn't say much, not to Maeve. She didn't know him very well. Then it occurred to her that *she* had produced a portrait of Willie for Harrison Riddles. She had described him in the big coat. Did Willie know that? Had Harrison read her letters?

"How exactly did this happen?" Maeve asked. Katrina revealed that she'd brought Willie with her, out for the burrito, that day Harrison called the library and asked for Maeve.

"It was like we all already knew each other," Katrina said, sighing happily.

Why didn't you invite me? You brought Willie but not me?

She didn't have to ask. Katrina, sensing it, put her hand on top of Maeve's. "If we had known that evening would be so fortuitous, I would have called you. I said to Harry, at the end of the night, 'It's really rotten that Maeve Cosgrove's not here.' I thought—well, that it might be salt in a wound, to invite you to come."

"Did you tell him I lost my job?"

Katrina nodded, looking pained.

After one dinner, one burrito, Harrison knew he wanted Willie to be the subject of a *book*?

No, she couldn't say that without sounding incredulous.

"People will judge me," Willie said. "Eddie will say I'm giving some white man my life. But I believe it's a reasonable decision." He looked at Katrina. "No one would question a movie. If Spielberg said, Hey Willie, let me do a biopic about you, and I will interview you, and an actor will play you, and the publicity will help your people—no one would fault me then. Is a book any different?"

They were picking up another conversation, Maeve saw. Katrina said, archly, mysteriously, "Power concedes nothing." She stroked his arm. "And *yes* they will fault you if you sold out to Spielberg! Are you kidding? You will be faulted for everything. No matter the choice. No matter the outcome. Aren't you always saying that? That you'll never make Eddie happy? Someone is always pissed off about something."

Maeve felt dizzy with information, missing information. Who was Eddie? she wanted to know. His old friend from Sudan, Willie said. He lived in Atlanta. But he wasn't telling Eddie or anyone else yet. Not yet.

"Only Maeve. Only you, Maeve."

"Only me?"

"People will love this book," Katrina said. "They love anything Harry does, and this is *Willie*, amazing Willie, our Willie, in his hands. This is gold. The publisher's in heat, evidently. We have to prepare for it."

Maeve could hold back no longer. "I'm the one who invited him. And now I'm fired. It's bullshit."

"It's bullshit." Katrina didn't miss a beat. "Totally unjust."

Willie knocked the table. "I like hearing you swear, Maeve."

"I want to fight back," she told them.

"Fuck the board," Katrina said.

Willie said, "You were the heart of the place, that's for sure." He took a deep breath. He wore a studious expression now, the look of a young person wanting something from an older one. She thought he was going to talk about fighting back for Maeve, but he said, "I am not a child. I am old enough to know how an operator works. I've had experiences. I want to trust Harry and I think I can. But it's happening quickly. I would like another set of eyes. I would like you to have dinner with us. Tomorrow. With Harry and his wife and us. At his house up the coast. Would you come?"

"I'll drive," Katrina said. "It's not too far."

"You want my eyes? On Harrison Riddles?"

"*We* do," Katrina said. "Me too."

Willie said, "You can tell us about the injustice at the library."

"I never said 'injustice' . . ."

"I said it," Katrina said. "And I stand by it."

"We can talk it all through later," Willie said. "I really want you there, Maeve. Harry does too. He liked your letters a lot. He wanted me to tell you that."

Something happened to her eyes, or to the room, as if the brightness had been adjusted.

Maeve? Did she hear what he said?

The coffee grinder again, roaring.

"Of course I'll come."

"Oh good." He seemed genuinely relieved.

"I knew she'd say yes. We can count on Maeve."

He added, "And don't worry, Maeve. I'm not asking you to be my mother. Just another set of eyes."

16

SHE CALLED HER BROTHER. He didn't answer either but called back five minutes later—"How's the vagina?"—and she told him breathlessly about the meeting at the café. Had to tell him.

"Holy Christ. Riddles!" She explained the circumstances, the book about Willie, but Deacon only said, "You think he still has that beard? On *Charlie Rose* he had a great beard."

"Promise you won't tell anyone."

"Take photos. The food, place mats, utensils."

"Oh God, can you imagine? Snapping pictures of my dinner plate? The humiliation."

"Find a way to use the bathroom where he keeps his deodorant. His Viagra and sleeping pills. His antidepressants. I want to know."

"I'm not snooping around his medicine cabinet."

"He's been on *Oprah*. He must expect it."

He'd sat on Oprah's famous yellow couch with his legs over-spread. She remembered that Katrina had forwarded her an article on Jezebel called "The Very Big Testicles of Harrison Riddles." The writer had used this one image, Harrison on the yellow couch—"thighs a proud V"—as a springboard for a larger discussion of over-spreading from a woman's point of view. Did it mean men had big testicles? Or wanted you to think so? Was it overcompensation or aggression or bodily necessity or what? She remembered feeling embarrassed for him, whose books moved her, who didn't deserve this pelvic scrutiny.

"I'm not photographing his prescriptions."

"I loved him in *Elephantine*." Deacon meant the cameo in the movie version of his first novel. It took place at an amusement park in Arizona, before his settings got global. "Will his wife be there?"

"Yes, Dora will be there." She felt powerful saying the nickname.

"In *People* she looked sort of plain."

"You're making me nervous. They're just people."

"Will you bring him a copy of *The Palest Winter* to sign? Please? To Teddy? He loves that book."

"I don't want to seem like a—" She shivered. "A *fan*. I want to come across as a professional. Not some sycophant begging for autographs."

"Small-town librarian kneeling at the hem of the literary king?"

She didn't like how readily he came up with that, for it was exactly what she feared. Was it so visible, or only that Deacon knew her so well?

She said, "Of course I'll have him sign the book," knowing she'd apologize for forgetting after the fact. She'd take secret photos to make up for it.

OK, Maeve, she told herself. Out with it.

"Listen, Deacon, I have to tell you something. I'm *not* a small-town librarian anymore. I got laid off."

She filled him in, budget cuts. Not the accusation, not Libby: she couldn't.

"Maeve! Poor Bug! Wait—why didn't you tell me? What the hell?"

"I'm sorry! You were in a sour mood. I didn't want to burden you with bad news."

"No, no," he said, "*I'm* sorry. I am. Fuck. I know what the library means to you."

She sighed.

"I think they're going to get married," Maeve said. "Willie and Katrina."

"I bet she's begging for a ring."

"Don't be such a cynic. They've been happy for a long time."

"No better way to ruin it than get married. Except for you and Jack of course. Nothing could bring you two down."

"Nothing," she repeated.

"There are other libraries, Maeve."

"Yeah," she said, but *no no no* went her heart.

"Listen, I have to go. Teddy and I are having lunch. We have to deal with his archetype deficiency disorder."

"What *is* that?"

"Hell if I know. We're going to eat oysters and talk about it."

"You know what? I love Teddy. Tell him I said so, will you? I know he's New Agey . . . and I know the bathtub thing. But he's—he's a wonderful person. I love him."

"I do too," said Deacon, sounding defeated. "I'm going to ask him to marry me."

"Marry! Oh! But . . . oh!"

Marry marry marry!

"Don't get your panties in a bunch, Maeve. Don't drop your vagina. I might break up with him or I might marry him. One or the other."

"Let's never talk about my vagina again."

"You brought it up," he said. "Listen, I gotta go. I want to see pictures, OK? Don't pretend to be shy."

It was unfortunate that she'd put that last letter in the mail. She regretted it, feared her complaint was petulant, self-righteous, needy. A transparent jab at the board. The coy suggestion—batted away but stated in any case—that Harrison Riddles decline the invitation as a protest against her firing . . . The letter was bitter, unbecoming. But what could she do? The blue mailbox only works one way—certain things can't be rescinded or retracted, try as we might. Anyway, she'd sent it where she sent all of them, to the P.O. box in New York City, and Riddles was here, in Maine.

As for Jack, she was not going to tell him until afterward. Jack would make her feel like a hanger-on. Jack would think Katrina felt sorry for Maeve, that the dinner invitation was conciliatory. He'd be mildly enthusiastic, sympathetic, but then he'd make a comment

about how it was time to move on. He would sniff it out in a heart-
beat: her hope that Riddles would pull some strings, help get her
reinstated to her post. She wanted it to happen before she told Jack.
She wanted to announce it, to see his shock, to see how wrong he'd
been in encouraging her to let it go.

"Would *you* accept it?" she'd asked him on the phone the night
before. "If you were fired for some bullshit reason, some totally fabricated reason, from the job you've worked all your life?"

"No," he admitted. "But a budget cut isn't fabricated."

"You know what I mean."

"Correlation isn't causation, honey. That girl. The budget cuts.
Two different things. I highly doubt there's a legal case."

If she told him about the invitation to dinner, he would be cheer-
fully suspicious. She knew the edge of worry he would not be able to
disguise. Nor his suspicion that this new turn of events would strand
her more deeply in a depression ("obsession," he called it once, and
she was not sure she could forgive him for this). Preemptively imagining his response, that combination of false cheer and genuine
warmth, she hated Jack, her meteorologist-souled husband, this
Mainer, this bumpkin with his calculator who was so smug about
human behavior, so certain he knew best.

"What should I move on *to*?"

"The job listings? That résumé workshop? I'm only being practical."

Boo hiss! She felt a desperate adolescent anger. You don't own me!
A tantrum, an old spasm of sovereignty; she even hung up the phone.

17

ONCE UPON A TIME you could live here without writing best-selling books or slaying it on Wall Street, but those days were no more. The earth rose and fell in gentle slopes, woods opened to a spectral meadow. The air was sweetly briny, pleasantly dense. The plushness of the moss, the mushroomy dampness, skittering insects, all gave the impression of stepping into something, the outdoors as a room waiting to be occupied. Between two glossy hedges was a slippery, winding path to the sea, the start of the sea, a corridor—a bay edged with rocks, the water in the distance dotted with islands.

At the end of the path, before the earth dropped to the sea, sat a house. This is where the Riddles family spent six weeks of their summers. More if they could. A sprawling structure, cedar-shingled, each room creakier and more wonderful than the next. For Maeve it was like walking into a store where you want to buy everything. You'd buy the air if they sold it in bottles. Yes, your body cries. I want to live with *these things*. Earthenware pottery, textiles from India, children's drawings matted and framed like modernist tri-umphs. There were side tables piled with magazines, a big basket full of yarn, faded kilim rugs scattered on wide, pumpkin-colored floorboards, records upon records on blond wooden shelves. She saw chunky wool sweaters tossed over the backs of mid-century chairs the way they are in catalogs, and on the simple mantelpiece—a Quaker mantel—a Freud action figure and a series of jagged sculp-tural animals in shining silver, and a trophy that turned out to be a Vietnamese humanitarian award.

Books, of course, everywhere, in every conceivable storage nook. The coffee table was a piece of wood, gnarled and polished, set atop neat stacks of his own foreign editions. Hooks for coats on the walls. A muddy mudroom. A woodstove, candles, a stick of incense burning, an air of camping.

She never wanted to leave; the moment she entered she could not bear to ever go.

A gin and tonic in a cold tumbler—a floating slice of cucumber—pressed into her hand. The wife put it there. The wife wore navy Keds. You had to start at her feet.

"I'm Dora," the wife said.

Navy Keds. Bare ankles. Loose, sexy jeans. An embroidered leather belt that looked Navajo. A white T-shirt, cropped to reveal a sliver of white belly, the fabric at its neck stretched out, misshapen, so you could imagine the hands that stretched it, the kids who owned her and tugged her.

"Maeve Cosgrove," said Maeve.

"Great point about the perversity," Dora said, her voice husky.

"Excuse me?"

"Willie's '*B*'!"

Willie! She had forgotten about him. They'd driven here together—Maeve and Katrina and Willie in Katrina's tiny hatchback shuddering in the wind on the highway, alarming Maeve, who clutched her armrest in the backseat—but she had already forgotten about them.

"Oh yes," said Maeve.

She took a sip of her drink. It was wonderful. Cucumber. Ice.

Dora was plain, just as Deacon had said, but what you couldn't tell from the *People* photograph was how beautiful her plainness was, how simple, painterly. And now came Harrison Riddles. He wore a faded plaid shirt with sleeves rolled to the elbows and wrinkled khakis. Neon green flip-flops like a teenage lifeguard's. His teeth were a bit gray. Age looked good on him. He was newly, delicately craggy. She fell in love. The totality, both of them, Harrison and Dora.

"Maeve Cosgrove! How excellent to meet you at last."

Harrison hugged her. He smelled like a more intense version of the house. He was large, bigger than Jack, more solid.

"So serendipitous, right? I mean, man! Your letters. I loved your letters, Maeve. I'm glad we finally made this happen. Can you believe this?"

At last. Finally. Love.

"I'm glad you read them."

"Your passion for the library is palpable. You brought me there."

She thanked him, blushed, her heart swelling.

"And now—well, Katrina told us." He shook his head. "I'm sorry to hear about layoffs."

"Just one layoff," she said, her voice small.

Dora gazed at Maeve meaningfully, took her hand. "You're heartbroken," Dora said, "I can see that. Of course you are. Harry said you wrote so beautifully about the library."

If Maeve had known she would be here now, no, she would *not* have sent him that last, petulant letter. But she didn't care anymore. It was on its way to New York. She would make up for it with graciousness, humility—

Then Dora hugged her too. Dora's hair smelled sweet, like vanilla, like a child's hair just washed. She was smaller than Maeve, but not much smaller.

"Your home is so beautiful," Maeve told them. She admired a painting of a girl with blond hair. She admired a giant glass vase, waist-high, full of paper cranes, which sat on the floor beneath the painting. Imogen folded all those cranes, Dora explained, and the painting was an Alice Neel, one of their favorite artists of the whole last century.

Harrison said, "We let ourselves be messy here. In New York we live like monks."

"In New York we have four cups, four spoons, four plates. I'm not exaggerating."

"She really isn't."

"We're minimalists there. I read a book about it. *The Low-Stimulation Home*. The city is stimulating enough, right? But here, to balance the serenity outside, we let ourselves be stimulated inside."

"I've seen that book," Maeve said. "Orange cover, right?"

Harrison lifted his glass. "To stimulation!"

Katrina and Willie were already on the couch, in socks, her feet tucked up under her, Willie's on the coffee table. Was she dreaming?

The children were called Imogen and Cy, towheads, seven and five. They were being homeschooled for the time being, though they attended Montessori when they were in the city. "Hey Immy! Hey Cy!" Willie called. Maeve saw his familiarity, noted the ease with which he called the writer's children to him—and they danced into the frame, introduced themselves in a fit of giggles, danced out. From speakers mounted on the ceiling came the voice of Michael Jackson.

You believed him, this house made everything credible, she was not his lover and never had been.

Crudités on a cutting board. Shrimp cocktail. An open jar of cocktail sauce. Green olives flecked with herbs, a saucer for the pits.

"We love Jacko, can't help it."

The kid is not my son.

"We believe in unlinking art and artist."

The drink went to her head. It was wonderful to be buzzed and hungry and about to be fed. And then a chime went off and the meal was ready. At dinner they talked about Oprah—such a kind woman, the Riddleses said, a Grade A purveyor of love. Really she's done as much for the project of love as the Dalai Lama. They talked about Imogen and Cy, their whispery school in New York City that cost a fortune but was totally worth it, and the genius teacher everyone called "Mama Z" (Dora: "I swear I don't know her real name"), and about rain and drought and the end of the world and California, where Harrison was spending next fall to develop a TV show. They talked about the crabby pride of Mainers, and Maine accents, their local handyman who says *ayuh*—and speaking of *ayuh*, about growing up on the television show *Murder, She Wrote*, its bad Maine accents.

"We came here because of *Murder, She Wrote*," Dora said. "I'm not even kidding."

"I love that show!" Maeve cried. "I watch it all the time!"

Harrison said, "Goddamn. I knew it, Maeve. I knew I could trust you." He pounded a fist on the table. "J. B. Fletcher. Most famous Maine writer after Stephen King."

Maeve felt a laugh surging from deep in her stomach.

"Who is this person?" Willie asked.

"It's a TV show," Harrison said.

"Before our time," Katrina said. She grabbed Willie's hand, and laughed when the old folks groaned.

"Jessica writes mysteries," Harry explained. "She lives in Maine. Cabot Cove—"

"We call this house Cabot Cove," Dora said. "In New York, when life gets crazy, I'll say to Harry—'I suspect it's time for a trip to Cabot Cove.' Which is funny, because of course the show was shot in Los Angeles."

"Wherever she goes—murders," Harry said. "She'll be on a book tour, a trip, or visiting a friend, and right away someone is killed."

Willie said, "Wait, this is true or fiction?"

"Fiction," Katrina told him. "Like *Monk*."

"I love *Monk*!"

"Before J. B. Fletcher, I thought writers had to be unhappy," Harry said.

"And widows," Dora added.

Maeve's mother would braid her hair while they watched the show. It was their Sunday night tradition. The plucky theme song came into her head. She hummed it, and Dora joined in. Their eyes held for a moment. That had been the sweetest hour of the week, having her hair braided.

Harry said, "When we decided to buy a summer house, we were torn between Montauk and Maine. That old show was honestly the deciding factor. I met Angela in London a while back, and I told her that."

"Who is Angela?" Willie asked.

"The actress," Harrison said. "The one who played Jessica."

This thrilled Maeve. "You met Angela Lansbury? What did she say?"

He paused, tapped his pursed mouth with his index finger. "You know what? I don't remember!"

Easy laughter. Easy hunger. No apologies for big appetites. They ate steamed mussels, slabs of grilled salmon, broccoli, heirloom tomatoes from the farmers' market. "The fennel! I forgot the fennel!" Dora ran to the kitchen, emerged with a huge wooden bowl held low against her belly, her arms around it the way a pregnant woman holds herself. Everything was simple, delicious, unfussy. They wiped oily mouths on batik napkins. They talked about Indonesia, where the napkins had been purchased on their backpacking honeymoon, and then about a poet she'd never heard of who began a poem: "Often two people must separate / to reveal they are inseparable," which is how, he explained, he and Dora had learned to celebrate his long absences.

The conversation moved freely, went everywhere, a river that met no impasse. Dora and Harrison had met and loved the Obama family, but even the bad stuff they talked about with energetic, optimistic wonder. ISIS. Bush. Gluten obsessions. Yankees versus Red Sox. Criminal athletes.

"Man, I love Mike Tyson." Harrison leaned forward. "He's my favorite of the jailbird jocks. *I am a peasant. At one point, I thought life was about acquiring things. Life is totally about losing everything.* I have that taped above my desk in the city. He sometimes dresses in old clothes and begs for quarters on the street." He took a bite of salmon, chewed thoughtfully, and said, "Ali has nothing on him."

Dora smacked his arm for that. She told the table, "He's prone to hyperbole."

The children were eating grilled cheese sandwiches and watching an animated Japanese movie in the other room. Occasionally their laughter floated to the dining room and Dora and Harry would smile, exchange a glance.

"When I hear them laughing I'm so damn relieved there are two," said Dora. "Maeve, you have a daughter, yes? Just one kid? Not that there's anything wrong with just having one!"

"Just one, yes. Paige."

"Paige! I love that. We thought about the name Paige for Imogen."

"You did?"

Harrison said, "We decided for a writer's kid it's just—too much." He made his hands into a book.

They wanted to know about Paige. Maeve told them how since she'd been a young child Paige loved flowers, seeds, earth, loved planting things and watching their mysterious business, root systems in transparent containers. Now she was working in one of the best undergraduate laboratories in the country, doing things to seeds. Maeve was thrilled and bewildered by this, hadn't understood you could do things to seeds that the girl did. Seeds, Maeve had imagined, were immutable, irreducible. They just *were*, she had thought, but it turns out they weren't.

"No indeed," Harrison said.

"Her plants are queer," she said, wondering how the table would respond. She felt cool, using that word. "That's what Paige calls them." She told them what Paige had told her when she finally asked what it meant, that gender is irrelevant or nonexistent in many plant species. That they propagate through asexual networks or hermaphroditic means. "Plants are at the heart of everything, is what Paige says. Right there for us, with all sorts of lessons. But as a species we're obsessed with our differences. This holds us back."

"Phenomenal," Dora said. The rest of them nodded.

Harrison was smiling, his gaze bearing down on Maeve in a new way. "Holy shit. Isn't that the height of success? That your child is doing what she loves to do? If Immy and Cy find that . . . I'll never need to write a book again. I'll rest in peace."

There was a pause, then Katrina said, "For a long time I didn't think I wanted kids. But now—" She glanced at Willie sweetly. "Now I want them. Two max. Just because I believe in the idea of siblings."

Harrison wanted to know if they had siblings and the birth order.

"Two brothers," Katrina said. "I'm the middle."

"I was one of five," Willie said. "But now I'm only one of one. The rest were lost in the war."

Dora, without pause, reached across the table and placed her hand on his. Low, rolling thunder moved across the sky. The children screamed in the other room, then laughed wildly.

"You, Maeve?"

"One. An older brother, Deacon. He's a trader on Wall Street."

"A vampire," Harrison said, winked.

"He's gay," she said—to correct the perception, or to balance it.

Harry drank, inhaled through his teeth, said, "I lost my only brother to a drunk driver. Vincent. That was ten years ago. Eleven, actually. He was gay too. He hadn't come out, but I knew."

Dora looked at her lap and said, "So sad. Dear Vincent."

"I hope he did not suffer," Willie said. "As a homosexual. So many do. Or in the accident."

"It was instantaneous. The coroner was certain."

Condolences now, but languid, relaxed. Where were the heavy pauses? The awkwardness? Wine passed around and around, but wine alone didn't account for the ease. Death was a guest, welcome as everyone, would be given the same courtesy. That's the trick of hospitality, Harrison told Maeve later: give it to those you fear and mistrust. You can soften anything with love. And everyone had lost someone. It came out that Maeve's mother was gone. That her name was Molly. Harrison asked what she was like and Maeve told the story of her mother and the knife and the rec room, of locking up the antenna.

"Good mama," Dora said.

"Sometimes," Maeve said.

"I love that image." Harry squeezed his eyes shut. "Can I use that? The antenna in the safe? It has metaphorical implications."

She laughed.

"No, I mean it. Can I, Maeve? I'm asking your permission for real."

A pause. The table waited.

"Sure you can." Her heart rose. "I mean, of course! I would be so honored," and he reached into his shirt pocket, removed a stub of orange pencil, a memo pad. He wrote something down and returned the materials to his pocket.

Katrina had lost her childhood best friend to cancer. Dora her father. They relayed the hardest moments in their lives with straight-forward, affectionate conviviality. The conversation moved without friction from death to sex. They talked about a new translation of Catullus, born at the end of the Roman Empire, ancient dirty poems. At last someone had translated him honestly, Harrison said, some-one without a moral bone to pick. He jumped up, grabbed the book from the top of a pile, read:

"Surround her! Capture my poems! 'Give back my lines, you filthy cunt, filthy cunt, give back my lines!'"

"They're very dirty," Dora said.

Harrison put the book down and said, "There's a Russian say-ing: 'Translations are like women. They're either beautiful or they're faithful.'"

"Ha-ha," said Dora, archly.

"Ha-ha," echoed the table.

Harrison's laugh was deep, rich, made Maeve think of a dessert cocktail, rummy and thick.

Dora asked how many languages Willie spoke, and he said four, give or take, and then she asked to hear something in his native tongue. "Can I ask that? I love new languages . . ." She leaned back, rested her arms on the back of the chair.

Willie looked shy, tugged his bottom lip with his fingers. Finally he spoke.

Dora said, "What does that mean?"

"It means: How are you?"

"Ah yes. It's pretty, isn't it? How do I say: 'I am wonderful, thank you! I have new friends!'?"

He told her, shyly, clearly pleased. Dora purred.

"I need to write something down," said Harrison. The notebook came out. They watched him scribble.

The movie was over. The children were sent upstairs to put on their pajamas.

Dessert: broken pieces of doughnuts left over from that morn-ing, salty caramel gelato, a sleeve of frozen Thin Mints from what

Harrison called "that most industrious of cults." Coffee, of course, and herbal tea from Bulgaria that a friend had sent, and a port wine from India, another gift, called Red Lips. "Red Lips for me!" said Dora, and they all followed. The children came in, drowsy, ready for kisses, each in a T-shirt to the knees, their father's shirts, from the road races he and Dora had run early in their courtship. Each child was given a bite of doughnut, and then Dora led them up to bed.

"This project," Harrison said when she left. "It's going to be exceptional."

Katrina and Willie nodded together. They looked like students, hungry to try their best, to be evaluated, ready for it. And at once Maeve realized how wise Harrison was—how gently, openly strategic. They had all talked about their sorrows to prepare Willie for the dredging to come.

"I want you to be totally comfortable. You call the shots. Whatever you need. I know it'll require a lot. A lot from both of us. Do you understand how committed I am? To my part?"

"I understand," Willie said.

"You're going to get to read it first. You'll need to approve the text before anything happens." He turned to Maeve, the other grown-up—"I'm making sure all this is written into the contract."

Dora came downstairs, worried now, hair mussed. In her hands, three pieces of ceramic: legs, torso, head.

"Oh no! The ballerina. Don't tell me. Shit."

"Immy's most cherished possession," Dora told them. "She got knocked off the dresser. The poor thing is in tears."

"Is it fixable?" Harrison took the pieces, turned them over in his hands.

"Everything is fixable," Willie said, leaning in to look at it. "You just need some power glue. You have some of that?"

"*Super*glue," Katrina said.

"Oh yes. We called it power glue back home."

"I like that," Dora said. "Power glue! I'm going to call it that from now on. You have some, Harry? In the shed?"

"Sure. I'll do it in the morning."

"Tonight. Can you, honey? I told her we'd repair it. That when she wakes up it'll be on her dresser in one piece . . ." She flashed a sleepy, apologetic smile for the distraction, for the sin of indulging a child, and said to the guests, "It's really her very favorite thing. It was a gift from her beloved aunt. My twin sister Penelope."

A twin! Hold up! Maeve could not imagine two Doras.

"I'll do it before bed," Harrison said, and Dora kissed his check.

"A twin?" Maeve said. "An identical twin?"

"Fraternal," Dora said. "We look nothing alike. Unluckily for me."

"Whoa," Katrina said. "Must be a looker."

Maeve wanted to see a picture but Dora went back upstairs to reassure her daughter.

Willie said, "Sometimes they put it in children's eyes."

"What?" Harrison asked.

"The glue made them blind. That's why."

"Oh Willie," said Katrina.

"They put it in other places, too. But mostly in the eyes."

Harrison took out his notebook again. Wrote something down.

After that she found no conversational opening to ask about her job. At the door, as they were leaving, she thanked him, and he said, "How can I get in touch with you, Maeve?" She wrote down her email address on a yellow legal pad. She knew it would be presumptuous to ask for his.

18

ON THE WAY HOME, Maeve again insisted on sitting in the back-seat. The wind had died down and Katrina drove slower. They were all full, tired, damp from the walk from the house to the car—the rain fell steadily. Maybe she was still a little buzzed. At first, none of them spoke. Once they were back on the highway, Katrina murmured, "Aren't they rich people who actually seem decent?"

"He's a good man," Willie said quickly, as if he'd been waiting for someone else to begin. From the passenger seat he twisted to see Maeve. "You think so?"

"*We* do," Katrina said.

"But do you?" Willie asked.

She heard his need; the mother in her perked up. The giantness of the question leapt at her. Should Willie trust Riddles? She was being asked to be another set of eyes, yet she was swooning. She needed to be careful.

"I think so . . ." Maeve began. "But you need to learn more. Much more. What kind of book does he want to write? And how will you be compensated? Will you have some editorial role? Or a role in the publicity? There are so many factors to consider . . ."

Willie looked forward again. The rain came down harder now; Katrina flicked her wipers to the highest setting.

"All of that can be decided," Willie said. "I'm talking about trust. Before all that. The gut."

A truck passed, and for one harrowing second the windshield was a gush of blinding white froth, then the road again, rippling dark-ness, the miracle of reflective strips.

Katrina said, "Your opinion matters to us, Maeve."

"Katrina tells me you are practical and levelheaded."

Maeve said, "Look, if I saw any glaring red flags, I'd say so. He's a very compelling person. But do you trust him, Willie? That's what matters. I think it has to be *your* gut."

Willie thought for a moment. He said, "I am very careful with my inner steering wheel. I try to avoid sharp turns. Look both ways before I go." He told her that Bob, his Christian sponsor father, had given him the steering wheel metaphor. It was one of the first pieces of advice Willie received here, when he was new to America, and he came to rely on it, installed this mental picture at a tender age and henceforth conceived of his life as a car. Which was funny, because he didn't drive.

"I need to trust him before I turn the wheel," he said.

Maeve thought for a moment he might mean Jesus.

"Him?"

"Riddles."

"Right. Good. You must. And what does your gut say?"

"To accept my luck. On behalf of my people."

"Will it be hard for you? To be interviewed like that?"

He thought about it. "Everything is hard if you try to do it well. So yes. But I like his books a lot." He paused. "Being in a book is not an opportunity I thought I would ever have."

Katrina said, "It's amazing someone who writes those books can be so funny and down-to-earth. I expected he'd be more, I don't know . . ."

"Confident," Willie said.

"I was going to say pretentious. Arrogant."

"He's anxious," Willie said. "He worries a lot. I can tell. I like that about him."

Maeve sensed that and liked it, too.

"It's better than if Spielberg wanted you," Katrina said, a little dreamily. "A book is a better thing, categorically. Did you see that photo in his den, Harry as a kid with his little brother? They looked exactly alike. Their matching ties. Did you see that one, Maeve?"

"Like twins. He was so cute."

"And Dora has an actual twin!"

Maeve felt connected to Katrina and Willie, linked in their awe. They all agreed the house was fantastic, agreed it had been the coolest dinner party they'd ever been to. Like being on a movie set, which actually it was—Harrison had let his nephew in film school shoot his thesis there. Maeve wanted to ask Willie—Is he paying you? How much? But she couldn't bring up money right as she was being dropped off, and now they were pulling up in front of Maeve's dark house and Katrina was yawning loudly. Maeve thanked them for including her. They told her she could come over and play Clue with them anytime.

Willie said, "We need three."

"Hang in there," said Katrina, blowing a kiss.

"I hope you have better dreams tonight," Willie said.

"Oh yeah, Maeve." Katrina laughed. "Hope everything stays in place."

19

WHEN PAIGE TURNED TWO, per the plan, Maeve had asked Dr. Mulligan to remove her IUD. Privately, she was afraid to have another, as she had grown preoccupied with a concern. Her daughter was perfect: a properly assembled girl, a good sleeper, no abnormalities. What if the next baby were ill? Or deformed? Or a terror? She had not nurtured such concerns while pregnant with Paige, not until the moment she held Paige in her arms and saw at once how many things had had to go right. Oh my God. She should have been terrified all along! She had not gestated the right feelings, she decided, had been vain and entitled, would pay for it next time.

Sex without the IUD felt precarious the way riding in a car without a seat belt does, but she went along. Cruel to deny her daughter a sibling. Jack's eyes grew soft whenever they spoke of another one, a boy. For her part Paige said, "I want a baby brother." Then she jammed a crayon into the mouth hole of her Baby Mine. A sadist like all toddlers, with violent eyes. Sometimes she tugged on her own eyelashes, which were dark and long and drew compliments from strangers.

"Be nice to your eyes!" Maeve told her.

Paige blinked.

"WANTA BROTHER," she intoned.

Maeve knew the girl had been coached by her father to want a sibling, knew it meant a lot to him, so they tried.

"Should we try a fertility specialist?" Jack asked after some time had passed.

She was honest now. "I think I'm happy with Paige," she told him. They were in bed, where all their important discussions happened. He didn't believe her at first. "There's nothing wrong with you," he said carefully. "There's no shame in a specialist. That's how the Walkers had Jeremy. It's how the Finners got Ella-Mae . . . Ralph told me. We're not supposed to know, so don't mention it to Donna."

"Donna told me that years ago."

"Oh."

"I'm not ashamed."

She planned to get another IUD but the first insertion had hurt like hell, so she made him use condoms again. Once he said, "Condoms? Is this my punishment?"

"Why would I punish you? For what?"

He only said, "Actually, it kind of turns me on. Like the olden days."

But after a few weeks she saw it was unreasonable, and she winced through another IUD insertion. She felt so happy when she got the job at the library rather than another child.

She never doubted this decision. But that night in the rain when she came home from the Riddleses' party to an empty house, fired from the library, returning to no one, she experienced the strangest flash of longing for another daughter, asleep in a twin bed across from Paige's twin bed . . . a girl with her own hobbies, quirks, her own cosmos to discover. Another to keep Maeve anchored, to do things for. To do anything for. And then to launch.

What do you do with that energy, the energy of *anything*, when the child has been launched? What do you do with the time and the space? She went inside. Made a cup of tea and waited for the sadness to pass. Which it did. Fast. Because she had the night with the Riddleses to interrogate. The rain came in fits and starts. She looked out the window at the greenhouse. Drank her tea and replayed the evening. All the fears she'd held back surged forth: Had she said something stupid? been adequately gracious? good with the kids? talked too much? But then, in her mind, Dora put her warm hand on Maeve's.

Before she went to bed, she turned on the computer, the desktop in the nook underneath the stairs. Of course he would not have written to her yet. Of course not. And he hadn't.

She called Jack to say good night but he didn't answer. "You'll never believe what I was doing tonight," she said to his voicemail. "In a million years you won't believe it. In a hundred million years you won't," and then she turned off her phone and went to sleep, and almost had a day without Libby Libby Libby—almost—but there she was, at the edge, between dreaming and waking, saying, What the fuck, Maeve? You're going to let them get away with it?

20

IN THE MORNING she found an email from Harrison.

> A gobsmackingly lovely night, Maeve. Thank you. I hope we can do it
> again soon? Yours, HR

She couldn't believe it.

That's when Jack called back, but she didn't pick up. "What won't I believe in a million years?" he'd say, and she didn't want to tell him right now. It would feel good to shock him, but that would mean it was over, the dinner feeling would end. For now, wondrously, Harrison was speaking only to her. His message had to be tended to before anything else.

She considered her response as she made her coffee.

> I thought I was supposed to send the thank-you note? Now you've
> put me in a difficult position—I need an adjective even better
> than gobsmacking.
> Yours,
> Maeve

What else? Nothing else. She sent it. It was seven forty-five in the morning. He wrote back immediately:

> Supercalifragilisticexpialidociously?

Trademarked, she replied. Hit send.

This was in real time. In their own houses, on their respective devices, they were having a conversation.

Disney rules the world.

OK, here's my proper note: The evening was beautiful. That's the only word & the right one. Dora, the children, your home, the food. It was such a pleasure, Harrison. I am grateful to be part of whatever serendipity is occurring. Thank you.

Harry. My friends call me Harry. Can I count you among my friends, Maeve? I'd like to.

Naturally, was her reply.

I loved your letters, he said not a moment later. I kept them. I'm sorry it took me so long to respond. I can't believe this lucky sequence of events. And I'm really really sorry about the library.

She thought. Then she wrote:

There's another letter coming to your P.O. box. One more. A more petulant one. I wish I hadn't sent it! I needed to vent. It hurt so much, being fired. You read my letters. You know how much I love my job. Isn't it odd they'd choose me to go? And they say it's not related, not connected in any way, but—she paused a long time, considered, finally decided she had nothing to lose—somebody wrote something about me that wasn't true. A troubled girl. It kills me! A girl I was trying to help told a lie.

She had meant this for the middle of a conversation, not its end, and so when he did not reply in five minutes, in ten, in half an hour, she felt weird. Why had she said that last thing? The statement gained potency the longer it sat without a response. She had written those sentences so quickly, caught up in the intimacy of the night before. *Troubled girl.* Why had she put it that way?

Finally, three hours later, he wrote back.

M—

Sorry for abruptly getting off. Had to say goodbye to D. She's taking the kids to her sister's in North Carolina for a couple of weeks so I can work on this project—Willie's project. And here I must thank you, with the deepest bow I can muster (my spine in this letter is still a boy's spine, capable of deep bows), for inviting me to come. I am gobsmackingly (yes, it's true) grateful. Do you like Willie as much as I do? Something in his eyes breaks my heart. Dora wanted me to tell you how much she likes you too. She hopes to cook a meal for us all again when she returns. She always leaves when I'm starting out. I'm a mess when I begin. I'm full of fear and self-loathing. With this project, I'm even more disgusted with myself. Disgusted by my own fear. I'M afraid? ME? After what Willie went through, that's obscene. The first few weeks are always the hardest. A book is like a war with yourself. If I get through this one I'll never try another. Great supervisor above, just one more and I won't ask for anything else. I'll never do it again. I make a vow, which I always break. I can't stop if I wanted to. Anyway I am insufferable at the beginning. Full disclosure. Dora takes the kids and flees. If you ever want to distract me from my misery, let me know. My wife won't stand me, but another writer might. I do go mad without a little company. —HR

p.s. A troubled girl? I heard only about budget cuts. This deserves more conversation.

She stepped away from the computer.

She picked up her phone to look at the photographs she had taken of his downstairs bathroom. The hand soap was French. *Savon de Marseille Extra Pur Olive Lavande.* In his medicine cabinet had been a single red toothbrush, a travel-size tube of Crest, and an old bottle of Coppertone sunscreen with a cracked label, that dog pulling down the girl's shorts. Demented, that dog . . . how was it allowed, an animal doing the very worst thing a person could do to a child, right there on the bottle?

This was not the official bathroom, not the most interior chamber where they performed their ablutions, but she had taken pictures anyway, felt a charge. The seventies-era towel, a faded floral, folded neatly in half on the towel rod. A simple linen window shade—she had pulled it to the side, noted the softness of the fabric. A round window, like a porthole, with a view to the driveway where Katrina's hatchback waited in the rain. She forwarded the soap picture to Deacon, and the Coppertone, and the window. And then she opened her email again and wrote: Anytime, Harry. Just say the word. To her amazement and delight, he proposed a plan.

21

MAEVE HAD NOT BEEN PREPARED for the pressure of freedom once her daughter was gone. The heaviness of time. She had not expected it to hurt so badly, all those open nights—and that was *with* a full-time job. Now, axed, time slowed. She knew she was vulnerable, unusually porous, needed to be careful. Keep busy. She thought about how nice it had felt to talk to that life coach. She considered another session but didn't want Jack to see the bill. He would want her to get a regular therapist. He'd say she should do it with a licensed person recognized by her insurance company, in a shared, real-life room.

It was nearly May now. The summer was coming again. Would Paige come home? She wanted her to come so badly. So badly she could not ask, was too afraid of hearing her say no. A therapist would want her to talk about Paige. About her mother, dead so long. Her father who—they learned after Molly died—was not a thriving family man married to his dental hygienist, as Molly believed, but an addict bumping between shelters. He died in a motel in Virginia a few years after Molly died. One of his ex-girlfriends found Deacon's number and called him with the news. None of that was worth regurgitating.

In the greenhouse, a dense air. Sweet and vegetal on warm days. Paige had written: The plants are tentative. They may even seem to be failing. Follow the protocol. It's part of their genetics to play dumb. Suddenly they're hearty giants and you won't believe it.

Like raising children, Maeve thought.

How much "raising" had Maeve really done? This one seemed to raise herself, with books and the internet. When Paige was twelve, Maeve sat her down for the birds-and-bees talk, but had only just begun when Paige looked hard at Maeve and said, "Mom, you don't have to worry about men."

"Men?" She blinked. "Oh. You mean boys?"

"Yes, Mom."

Maeve said something she had practiced, even before Paige was born. "If you're a lesbian, you know we'll love you. Uncle Deacon, he showed us—"

"I'm not a lesbian, Mom. I'm not anything at all."

"Not anything?"

"But that's nice of you to say. It really is." Then she said: "You look so worried, Mom. Yes I am a feminist. I believe in Darwin. I'm evolved. I won't fall into the hands of some backwoods dope. Or a taxation specialist either!"

Maeve felt always a few steps behind her daughter, even back then.

Paige reached over to hug her, then pulled back and looked her mother in the eye. Her big, long-lashed eyes had a loving sternness, as if she were the parent and not the other way around.

Paige always told her parents she had no interest in staying here after high school, or coming back after college. "I didn't think I would either," Maeve would say, and her daughter's expression was complicated—warm but pitying.

Maeve meant it. She had not in any way intended to return after college—had thought going to an excellent school out of state would prepare her for a career, a life, would get her to New York City with Deacon where her adulthood would begin. Free of her lonely bleating mother. Free of penny-pinching and the TV on all day and night and shelves of bad romance novels and fad diet books and the musty basement and Lucinda Lucinda Lucinda. Anyone with a brain goes to New York City, Deacon assured her. He'd majored in economics for the security, but she should do whatever she wanted. She should study what she loved, he told her—he would have enough for them both someday. He helped her get a scholarship to Mount Holyoke. Her plan after graduation was to join him in New York, but then, visiting Maine for the holidays her senior year, she saw Jack.

This was at a crowded bar called the Snug where recent high school grads hung out. Of all the old acquaintances she could have run into, all the plain-looking men made handsome by the glow of Christmas lights, it was him. She couldn't remember his name.

"Maeve Jordan? Hello!"

She blanked. They'd gone to a giant regional high school. But they'd been in a class together once. Biology? Why did she picture him holding a frog? Did he run cross-country? She remembered him wearing overlarge shorts, like all the boys.

"Hey! Nice to see you, John . . . ?"

James?

"Jack. Jack Cosgrove."

"Yes! Right!"

"No one remembers my name. I don't take it personally."

Pink and happy eyes. He was symmetrical, bright, like a boy in a brochure. He bought her a drink and told her he'd received a job offer from the biggest accounting firm in town that same morning. She lifted her glass and said, "To you!" and he said, "No, you!"

"To us," she offered, and he agreed, then shook his head in bewilderment, as if the day could not get better.

He was a little taller than her and very fit. He had a square face, a scrubbed look, brown wispy hair. He told her all about the job, which sounded frankly miserable, computational analysis and software systems and other words that made her space out. When she said she was a humanities person, an English major, he smiled and said, "The world needs people like that even more," which was not the response of most people.

Before the end of the year they were engaged, and no—she swore to her brother—she wasn't pregnant.

"I don't understand," Deacon said. "You'll be stuck in Maine. You'll be stuck with Mom!" He actually cried, imagining it. He had groomed her to leave. The most important thing he had done for her, and she was about to squander it.

But it turned out to be the best decision. It meant Maeve was living in Maine that next August when her mother had the stroke. Could be there by her bedside. Held her hand when she died. And in time, as the years passed, Deacon came to see how wonderful Jack was, how steady and competent and kind. Jack, graduate of the local university, hometown kid at heart—look how well he did. Look at the house he bought for them, such an upgrade from their childhood. A Volvo, top-of-the-line, and a greenhouse for their kid, all the trappings of a higher class, all the things their mother screamed had been stolen from her by Lucinda, Maeve got in spades.

In time Deacon came to adore Jack, to say he could have imagined no other life for his sister. Which Maeve didn't quite like either, but she knew what he meant.

Time to tell Jack. She waited until it would be weird if she didn't, and then called him in Ohio and spilled everything. It felt guiltily good to shock him, to hear him flummoxed.

"Harrison Riddles loved my letters. He called the library asking for me."

"What?!"

"I know."

She told him about the evening, the dinner. She felt close to crying, heard straining in her voice. He stammered and gasped and then laughed.

"Holy shit, Maeve. Wow. This is wild. But I don't understand . . . he's writing about Willie?"

"You cannot tell *anyone*. They swore me to secrecy."

"Is he paying him? Is it a biography?"

"I can't really say as far as genre—"

"Wait, does Willie have a lawyer?"

She wondered too, had been considering how to inquire, but she found something crass in Jack's saying it outright.

"Not everything's about money."

"Of course not. I just want him to be careful. He's a sweet kid, Willie. Remember how we met? When the lady caught on fire? He came up after me and shook my hand. I found that very touching."

Jack had been the hero that day, rushing the woman and wrapping her in a picnic blanket, this elderly aunt of Nina's whose dress ignited when she stepped too close to the grill. That barbecue was a source of much discussion through the years, a joyous family memory, a horror averted, and their man—Maeve's, Paige's—the star. It made her happy that Katrina and Willie had been there, as witnesses.

She missed Jack suddenly, a big galloping longing, and said, "I miss you. I'm sorry I'm a bitch. I really am."

"Don't talk that way about the woman I love."

She would be up-front. "I'm going to Harrison's house for lunch tomorrow."

"A social visit?"

She didn't quite know, but said, "A planning meeting. He asked me to be there. Willie wants me there too. Another set of eyes." Though that wasn't true—Willie had asked for Maeve's eyes at the dinner, not now. Now she would go at Harrison's request, for lunch, before Willie came.

"Good, yes. Keep an eye," Jack advised. "If Willie needs a lawyer—"

"I'm sure Katrina's on top of it. I'm sure *he's* on top of it. He's perfectly capable. A grown man."

"I can connect him to an entertainment guy I know. Just for another set of eyes."

"You know an entertainment guy?"

"From college. He does movie rights."

She felt somehow Jack was missing the point. Harrison Riddles had loved her letters. He had been moved by her. By Maeve. That was the larger point.

"Listen, Willie's fine."

"Well, I'm glad to hear it. He's a good kid. That's a lucky strike. I'm not a reader and even I know Harrison Riddles."

Then Jack filled her in on his mother's condition. He was leaving Ohio, flying to Tampa in the morning. Think about it at least? About flying down? He'd fly her first-class. He had a million miles. He'd buy her a daiquiri poolside.

22

YOU ARE THE LAST HUMANIST, *it seems to me.* That's what she had written to him in one of the letters. She wasn't sure what she meant by that anymore. Now that she had met him, been hugged by him, *humanist* seemed like a very embarrassing thing to say. She had also become concerned that her excessive praise of Aina and *The School for Seeing* made her seem a fangirl.

Aina had come to him one day on the subway in Manhattan. "She channeled me," he'd said in his TED Talk. "Shook me. The voice was so strong. It was almost against my will." Maeve, too, had been shaken by the voice of that girl. It had done something to her, pulled a feeling up, bigger than she had expected, the way a root sometimes comes up and keeps coming.

When she got to the property she rolled down her windows, breathed the analgesic air, let the soft rain touch her face. The pasture was greener today, brighter. A bank of fog, so she could hear but not see the ocean. Harrison greeted her at the door.

"Maeve!"

They embraced. He hadn't shaved since their dinner. He wore a Princeton sweatshirt, beat-up moccasin slippers, jeans. A hank of thick salty hair stood upright, somehow reassuring.

The kitchen was fantastic. Original wood floors and rafter beams, with a modern slate-colored island and shining industrial appliances. White subway tile behind the sink, whose giraffe-necked faucet could turn in any direction.

He put on the kettle. The amazing spread had been all Dora's. Now there was an open bag of chips, a couple of mandarin oranges. He was abject, he'd told her, without his wife. A beast. He was a junk-yard dog, an eater of scraps. He opened a box of crackers, frowned, tossed it in the trash.

Willie was coming over shortly for the first interview. In a little over an hour. Harrison and Willie had gone on a hike yesterday and made a plan. Decided: strike while the iron is hot, during Willie's spring break. Harrison said it might be good for Maeve to be there. He had asked Willie not to bring Katrina, but he did think a familiar presence could be helpful, and Willie had agreed.

"Someone pleasant and neutral, to keep things steady. For the first day or two or three, just until we get into a routine."

Maeve said, "I'm happy to be pleasant and neutral."

"I hope I didn't offend. You're—" He seemed to struggle for the word, bit at his thumbnail, smiling. "A librarian."

"Actually, I'm *not*. Not anymore."

He frowned. "You will be again."

The opening. Take it. Ask him to intervene, to write a letter—

She wasn't fast enough. He answered another question she hadn't asked: "Katrina came along on the hike yesterday. She wanted to come today too. But I know from personal experience it's no good to be interviewed with your wife—your significant other, whatever—in the same room. Even in the same house. It's a disaster waiting to happen."

"It is?"

"Well, worst-case. At best things stay thin. It's hard to relax, to sink into that stream of consciousness where you say stuff that's smarter than you are. Smarter, stranger . . . for both the inter-viewer and the subject. Which is, in my view, the principal goal of any interview. When Dora's nearby it's harder to relax. I'm talking to *her*, no matter what. I can't stop it. A sort of editing goes on when your wife's within earshot."

He got up and began looking through the cupboards again.

"It might be most ideal if you're out of earshot . . . but still pres-ent? Making noise in the kitchen? Banging pots? That sounds awful. I swear I'm not trying to put you to work."

He laughed; she did too. He sat down with her, looked directly at her.

"How do I show him I'm trustworthy? How do I create a sense of comfort? I learned from a superb therapist: you borrow the boundaries of others. Willie trusts you. I have you near, we borrow your boundaries, we're saturated in that atmosphere. A transitive power."

He made a face she could not quite decipher—his eyebrows coming together.

"Are you willing? It worked superbly in Vietnam for *Enter Hope Now*. This nurse from the village was the go-between. She fostered the interaction, you could say."

It seemed to Maeve that Harrison and Willie had already developed quite a tight rapport. She recalled Willie's feet propped up on the coffee table, how he'd called to the children with such casual confidence—did they need help fostering an interaction? But she was flattered, and curious, and said, "I'll help in whatever way I can."

"Wonderful."

"I'd love to know more about the book."

He grimaced. "Oh God. No. Even you saying that—'the book'—as if it's a *thing*—I wasn't exaggerating, in my email. I live in fear, Maeve."

He did seem afflicted, blanched, pressed a hand to his chest.

"Poor you!" she blurted.

He lifted an eyebrow. "You're mocking me."

"Not at all." She shook her head. "It sounds awful. I mean it, truly. As far as I can see, it's all relative. You're in the most difficult moment in your work. I had some difficult moments." She paused, decided she would bare herself. "I'd never mock you, Harrison. I never would. You read my letters—you know what your books mean to me. I believe in your work. If there's anything I can do to help, I want to do it."

"*Harry*, please," he said.

"Harry."

"Thank you, Maeve. But I didn't invite you just to ask you to help." He looked at her steadily. "I wanted to thank you. Your letters made me think about libraries. And about how communities form. How books nourish us."

But *nourish* seemed to distract him. Lunch! He smacked his forehead with the heel of his hand. Found a frozen pizza. Big enough for two, not more. He was supposed to go shopping yesterday. He had told Dora not to shop before she left, he'd do it, but then he'd had a deadline, a column he'd agreed to write, and then a couple of drinks (he admitted sheepishly), and it was too late anyway, the store closed at six.

He preheated the oven for the frozen pizza. It occurred to him that he didn't have anything to feed Willie.

"See what an idiot I am? How truly helpless?"

"He can have this pizza."

"Oh no, no. I invited you here for lunch. *You're* eating the pizza. How about we eat. You and me. And then Willie arrives and we'll greet him together . . . and then you run out to the store? I can put the order in, and you can pick it up for us later. I'll give you my credit card. It's right off Route 1. Twenty minutes away. You can see the oldest bridge in the county."

"Sure. I'd be happy to."

Once this problem was resolved, his affect changed. He became thoughtful, more relaxed. He pulled on a thread from the wrist of his sweatshirt. He said, "Dora calls it 'learned helplessness.' She wanted me to tell you that."

"Oh, it's no problem."

"She wanted me to warn you that I can be needy."

He offered her a choice of lime or melon sparkling water.

"Lime."

"I drink still water. Sparkling triggers my IBS."

It was hard to know how to respond. This was a detail Deacon would love—the bowels of the great man—and yet it made her nervous, his digestive system before them as a conversational possibility.

There wasn't too much time before Willie came.

"Tell Dora—" for she felt it important to say something back. His wife was communicating with her, knew she was there. That was the point. There were no secrets, no subterfuge. "Tell her I appreciate her warnings. Tell her I understand husbands."

Though her own husband was in no way helpless.

Harrison said, "She'll love that."

He called the order into the store. As he gathered things to set the table—plates, the batik napkins, silverware—he talked about providence, the miracle of waiting, not knowing, trusting something will show itself. More will be revealed, that was his motto, and look at this. This would be his first novel connected to Maine. He'd wondered what that book would be, and now he knew, or sort of. He tried not to know too much at this stage in the process. But then of course now he had Willie, a real person, whose life circumstances would determine, to some extent, the content and form.

"I was wondering about that," Maeve said. "About the form. The genre."

He pulled a bottle of eyedrops out of his pocket, tilted his head, and delivered a drop to each eye. "Hydration," he said, replacing the cap. "My eyes are wildly sensitive to Maine. Every other part of me loves it." He blinked a few times. "Go on."

"Well, you said 'novel,' in your email."

"Indeed."

"So a fiction?

He nodded.

"Like Aina . . ."

"No. I invented Aina. I mean, as much as pure invention is possible. I'd been in Afghanistan for three months doing the United Nations thing. I was back in New York for two days when she came to me, on the subway. I'm sure I unconsciously borrowed a hundred details from a hundred little girls, but everything was so finely distilled. I saw it like a movie in my head and just wrote it down."

"I heard your TED Talk."

"I repeat myself, I know. I'm a bore. Ignore me. Mute me."

"I didn't mean—"

"No, no, it's fine. I appreciate your interest." He thought for a moment. "I'm doing something new with Willie. New for me, I should say. But maybe also new? Radical character-making. With Willie's cooperation and consent. Openly. In the spirit of *In Cold Blood*, broadly speaking. You know it?"

"Of course I do. Capote."

"The comparison is crude. Unfair to me and Truman both."

"A *non*fiction, then. Like New Journalism?"

She wanted him to be impressed that she knew these terms, but he frowned and said, "These are blurry categories, Maeve. They get blurrier every day."

She understood this. She read the *Times Book Review* and articles on Lit Hub. She had read lots of Harrison's reviews, even academic articles, understood hybridity. She didn't want to be one of those hysterical labelers. She feared she was coming across as hectoring, that her anxiety made her seem a know-it-all, so she said, "Look, I know nothing. I can't imagine writing a book of any kind."

"Lesson number one. Deflect. Make your very intelligent and generous interlocutor feel like she's crossed a line when she has done nothing but ask a pertinent and highly reasonable question."

He smiled. She loved his teeth with all her might.

"Sorry," he said. "See? I told you. I'm a dick when I start a book."

He went to the tap, filled a glass. Took a long drink.

Then he came back, sat down. "Can I be candid with you?"

"Please."

She waited. Her heart sped.

"I feel stupid at the beginning. I hate that. I'm on a plane way up high. Every day I descend a little. Every day, if I work on it, the things on the ground get more thing-y."

Thing-y. She liked that. She looked around the room, collected things with her eyes, things she could show Deacon if she described them well enough: the red enamel colander, the bouquet of spatulas in a ceramic pot, an oil painting of an oyster over the table, light yellow and green, briny colors, and on the windowsill, a small potted cactus with a fleshy red ball sitting on top.

"In any case," he said. "It's not my story, this time. It's his. Willie's. The plot is there. It's the voice I have to find."

She felt a maternal pull to ask more about Willie, his psycholog-ical welfare, how he would be compensated and protected. But her time with Harrison was limited. She'd check in with Katrina on this point later—because there was another pull. "I need to talk to you about the library. About my situation."

"It's maddening. No more culture at the library, huh?"

She liked that word: *maddening*. A Maddening Abomination. That could be the title of her memoir. Not that she'd ever.

"I'm sorry about it," he said, messing with his eye, using his pin-kie to free a trapped lash. "I've been doing these benefit readings all over the country. All these little town libraries, operating on a shoe-string, going under. But yours seemed to be thriving."

"We *are* thriving. In large part because of my work. I started a dozen initiatives. I got us three grants in the last two years. And I got—"

She could not say what she wanted to, which was: I got you. I got Harrison Riddles.

He blinked a few times; his eye was pink. Then his eyebrows pulled together again, that expression she wasn't sure about.

"I was there for fifteen years."

"Fifteen. Man. I'm thinking about that." He swayed his head back and forth. She sensed the eyebrow thing meant he was curious—something happening in his mind, a diving at an idea. She felt him moving away and toward her at the same time.

"Devastating," he finally said.

"Yes."

"'To love and to work are the cornerstones of our humanness.' That's Freud. The penis stuff is bananas but he was right on the money there. To love and to work. *Liebe und Arbeit*. I'm sorry, Maeve. Fifteen years is a long time."

"They say budget cuts, but it's more complicated."

"No one reads anymore," he said, looking heartbroken.

"Yes, that."

"And a troubled girl, you said in your message."

She felt her breath catch.

"Too many stories start that way," he mused. "It's a device. I've been thinking about that."

"Do they?"

"People can't get enough of girls in trouble." He added, "White girls."

"She was a patron, this one."

"And white?"

"White, yes."

"How old?"

"A teenager. Katrina says she has borderline personality disorder."

He sniffed. "Is this your diagnosis too?"

"I don't know anything about her."

He waited, looking at her. Curiosity brought a deeper, rutted handsomeness to his face. She felt her face warm. She felt curious too, as though it could be shed, like a virus, could infect her. She said, "Did Katrina tell you what happened?"

"Budget cuts. She said it's heartbreaking to lose you."

"But before the budget cuts, a couple of months before."

It was too embarrassing.

"You alright, Maeve?"

"I'm fine." She took a sip of sparkling water. The lime flavoring had a metallic undertaste, a mineral zest. As if in commiseration with him, her own stomach seized with hurt. But then it stopped. Settled. She decided to speak the truth, in generalities. It would be implicating and neurotic not to say it outright.

"This troubled girl, she was in foster care, told a story, a lie about me, that I was watching her and a boy in the bathroom—and even though the whole thing was dropped, I can't help feeling it played some role."

"Wait—what did she say?"

She swallowed.

"She left a letter in my boss's mailbox in the staff room, naming me. She said I watched her and some boy, from the next stall. Through the crack. Regularly."

"You mean sex or drugs?"

"Sex," she said, and found she was shaking. "It's horrifying. She said that I watched."

He cocked his head.

"Sex? No way." He swept the word off the table with his arm. "Drugs, who knows. Drugs get good people caught up."

"I wouldn't have done either!"

"Of course not." He laughed, clapped a hand to his mouth. "I wasn't suggesting it."

"It was dropped, naturally. The girl was hospitalized. She's a famous liar, evidently. But it still bothers me."

"You should write about it," he said, softly, serious now. "Have you done that yet?"

"I'm thinking about a letter to the board. A formal complaint."

"For *you*, I mean." He leaned toward her. "To understand it better."

"There's nothing to understand. She's nuts."

"If you're a writer, there's always more."

"I'm not," she told him.

"Too late. I read the letters."

She said, before she could think better of it, "You didn't write me back."

"No," he said. "I called."

"I wasn't there."

"You weren't. So I conceived of a dinner party."

She smiled. The timer dinged. He donned a bright orange silicon mitt and retrieved the pizza from the industrial oven, and God it was delicious, mushrooms, truffle oil, roiling with earthy flavor—impossible to taste that good after being frozen. How could it taste that way? The Riddles home magnified things, granted access to more receptors.

They didn't wait for the pizza to cool. Both burned their mouths. Later on, touching her tongue against the roof of her mouth, she'd feel what the roof of his own mouth would feel like.

"I wonder if you can help me," she made herself say when the pizza was gone.

"I have less clout than you'd think."

"You're doing the event, right?"

"Wednesday."

"Gloria will be there. Our director. You might have a word with her."

She waited for him to ask what he could do, what kind of word, what shape this might take. Waited for him to announce his intention to sing her praises, assist in any way he could, but he didn't. All he did was nod and say, "Got it."

She sensed it would not be a good idea to push more. He seemed nervous about Willie's arrival, any minute now. He said, "Katrina might be pissed. She wanted to drive him. He doesn't drive, you know. So I hired a car. I was trying to spare her." He thought for a moment. "I wonder why he doesn't drive. Do you know why?"

She said she didn't.

"It's odd, for a man . . ." Harrison began. He lifted a finger, pulled the notebook and pencil from the pocket on the seat of his pants. He wrote a quick, furious note, then put the notebook away and returned his attention to her.

"I told Katrina no need to drive. I didn't want her stuck here all day. I didn't want to feel like I was on the clock with Willie, right? So I ordered a car from a service."

"I can't imagine she was pissed."

"Will you check to make sure? I want to make sure she understands."

"I will."

Their eyes were holding now. She did not pull away. Lovely eyes. The dark green of expensive mud, deep, rich mud that clears the pores.

"I bet it hurt," he told her. "This thing she said. It's hard being lied about. People say things about me all the time that aren't true. You wouldn't believe it."

"It hurt," she said, feeling close to him. "It very much did."

That's when the hired car arrived, a black Town Car, and his focus swept across the room to the window.

Willie emerged from the car wearing his red backpack facing forward on his chest and a Sea Dogs hat. The Sea Dogs were the Red Sox farm team, Double-A. Years ago, his youth choir had gathered around home plate to sing the national anthem at Hadlock Field. Lots of New Mainers sang in that choir, children from all over the world, and many of the librarians had gone to listen and cheer.

It was raining but warmer now, humid. Willie didn't wear a coat, and Maeve was surprised to see his arms had become quite muscular.

"Will!"

"What's good, Harry?"

The men embraced. Maeve and Willie waved to each other shyly. They all chatted for a bit in the kitchen, about the weather, about a famous old tree in a cemetery that had been uprooted by the wind last night. Eventually Maeve said, "Well, you two get started. I'm going to run to the store and get you some snacks," which Harrison had asked her to say when the moment was right, as if they were collaborators too.

The store was called Foster's General & Sundry, had beautiful wood floors and smelled like cinnamon and coffee. You could buy pâté here, organic wine, and also live bait from giant coolers and buckshot and Natty Light. The proprietor, French Canadian, a woman in her sixties, said, "Tell Mr. Riddles I threw in an extra pint of Rocky Road. I know Dora's away."

She wore a plaid shirt and neon vest and had cheery red cheeks, like a crossing guard.

"You his new assistant?"

"Just a friend."

"Ah, I see. Grab one of them fiddlehead bundles. On me. Tell him that. On Jeannie, tell him. He loves them."

"That's kind of you." Maeve placed a bundle of fiddleheads, green and hairy, embryonic, not quite plant or animal, on top of the eggs. "I'll tell him."

"What's your name, can I ask?"

"I'm Maeve."

"You got a very nice new friend, Mavis. You know how nice he is?"

Maeve waited for the answer as for a punch line, but the woman said nothing else, just looked at her.

"He's very nice," Maeve said.

"You can say that again."

On the way back Maeve paused at the oldest bridge in the county, but it wasn't much, a simple wooden platform over a reedy brown creek, not as interesting as his house, so she didn't get out of the car. She drove back to his house. On this occasion didn't knock, let herself in, a bag of groceries on each hip. She felt like an actor on a set. She took off her rain boots. She heard them talking upstairs, low, smooth murmuring. She followed the plan. Unpacked the groceries, let the water run, hummed. Carry on as you would if you were alone, was what Harrison had asked her to do.

Did she know how nice he was?

Pretend to be alone at my house.

Very nice.

Interesting to see what groceries he'd picked out for the afternoon with Willie. Several bags of frozen French fries, hamburger patties, a bottle of Heinz, Hershey bars. She heated the oven for the fries, as discussed, and put the staples away. All the while, without quite meaning to, found herself pretending she was Harrison's lover. It wasn't a stretch. She was in her socks doing the dishes in his kitchen. Putting away groceries. Eggs and milk and cheese and bread. Lover or wife. Dora. She moved around the kitchen, tried to be light on her feet, lithe, to cultivate Dora's way of moving.

She made a pot of tea as he'd requested, carried it up to the men while the fries cooked. His office was up the back stairs, which she took slowly. The narrow staircase turned twice, the creation of another era, when houses were stitched together weirdly, full of hiding places and funny joints. As she came to the top of the stairs, she heard Willie say, "I never understand why they call it that!" and Harrison say, "Puritans!" The men faced each other, each in a dark leather chair, each in his socks and holding a brown glass bottle.

One enormous space, the whole top of the house. Once it had been lots of little rooms; she could see on the floor a map of where the original walls had been, lighter wood demarcating the old arrangement, the servants' quarters. One wall was full of newspaper clippings, postcards, maps, like a madman detective on TV. (No red string, she'd tell Deacon later, but that was the vibe.) On the other side, more orderly, hung a couple of framed art prints and some photographs of his kids. There was a mini trampoline. An exercise mat, unrolled. A big desk against the farthest wall, cluttered with papers and curiosities, a brass banker's lamp with a green glass shade, a statue of Mickey Mouse with his finger in the air.

Next to the desk was a piece of furniture that made her catch her breath—an antique card catalog. It looked like mahogany. Five boxes across, four down, shining brass knobs. It stood on long legs, elegant, like a crane. Stunning. On top of this, a globe.

"Hey! Thank you!"

Harrison rushed to her, relieved her of the tray, and she hurried back down for the fries. It was harder going down the quirky stairs, even without the tray.

He joined her in the kitchen a moment later. "You've been more helpful than you'll ever know," he whispered. "I've got this now. You were perfect."

"Oh good!" she whispered back. "I'm glad it's going well."

Returning to normal volume: "Tomorrow too? Lunch? I have food now, as you know. Let me make you something proper."

Her days of course were free.

"Come a little earlier, so we have more time to talk before Willie arrives?"

She said she would. "Oh, and Jeannie said the fiddleheads are on her. She put in some extra ice cream, too."

"Jeannie. She's a doll. You know how nice she is? That's it then, fiddleheads! Tomorrow. You like them? It doesn't even matter. I have this thing I do. I swear, you'll think I'm Indigenous."

23

ANOTHER WAY TO UNDERSTAND borderline personality disorder is a response to trauma, to abuse, to the wickedness that happens under so many roofs. Mostly females get this label. They are called attention-seekers, malingerers, dissemblers, manipulators. Maeve discovered an online forum where people argued against victim-blaming psychiatric labels. Borderline has become a slur. A borderline is a girl who is blamed for being crazy, who somehow bears the responsibility, pushes people to their limits, brings out the worst in others. An essay by a psychologist with a thrilling white streak in her dark hair said that the diagnosis serves to blame, stigmatizes, and so the clinical category exacerbates the behavior and the behavior begets the reputation, a good old ouroboros of suffering. Projective identifications abound. We should not be shocked by anti-social behavior in those with trauma history. When others wound your body so regularly or violently that it is no longer your own body, that the concepts of "own" and "body" have been canceled, obliterated—how to get what you need to survive? How kaleidoscopically dysregulated life feels, how frightening basic interactions. Rather than blame the behavior, the writer concluded, we must change the system. Her website said she was writing a book called *On the Hatred of Girls*, but there was no record of the book's existence beyond that.

Maeve thought about Katrina's scorn. The way Katrina positively sneered at Libby, and at her mentally ill cousin, and in fact—now that Maeve thought about it—at many of the more troubled-seeming girls who came in the afternoons, the girls who smoked by the bike rack, the ones who sneered.

When you looked at it this way, it was *Katrina* who became the bitch.

Maeve left Harrison's house that afternoon and, out of habit, drove by the library on the way home. She saw a pale girl, blond hair, smoking on the bike rack—but it was not Libby. This girl wore a giant sweatshirt. Her backpack slumped on the ground next to her like her depressed dog. She wasn't Libby, but she ran in that crowd.

If there hadn't been an available space, right in front of the bike rack, Maeve never would have stopped. But there it was. The meter even had time left on it.

She got out of the car.

"Excuse me."

The girl stiffened, prepared herself for trouble. She had a round, pretty face, lots of mascara. Now that Maeve was closer, she saw that her hair was black at the roots, that the blond had a green tint.

"I just lit this. Please don't make me put it out."

"I won't," Maeve said. "I promise."

The girl looked dubious, brought the cigarette to her lips.

Maeve said, "Are you friends with Libby Leanham?"

"I wouldn't say *friends.*"

"Has she been around lately?"

The girl gave Maeve a long, vague look. She exhaled a stream of smoke off to the side.

"I heard she was at the Harbor." That was the mental hospital. "But Dax came back from there and said he hadn't seen her. Why do you want to know?"

"I wanted to ask her something. I wondered if she was back yet."

"You heard about the teacher, huh."

"What teacher?"

The girl lowered her eyes, as if realizing she'd made an error.

"I gotta go," she said.

The hand without the cigarette rested on a piece of hinged metal. Maeve had mistaken it for part of the bike rack. In fact it was a scooter, slim as a broomstick, and in a flash she pushed off and flew down the street, dark clouds mounting in the sky.

Later that night, an odd thing happened. The bathroom light was off but light came in from the bedroom, and she found, washing her face before bed, that she liked seeing herself in this particular dimness. She saw her cheekbones as Katrina had for a moment. She applied a lotion that Katrina had once recommended. Then she sat in the upholstered chair in her bedroom, in her sweatpants, a bra, wearing Jack's old chambray shirt unbuttoned. The rain slammed the gutter. The TV was on, a documentary about the seacraft of the ancient peoples, the first brave citizens of earth who ventured across the ocean. She sensed that something was going to happen. When the phone rang, she turned off the TV.

"Willie's not back yet from Harry's," Katrina said, sounding tense. "He texted me almost two hours ago and said he'd be leaving soon. I haven't heard from him again. Did everything go OK today?"

So she knew Maeve had been there.

"I didn't stay long."

"But he seemed OK?"

Maeve described what she'd seen.

"Oh."

"What?"

"Beer?"

"It might have been root beer," she said, "or soda," having an impulse to protect them, but Katrina said no, it was alright. A beer was an expedient. A little lubrication. "We decided one beer."

We? She didn't say.

"It's nice that Harry got him fries. His favorite. I thought Harry was going to ask you to stay the whole time. But—no, it's fine. He'll be fine."

"You're worried?"

"It's an incredible opportunity, an actual good for the world. I'm totally on board." She sighed effortfully. "It's only . . ."

"What, Katrina?"

"Him being gone so long. This car picked him up this morning, this black car—I only started getting nervous just now. Just at night."

"When I left they were laughing."

"Laughing?" Katrina inhaled sharply. "I've heard it, Maeve. They won't be laughing long. It's not a pleasant story. You know that."

She knew cursory details. A civil war, a refugee camp in Kenya. *Harrowing* does not come close. One day, when she finally reads the book, she will find it difficult to talk about what it does to her. How close it will bring her, again, to Willie, to Harrison. How moved she will be, how deeply moved—which will only complicate everything. A book that good. A boy asked to do so much. The dignity of children in a world so rotten.

"Poor Willie."

"He hates that. He hates 'Poor Willie.' He hates 'Lost Boy' too. Harry insisted the girlfriend can't be there for the interviews. He was very explicit." Then she stopped. She said tightly, "Willie makes his own choices. Maybe it's freeing, without me there. I get that. I'm not his parent. I'm not his therapist."

Maeve remembered how nervous Harrison had been this morning. She wondered, Might it be irresponsible? Even damaging? They had only just met—wasn't a book an awfully big commitment? She asked Katrina if they had discussed provisions for Willie's mental health.

"Harry said it wasn't his business how Willie addressed his own mind. He said he knew it might be tough. He said that all he could do was give him money, which Willie could spend or give or invest however he wanted."

"Oh! He's being compensated."

"Money is the ultimate respect, Harry told us. He said Willie could have someone there, just not his girlfriend. I wanted Willie to demand I be there. I am certain he would've agreed if Willie had insisted. But Willie said, 'Let's follow his plan.'"

"So it was Willie's decision."

"Yes," she sighed. "Exactly right, Maeve. And I respect it. I really do. But his story. I mean, as he talks about his—while he goes into all this detail about—"

She could not say what because she was crying.

"Oh Katrina. Oh honey."

She cried for half a minute, gasping sounds that Maeve had never heard her make before, and then pulled herself together.

"I can't do his suffering on his behalf. That's what my therapist says."

"You have a therapist?"

"God yes," Katrina said, sniffing. "Are you kidding? I used to have Kimberly but now it's Janet. I'd die without Janet."

Maeve was surprised she had not known.

Katrina said suddenly, laughing, "I bet I'm being paranoid. He's the steadiest person I know. He makes good decisions."

"He's being paid fairly? I realize it's not my business, but—"

Katrina cut her off. "Riddles is giving him half the advance. Plus eighty percent of royalties. The other twenty percent will go to a program supporting South Sudan. It's not formalized yet, so we're not supposed to talk about it. Don't say *anything*. I could get literally sued for saying this."

She said a pretty staggering number. It was more than Jack's annual salary.

Thinking of Jack, of a number that big, Maeve said, "Does Willie have a lawyer?"

"No, but he needs an accountant. Maybe Jack can recommend someone."

Why didn't you invite me to the dinner with Harrison, after he called? It would have taken only a moment: Come get a burrito with Harrison Riddles!

Did you really stand up for me, Katrina? Did you *really* make a scene with Gloria?

She didn't ask. Not yet.

Nor did she tell Katrina what she'd learned about the sexism in the mental health industry, about how ruthlessly the world comes down on girls like Libby. Borderline: like spitting on a baby for having been left on some church steps. Yet another vector of misogyny. But she didn't say so now because she heard grief in Katrina's voice, and because it did seem rather odd that Harrison was so certain the partner should not be present. Now she felt nervous for Willie.

Katrina had to go now.

"Hey Maeve? Thanks for being here for us. You're such a trooper."

Sometimes Maeve wondered what it'd be like to have a spouse whose background departed so wildly from your own. Jack and Maeve came from the same mold—latchkey children of working-class southern Maine, white kids with absent dads. Their main difference was he'd gone to a state school and she to a fancy liberal arts college. Katrina grew up in beachy middle-class suburbia and hosted a radio show and picketed Ringling Bros., while Willie as a boy had been witness to atrocities, actual crimes against humanity. Unfathomable.

Generally, Katrina said very little about her life with Willie. She was protective, and Maeve respected that by not inquiring. Maeve realized how little she knew about their life together. In her mind they lived in a dim, sweet cottage at the edge of the woods, white-seamed like a gingerbread house. Their board games. Their books. They were the lucky, bonded occupants of that dream house, connected by a force much bigger than statehood. She had not yet been to where they really lived.

She called Deacon. "Do you get a finder's fee?" he said when she told him how much money for the talking part.

"Harrison wants me back tomorrow. He's making fiddleheads."

Deacon said, "He's paying the dude for his trauma." He said this neither with scorn nor with approval.

"For art," Maeve said. And then: "For *us*."

"Us?"

"His readers. For posterity. It's a reckoning."

"With what?"

"War, Deacon. Genocide."

A pause.

"Well, I can't wait to read it." Then he said, "I bought the hand soap. It's fucking divine."

Maeve said, before she could rethink it: "Harrison thinks I should write too. He remembered my letters. He loved them. He thinks I should write about—this thing that happened to me at the library."

She had not told Deacon about the girl. She waited for him to ask about the thing, but he said, "I didn't know you wrote, Maeve."

"Just those letters."

"They must have been impressive."

"It surprised me too."

"I didn't say I was surprised, Bug!"

When he didn't ask what happened at the library, the will to say it vanished. She felt exposed. Off balance.

"Teddy and I are going to the Poconos and it's supposed to rain all weekend."

"The Poconos. Very romantic. Tell me if you're going to propose."

"Eww," he said. "Don't drag me in."

She was exhausted, lay on the mattress on her back, shoes still on her feet. "I'm going to fall asleep with my shoes on," she said.

Deacon said, "Fiddleheads will give you genital dreams. Don't be surprised if that happens. It's just the plants."

24

THE PLANTS. MAEVE WAS VIGILANT. Paige would be pleased. For Maeve, for now, plants remained what they'd always been: facts of the earth, to be studied and known, apolitical. She had no idea that a plant, like a sentence, might be edited, bred for certain characteristics, no idea how the simplest interventions might beget great changes. Last summer, before she broke her mother's heart when she left for Uganda, Paige had planted the special seeds she'd brought from California in a plastic bag, the seeds with the long latency period. Maeve had been vigilant, precise. Sometimes she had even sung to these plants. Now, after all this time, they were doing something.

That night the email came from Paige, and more instructions with it. Maeve had been expecting a message like this, but the timing was terrible. Because she had not told Paige her own bad news, Paige had no reason *not* to send the email, no reason not to be so casual, and therefore Maeve knew it was unfair to call her daughter insensitive. But the tone. The email not an invitation to a discussion. Not an apology.

Hi Mom,

Hope all's well. Sorry to be brief—up to my neck in research. GONZO deadline on Friday. Have you been tending cultivar #3? Can you see if it's sprouted? And if it has, can you give it some water? Not too much— prefers dry soil. Once it starts leafing, can you send me a picture? And can you give it a quarter gallon every week or so? Spread out over three or four days? Mist, preferably. Please DO NOT overwater. It's critical that you do not overwater. This is a highly important one. Hey I'm sorry it doesn't look like I can get home this summer. This project is game-changing. Mitchell working me and Joe like dogs. Dad says he understands. I hope you do too! Of course I know you do. Thanks for everything, Mom. You're the best. Let's talk soon.

    Love,

    Paige

She read it twice.

Not even twenty and already so adult, already that vibe of over-worked responsibility. *Gonzo deadline* was something Deacon would say. In her daughter's mind, Maeve still lived her old life. In her girl's stream of subjectivity, Maeve remained a librarian.

Sometimes she felt jealous of Paige. Of her curiosity, her clarity of mind. Of how content she was just to look at things, soil and trees and flowers and squirrels, ever since she was small. How she spent hours in that greenhouse wearing giant dirty track shorts, her father's old Birkenstocks, too big. Then she'd come in and shower and sit at the computer under the stairs, typing messages to like-minded young people all over the world. Back when she was in her proximity, Maeve had loved Paige's inwardness, her righteous focus, the way she'd lose herself to a task—but with thousands of miles between them, these qualities had lost their wondrous charm. Maeve couldn't oversee, couldn't set a plate of food before her or nudge her up to bed. Had no idea what went on in a lab.

Maeve had been upset for several days after Paige flew to Uganda last summer. It was hard to explain how upset. She did not like to think back on it. But pretty soon she stopped crying and settled back into her routine. The library helped.

This time the library would not help. Maeve read the email one more time, then went to the greenhouse and did what Paige told her to do. Rain beat on the glass roof. One of the plants, which had indeed sprouted, had been partly eaten. A gray mouse lay on its back, next to the plant, dead. Not dead, no, it was breathing. In fact sleeping, for when Maeve put her hand down on the counter, it rolled over, got to its feet, alert but not alarmed. It looked at her. Perhaps it was sick? The tiniest thing. The puniest. A little gray finger. It lay down again. She watched it breathe. It did not seem troubled, so she let it be.

When she arrived at his house the next day, for the fiddleheads, Harrison had shaved and combed his hair yet seemed tired. He hadn't slept well. Had dreams of circles. Circles sounded good, as symbology went, but they could be problematic. A ring of fire was a circle.

Rainy still, chillier today. The woodstove crackled. He was playing a record, a folksinger, a rough voice crackling about hard traveling. Coffee brewing.

He said, "I take my coffee black"—winked—"with a little cream."

"I take it that way too."

They sat at the counter again. They watched the cream swirl through the coffee.

She asked how it went yesterday with Willie.

"Brilliant. Thanks to you, Maeve."

"I can hardly take credit."

"You got the groceries. And you made me feel better."

"Good, then."

She told him Katrina called her when Willie wasn't back yet.

"Was she pissed? I bet. He didn't get home before midnight."

"I tried to reassure her."

"Thank you. Good to have an ally."

"Katrina's an ally."

"Sure she is, yeah." A pause. "But it's hard, being the girlfriend. I get that. She might feel left behind. Find it threatening. I probably would."

"Katrina's not like that," Maeve said. "She's bigger than that. She just wants Willie to be OK."

"Sure," he said.

They looked down at their mugs. His proclaimed his global superiority as a father. Hers was glossy red, squat, appeared to be handmade—he said he wasn't sure he'd ever seen it before. It must be new. Meaning *old*. Dora was always picking up odds and ends—she was a crow, a scavenger, loved rural flea markets and backwater Goodwills, loved intuiting beloved things and bringing them home to experience their energy. That had been one of the appeals of Maine, in fact, a state of old people discarding their treasures. He got into it too.

"In any thrift store we head straight for the mugs. A breast. Never not a breast. That's why people get attached to specific mugs."

In the dish rack was Dora's favorite, a bunch of bears, each holding a balloon that said *I Love You*. On the inside, along the lip of the mug: *It's a Sentiment That Bears Repeating*.

"We go to Goodwill. We have a pact, me and Dora, we only buy each other presents secondhand."

"That's sweet. And environmentally sound."

"I break the pact all the time. She'd kill me if I didn't."

Harrison proposed a plan: After the coffee, a quick walk to the water. Then fiddleheads. Then Willie would arrive and she could putter as yesterday until he came down to relieve her. Would that work? It helps his anxiety.

"I'll leave when you want me to."

He smiled. His imperfect teeth, jaw like a bullfighter's.

"I knew you'd get it."

Later Deacon would say she had been playing the emotional babysitter. Except she was the only one who didn't get paid. Everyone else got paid but Maeve. Did she notice that? Did it bother her?

Not everything's about money! would not be something she said that time.

But that day with Harrison she was still startled by his face, and by the openness of her days. It's hardly shocking what happened.

"Let's walk," he said. "How about it?"

25

HE LENT HER A RAIN HAT of Dora's with a wide yellow brim, and he wore a bigger version in blue. The air was complicated and lovely, woodsmoke, pine, sage, like a hotel spa. They walked in the drizzle, took a thorny path through swaying woods, green and silver. Slabs of ancient rock jutted into water. Shell middens, he told her, piles of the smallest shards of oyster shells, oysters consumed by the Wabanaki people. The very oysters that nourished the rightful owners of this land. He put his hands in the pile and took a long, meaningful breath.

"Have you heard about Malaga Island?"

She had not, so he told her the terrible story. It was an island here in Maine.

"This is recently, only a hundred years ago, not far from here. An interracial community lived on the island for generations. All through the Civil War, peacefully, but then one day the authorities came and took everyone off. Kids away from parents. Murdered them or put them in institutions. The governor of Maine authorized the whole thing."

"Wait, *when*?"

"Early 1900s." He gestured to the water before them. "Crazy no one talks about it. What Willie went through happened here too. More than once."

She shook her head sorrowfully. For a few minutes they looked out at the water together. Then he said it never seemed fair to him, how hard it was to swim. All these rocks, the barnacle shore. The beach had been a point in favor of Montauk, though he would never have met Maeve in that case, or Willie.

———

Back at the house, he made the fiddleheads. He sautéed them with lemon and garlic, sprinkled a spice from an unmarked jar. He told her he had an idea. "I hope I can trust your confidence."

"You can," she told him.

He spoke to her gravely, as though contemplating an actual danger, when really it was only whether he should use the pronoun *I* or *he*. The disclosure disappointed and pleased her at the same time.

"The standard assumption is that I tell it in the third person, especially since it's based on a real person's life. But I have this idea. I don't know if Willie will go for it or not. He has final say on craft matters. I made sure that got written into the contract. Taste this"—a fork coming for her mouth, a buttery green curl—and she took it between her teeth.

"Delicious," she said. "Goddamn."

He liked that, she saw. She swallowed and said it again: goddamn. Woodsy and asparagusy and better than any she'd tasted before. The Wabanaki used the fiddleheads in medicine and in art, he told her. They cleanse the body of impurities and toxins. He showed her a birch basket, fiddlehead shapes on its side, a gift from a Wabanaki leader called Al who was his very good friend. She remembered what Deacon had said, the genital dreams.

He served toast too, smeared with dill-specked goat cheese.

He told her he wanted the urgency of the first person, the intimacy. He wanted to create that experience for the reader. To shock them into a reckoning.

"I mean, it's risky, taking on Willie's identity. I'll have to be sensitive. Culturally sensitive to the extreme. And some people, hard-core types—they'll come down on me no matter what I do. But you never really know. I expected the response to Aina to be much angrier. White American guy channels Muslim girl? I got away with it, pretty much. It makes me want to be bolder, or more radical, more unrelenting. I don't know. Is that fucked up? I can't tell. Some desire to wear another person's skin. Like Buffalo Bill. What do you think? Can I pull it off?"

"You can pull off anything, Harrison."

"Harry," he said again.

"Harry."

"You're very proper, aren't you?"

To show him she wasn't, she said she wondered if he might help her. A favor.

"What kind of favor?"

"Would you write something on my behalf? A letter. To help me get reinstated."

A flat, unmarked expression. She couldn't read it.

She said, "Not to the *Times* or anything. Just the library board."

"If you'd think it'd help, sure. Yes."

"I *do* think it might. I really do."

He smiled. "Can I admit something? I thought you were going to ask me to fix the budget. And I plan on giving a donation, but more like five grand. I haven't told them yet."

"Oh, that's nice. That's wonderful, Harry."

"So that you can bring more writers. More of the youth programming."

"Gloria will be thrilled."

She felt a burning behind her eyes. Money to the program she had invented.

"But not enough to bring you back. Not that it's my business how much you made. But I know the budgetary issues are—beyond what I can do."

"It's not about the money."

"That girl, right? You think she had something to do with it."

His arms were around her as soon as she started crying. Heavy arms, heavier than her husband's. He hugged her and then pulled back, and did that thing to her shoulders the way Jack did, trying to level them, a shoulder under each palm. He was professional about it.

He said, "You might need a chiropractor."

"I've always been like this."

They heard the sound of the car coming through the meadow.

He took his hands away.

———

Willie looked tired too. He was embraced, given a cup of coffee. Willie actually took it black. He had a sip, another, then put it on the counter and said, "Harry, I have thoughts to share."

And the men went upstairs.

She puttered for a few minutes. Then did the dishes, swept the floor. She opened the drawers and touched all their implements, their whisks and tongs and spatulas and kebob spears, just like hers. The original house was from 1840 but had been added to over the years, new wings, new windows, so the property was half modern and half tumbledown, whimsical and clever and accidental. The illusion of accidental—later she learned a well-known architect had had a hand.

Harrison came downstairs again. The dim, stormy sky made it hard to tell the time. He said he was glad to have shared the fiddle-heads with her to make up for his horrible manners the day before, but he didn't want to take up her whole day. She should get home before the rain picked up again. He hugged her, pulled her close.

"You soothe my nerves. Thank you, thank you. Come back tomor-row and tomorrow and tomorrow."

On the way to her car, she passed the hired driver, a Black man, sitting at the wheel. Another helper. She raised a hand to him, and he did the same.

26

IT'S POSSIBLE SHE wasn't yet over what happened last summer. That she was still grieving. She knew that Paige's casual email saying she wasn't coming this summer was not the cruelty it felt like. She wrote back: Darling, of course I understand. She would not argue with her this time.

Maeve's disappointment last summer was made worse by the fact that she had done a good deal to prepare for their time together. She had replaced the screens on the back porch, purchased a two-person kayak, arranged a long weekend in Acadia in July and a week on Tenants Harbor in August, had put deposits down on these plans— said this many times until Jack told her to stop talking about the deposits. They would still take the trips without Paige, didn't she realize that? "I don't want to anymore!" she'd cried, like a child, feeling her pout, hearing her mother say, "A little birdie could land on that lip."

Maeve had lost herself in a dream of the months ahead, had imagined working in the garden and greenhouse, iced tea on the patio. Long evenings around the fire pit, stargazing, Paige's old friends dropping by, Katney and Georgia. Top of Munjoy Hill for fireworks on the Fourth, sitting as a family on the plaid blanket, sharing a fried dough, a snow cone, popcorn so salty it wounded the gums. One last summer.

But it turned out Paige would be gone by the second. Of *July*?

June.

Meaning she'd be gone again in two weeks. Would spend the summer in Uganda, then fly directly back to California for the start of the academic year. It was a last-minute invitation. And to make everything even stranger, Paige had brought someone with her: the graduate student, Joe Hess. Maeve saw them walking together down the airport corridor and her first thought was: Oh dear, does Paige need help extricating herself from that grubby guy?

"This is Joe," Paige said as she reached them—before she said anything else. "My boss."

"*Supervisor*," he said quickly. "She's smarter than all of us. Joe Hess. Great to meet you, Mr. Cosgrove. Mrs. Cosgrove."

Jack, thankfully, never got ruffled.

"Wonderful to meet you, Joe," said Jack, shaking his hand, patting his arm, as if it were no big deal to find his daughter in the company of such a filthy person. He wore brown pants with a dozen pockets, a hunter green jacket, a backpack with a metal frame that rose up over his head like a seatback on a bus. His mossy beard didn't hide his pockmarks. At the center of his long, thin, red neck was a prominent Adam's apple, like a mouse-bulge in a snake.

"I've been in South America," Joe Hess explained. "I've just returned from two months in the Amazon. Please forgive me, sincerely. I don't usually look like this."

"Or smell," Paige said, dryly. "Hi Mom!" and she wrapped her arms around Maeve, who smelled on her daughter something spicy and foreign, not native to her.

Joe and Paige talked nonstop in the car. It all came out: the project, a seed study on the outskirts of a small, very safe city. An incredible opportunity. A grant had come through—a substantial grant. Work that required deep understanding of the needs of a population, required the team to be *on* the ground, learning about people. On as well as *in* the ground, examining the soil and bugs and all sorts of excretions.

You're going to Africa to study poop?

She did not say this. The hurt throbbed. She wanted to say: Poop? To say: You are not allowed. But Maeve did not have this power any longer.

"Your daughter has already become a great asset to our project. I've never met an undergrad with such chops." For a person so young, he explained, to be invited along on a thing like this—it could not be overstated how significant the invitation.

Joe had a plane ticket to New York City tomorrow and asked Jack to drop him at a motel, but Jack said nonsense, Joe could sleep in the guest room for a night. He and Paige would fly together from JFK in early June.

"I told you they'd invite you to stay overnight," Paige said.

For her benefit, Maeve supposed, it was repeated several times that this plan had just come together. Paige said she wanted to explain it all in person, so they could celebrate together. She was smiling faintly, looking out the window. They passed her high school, the cemetery. "Look at this place. I forgot how pretty it is."

"You haven't been gone *that* long," Maeve said.

"Beautiful yard," Joe Hess observed. "Terrific rhododendron."

"Where did you grow up, Joe?" Maeve asked.

"His parents were hippies," Paige said with a smirk.

"It's true, we often lived in a VW bus."

"Is that so?"

While Joe bathed, Maeve helped Paige unpack, though not really—Paige just wanted to wash everything. Maeve did not like this. Unpack, she said. Settle in a little! You're home! But Paige wanted to continue to live out of her suitcase for the next two weeks. She might as well get used to it, she told Maeve. She would make an effort to live as simply as possible to prepare herself for the transition to come. She wondered if she could borrow Maeve's blue duffel bag?

"You can have anything."

"You know that old Bean slicker? The red one?"

"It's in the attic. I'll bring it down." Then she said: "What about shots? Don't you need shots if you're going to Africa? The McKendricks, before their safari, they had to get—"

"I had them. On the off chance." She pulled a pill bottle out of a handbag, shook it. "And malaria pills."

Then she put the pills down on the bed and took her mother's hands in her hands. She liked the feeling of their hands together. Hers had been cold, she realized once they were contained in her daughter's warm palms.

"I wished I'd known," Maeve said, a moan, her throat clenching.

"I know," Paige sighed, and let go. She sat down on the bed again, put the pill bottle back in her bag. "I'm sorry. Now I wish I'd told you beforehand."

Then Maeve asked: "Is Joe your boyfriend?"

A startled laugh, and, "God no."

Maeve sat next to Paige on the edge of the bed. "Tell me everything," Maeve said, "please," and Paige gushed like that sixteen-year-old seeing the crates that would become her greenhouse. She promised she would be safe. She showed Maeve a slick website describing the institute where she would be conducting her research. There was an important scientist there who'd founded a collective, who was working to implement a regional food program, a way to bring optimized nutrition to the most vulnerable. A plant they'd been working on, genetically spliced with another plant—an idea *she* had, in fact—might be an economic and social game-changer. Plus it was sustainable. Grown easily. Local leaders were interested, but needed reassurance, needed to see the face of their partners. All this was delicate beyond words.

Her face, Paige's face. That was the reassuring face they needed.

"You sure you'll be OK?"

"Yes," Paige said. "And you will be too."

Joe Hess barely looked cleaner at the dinner table. His hair shone with oil. He wore a white T-shirt with yellow armpits. Maeve drank too much wine and listened to them have a conversation about their project.

"How can we optimize? How can we infuse the food we eat with the conditions for our continued survival?"

Jack kept saying "Ah" and "Wow!" and "Say that one more time?" But the conversation might as well have been happening in another room. Maeve could not stop watching Joe's mouse-bulge bobbing, and his worshipful gaze toward her daughter, whose own face was thoughtful and unperturbed and, though young, girlishly freckled, seemed older in the eyes. Of course he was in love with her. She was spectacular. But this nagging, pesky thought: Was Paige unusually thoughtless?

No. She was brilliant. She was self-possessed and inspired and autonomous and all the things a person dreams her child will be. She was better than Maeve, that was the plain fact.

After they had dropped Joe at the airport the next day, Maeve went to the guest room and collected the sheets. She remembered it gave her a queasy feeling when she saw what he'd left behind: one dirty white tube sock with a band of orange at the top, orange capping the toes. She felt insulted, or disrespected, as if it were a condom. She pictured him standing in tall grass, wearing one sock. She put the sock in the trash can out in the garage. Then cleaned the room, sprayed its surfaces with bleach.

Soon Paige left too. That whole summer, after Paige left, Maeve hadn't been herself. Jack noted it. Her friend Zoë sent her a concerned email. Jack wondered if she needed a doctor—a therapist. He had a name, someone his colleague's sister recommended. That's not my style, Maeve said. She hated the idea of speaking directly to someone about her life. A stranger, sniffing around, finding sorrows, naming flaws. No thank you.

27

DAY THREE. He was a creature of habit. She was out of work. Rain, unrelenting. Today, the meadow was a denser, darker green. Even the sky had a greenish cast. "It's Ireland out there," Harrison said when he opened the door.

He took the bags of food from her hands. In the early days of writing, thinking, talking, whatever the hell he was doing—the early surreal selfish ugly days of a new book—he needed *salt*, he had told her, fried things and soy sauce, big sizzling flavor. He had asked her to bring Chinese from Portland, from a place he liked near the mall. He wanted enough to offer to Willie when he came later, and for leftovers.

She loved so much the subway tile in the kitchen. Loved the metallic-faced appliances and raw wooden ceiling beams. He wore the Princeton sweatshirt but different pants now, white utility pants, a loop where a hammer goes.

She sat at the counter while he unpacked the food, reheated it all in the microwave, lo mien, sweet and sour chicken, moo shu pork. Coffee again, always, even with Chinese food. God put that plant on earth for a reason. They ate in the living room, in the cedary heat of the woodstove. The blocks and toys that had been strewn around the floor during the dinner party sat in red plastic crates along the baseboard. Too hungry for chopsticks, he said, and attacked his plate with a fork, but she enjoyed how they slowed her down, gave her a task.

He began with a problem.

"Willie's uncertain about the first-person point of view."

"He is?"

"It feels invasive. Ventriloquizing. He didn't say it that way. He just said weird. You can imagine of course."

He had been saying that to her: You can imagine. A person like you surely understands. Could she? Could she imagine what Willie was feeling now? No one had spoken from her voice, no one who wasn't her had written the great trauma of her life as *I*, but she said, "Yes, I can see that."

She took pictures with her mind. Small things she'd missed before. A photograph of Dora and the kids on a high shelf. She was wearing a red coat and earmuffs, an arm around each child. Her eyes were too much.

Maeve wondered if the twin sister had the same eyes. Penelope. Fraternal. She couldn't imagine two sets of those eyes. Maeve wanted to see a picture, to ask, but Harrison wanted to talk about the book.

"He has the right to refuse," he said after several bites, seeming to have settled the furor of his appetite. "It's in the contract. It's also in the contract that I read Willie the early pages, that he gets to read along. He wanted that. I understand it. I believe in a contract that favors the subject." He shook his head. "He can pull the plug, if he wants to. Now I think I might have got myself in trouble."

"Trouble?"

"I started it. Longhand, like everything. Now it'll be hard to stop. I only have maybe ten pages so far, but—" He shook his head. "How real it is. This voice in my head. I feel it happening. Like with Aina."

"You hear *Willie's* voice?"

"I haven't even received the books I've ordered yet. I have so much to read. So much history! So much more politics! But just like Aina, the voice comes first. It's the voice that brings me to politics. The voice makes me care, and see. I hear Willie speak in my office and then—when he's silent, when he's gone—another voice. Another Willie."

She remembered how Aina had sprung her spine. The girl, Aina's voice, like a dream of Maeve's own self. She'd read it in a kind of trance, hours in the bathtub, and when the water got cold she got out and dried off, fell onto the couch, just a thin blanket over her, no clothes, too engrossed even to put on her underwear. Naked and chilly, as if the character's pain commanded its reader to suffer.

"I love Aina. I told you in my letters."

He nodded abstractedly.

"She's one of my very favorites." She wanted to make sure he understood. "Emma Bovary. Mrs. Bridge. Jean Brodie. Mrs. Dalloway. Aina."

He said, "Jesus, Maeve. That company. I definitely don't deserve it."

"Well, *I* put her in that company."

"Aina just arrived. A close third person. The closest. Like a shadow. She wasn't real so it didn't matter. I invented her, whole cloth. I could do anything I liked with her."

That last phrase disturbed the waters of her mind, but barely, a ripple.

"I mean in a certain way every character is a little bit real and a little bit invented. But Aina at her roots was a fabrication. Willie will be Willie, decisively."

He reached across the coffee table, his arm lightly touching her own arm, grabbed a wax paper bag of fried wontons, dumped two on his plate, one on Maeve's.

"I'm telling it straight," he said. "A to B to C. Simple. Organized. Willie said that would be a good correction. In his mind it's tangled. Presenting it chronologically may be therapeutic, we decided. Which may or may not be good storytelling. The aims of therapy and the aims of art aren't the same. He's fully aware of this."

"Can't Willie be a *he* too, like Aina? If that's what Willie prefers? Can't you do Willie that way?"

He winced. "It's not like that, I'm afraid. I'm at the mercy of the voice." He said more things about point of view, about means of perception. You make a contract with the reader. Focalization, perspective, it's the core of the book, determining its dimensions the great challenge of any project. He couldn't imagine anything else until he heard a voice, and once he did it was as good as done.

"Which means I really don't want Willie to pull the plug on it."

He squirted some mustard on his food, then on his plate, then sucked the remaining mustard from the end of the plastic sleeve. She remembered the IBS and worried for his stomach.

"Junkyard dog," she said.

"I disgust myself."

"Well," she said, turning to look at the fire in the stove, "you don't disgust me."

When she looked back he was smiling quietly.

He said, "Maybe you can talk to Willie."

"Me?"

"He trusts you. You have a way."

He poured himself more coffee from the steel carafe, offered her some but she put her hand over the top of her mug. Today her mug featured a line drawing of two polar bears, their noses touching, and his was the red one she'd used last time.

"If the moment is right. Tell him to let me try it—or, no, I don't mean talk him into it. Just help him get used to the idea."

"I don't know how to do that."

"You're magic with these kids."

Again it occurred to her that he was under a mistaken impression—about how close she and Willie were, about her role in the community more generally. She was not "magic" in any way. She could not convince a young refugee that a famous writer should be afforded use of his identity.

She said, "Katrina's probably the one to convince him. If anyone is."

He bit the egg roll, chewed and swallowed, and then said, "I fear she's become a bit suspicious of me."

"I don't think so." Her impulse was to smooth things over, though she too sensed a change in Katrina. "Maybe *you* should talk to her?"

"I can't deal with the social stuff when I start writing. I get anxious about the most basic social interactions. Not with you, Maeve. It's hard to explain. You'd be shocked how nervous I can get."

"I get nervous too, Harrison," she said, but likely this did not shock him.

"It's like I'm getting in trouble!"

She didn't understand.

"When you call me Harrison," he said. "Dora does that when she's pissed. Harry, please. Can you agree to it? That you're my friend?"

"*Harry*," she repeated.

"Is there a nickname for Maeve?"

She shook her head.

"May?"

"No one's called me that."

"It's pretty," he said, his eyes on the fire now. "You feel like a May."

"Bug. My brother calls me that."

He turned back to her.

"A cockroach?"

"I pictured a ladybug."

He smiled. "Naturally." Then: "I'm only thinking of Kafka."

"I love Kafka."

"Dora is writing a play for the kids to perform in. She wants me to fly down and see it next week. But I can't. She's angry about it, but I *can't*. Out of respect for Willie."

She told him her husband wanted her to go to Tampa, to oversee the repairing of his mother's hip.

He said, "Don't leave me here."

"I hate Florida. I'm not going."

He said, "Can I tell you a secret? I hate Dora's sister."

Her pulse revved. The confession hung in the room like the reverberation of a bell. When he said the minimizing things afterward—Oh, hate's putting it too strongly, she's a doll, the kids love her—she knew not to believe him, don't fall for it, and had the impulse to ratchet it up, up the ante, so she said:

"I hate my husband's sister."

She wouldn't take it back.

"Her name is Kelly-Anne. She wears an American flag bikini."

He leaned in conspiratorially. She saw a speck of mustard on his cheek.

"She's a lot," she went on, before her bravery faded. "His mother also. They're like one person. They live in the same complex in Florida. One of those churchy Republican enclaves."

On account of his mother's asthma the doctor advised a warmer climate, she explained, and Jack had helped buy them a pair of condos down there in the same complex. Thank God for the asthma, Maeve never said aloud. Never. She almost said it now, almost did—but then, miraculously, Harry said it first. "Thank God for the asthma," he said. "Huh, Maeve?"

Harry, too, had read her mind. He had forgiven her for this nasty thought by having it too.

He hadn't eaten like a person with IBS but now his face grew worried and red, and he jumped up and bolted upstairs, and she heard his footsteps pounding across the old boards above, comic thuds, as he yelled, "Be right baaaaaack!"

The bowels of the great man, Deacon would say to her.

The bowels of the great man, she would say to Jack.

That's really gross, Jack would say. That's just filthy.

Willie's arrival that day coincided with a downpour—he got soaked in the dash between the Town Car and the house, dripped contritely on the floorboards. Harrison got some towels, a fresh sweatshirt. It said UNC, where Dora studied theater. The light blue looked lovely on him. He had just gotten a haircut that morning. It seemed he had grown older, in just a few days—his expression was older, or maybe more serious. The haircut contributed to the effect.

Maeve felt suddenly self-conscious. A third wheel. *Did* Willie actually want her there? At one point he had, but now? Still?

"I'll get out of your way," she told him. "I drove up because Harry asked for some Chinese. It's from Chia Sen by the mall. There's a ton."

Willie said, "Can I bring some out to Jarvis? He's the driver."

"Sure," said Harrison. "Just don't give away all the egg rolls. I'll need one at midnight."

Jarvis was cool, Willie told them. He was putting himself through school with the job.

She said, "He sits out there the whole time? Waiting for you?"

Willie shrugged. "He reads and does his homework. He goes sightseeing. He can do whatever he wants. It's a really good job."

Harry said, plainly, "I told the service I wanted a Black man."

It surprised her, how matter-of-factly he spoke this.

"He's African American," Willie added, to Maeve.

She nodded. The men shared a knowing look. They went upstairs to get started. Maeve was charged with bringing a plate of food to Jarvis, but first she went to see what he wanted to eat. Perhaps he was a vegetarian?

He was practically a boy, acne on his cheeks, and wore an orange nylon jacket and a bright orange beanie, like Raul's. He was gazing out the front window when Maeve, under her umbrella, knocked on the window. He rolled down the window and said, politely, "Hello, Mrs. Riddles."

"Oh no, I'm not Mrs. Riddles. I'm Willie's friend. The librarian. Maeve."

He nodded. Frowned. There was a book facedown on his lap: *The Autobiography of Malcolm X*.

"You're another one cashing in?"

"What?"

"I'm kidding. It's a good gig. I took it too."

What to say to that?

"Are you hungry, Jarvis?"

"Naw. No thanks. I have bars."

"There's Chinese food. Willie thought you might want some. If you're hungry, I'll bring some out? There's a lot."

In that case, he said. If it wasn't trouble.

"You eat meat?"

"Everything."

She warmed a heaping plate in the microwave, grabbed a fork and knife, as well as a pair of chopsticks in a crisp paper sleeve. She went back outside.

"You can put this stuff back on the porch," she said, of the plate, of the utensils, "when you're done." She was only tracing the next steps in her mind. But she felt him look at her, an injured glance, as though she were reminding him not to steal the silverware.

A great cawing of birds overtook the air.

It's possible she was imagining the injured glance. She might have been. In movies, novels, on TV, small misperceptions like that, injured glances, grow to outrages, name-calling, momentous shame and catharsis. Life of course leans toward the boring and undramatic. Except in Harrison's proximity it didn't feel like life, which meant anything, good or bad, might happen suddenly.

"Can I bring you something to drink?"

"No thank you. I have water."

The loud birds grew distant.

She wanted to tell him he could use the bathroom in the house, but stopped herself. It wasn't her house to invite him into.

She went back inside. They were talking animatedly upstairs, happy voices. She called up—Excuse me? Again, louder, until finally the talking stopped. "Should I tell Jarvis he can use the bathroom in the house? Is that OK?" It was the kind of detail men forgot about.

Silence, then Harrison's low voice, speaking to Willie, and then Willie called, "We've got it, Maeve. Don't worry about him."

Walking to her car, Jarvis called out, "Library lady! You have another egg roll?"

"All gone," she told him.

She pictured Harrison in a bathrobe, in the middle of the night, thinking about her as he eats the last one.

Driving home in light rain, she listened to the classic rock channel. In middle school, she had thought the most romantic song on earth was Journey's "Faithfully." When it came on now it made her happy. Oh little Maeve. Wary, dreamy, avoiding dances, preferring to hide in the basement, her heart exploding when a song this romantic came on the radio. Loving a music man is hard, the song says. A man on the road. Jack was a man on the road too, but a rock star on the road isn't the same as an accountant.

When she got back to town, the rain had briefly become a mist. She passed the library.

Two spots.

How brave she has become. How uncharacteristically bold.

Now there was a pretty girl in a deep maroon hijab. She wasn't smoking but leaned against the bike rack, busy with her phone, waiting for the bus.

"I'm looking for Libby Leanham."

The girl shook her head. "I don't know who that is."

"Tall? Blond?"

"I just moved here," the girl said, and went back to her phone.

"Hey! No smoking thirty feet! Hey!" called Raul's voice in the distance. Maeve spun around, wondering who he was calling to, but didn't see anyone. She hurried back to the car, did not want him to see her there, being strange.

Stop it, Maeve, said everyone whom she would have told, if she had told.

28

ON *MURDER, SHE WROTE*, the person behaving most badly is the one likely to be murdered. Good people don't die on the show, or rarely, and in that case they're old, have lived long lives, and their death exposes corruption. Most victims are surly, backward, money-hungry, impudent. You can play a game with yourself, in your own life. Ask, as you go about your day: Would this person be a victim? Is this the sort of venal soul whose death might power a melodrama for another forty minutes? The first time Maeve had this thought about a person, a crabby library patron—You'd be toast in Cabot Cove for sure—it gave her an inward chuckle, a sense of authority and remove.

Harrison had met Angela Lansbury in London. He called her "Angela" and did not remember what she said. Wasn't it a wild coincidence, their shared appreciation for the show?

After Harrison's that day, she got home and puttered around the house. She made scrambled eggs for dinner. She got in bed early, put on the episode where Jessica gets locked inside a women's prison. It had barely started when the phone rang.

It was Katrina again. She said Willie was still at Harry's.

"There's a pause in the rain. I watched the weather forecast. It's wild out there right now. Foggy. Like a noir. I want to be in it. But we have to go now. Another system is working its way up the coast."

Maeve didn't admit she was already in bed. She sat up.

"How about my elementary school?" Katrina said. "I'll bring towels to dry off the swings."

This had been Paige's elementary school too—Katrina in her

last year there while Paige was in her first. Maeve had not known Katrina then. Maeve's first instinct was to say no, no, that the school would make her sad. But she reconsidered. This was sadness she could handle, a near-to-Paige sadness, a variety of closeness.

"I'll be there in ten."

"Thank God. I really need to talk."

Maeve dressed in her rain gear, drove in the fog to Gordon F. Braeburn Elementary. She saw the building under the dark cloudy sky, the Helvetica lettering, the jungle gym, and immediately regretting coming. But a few minutes later Katrina arrived. Now it was a shared nostalgia, and Maeve's pulse settled. Katrina wore a yellow slicker and hot pink rubber boots, lipstick, held kitchen towels in her hand.

"See? Isn't it creepy out?"

The sky oozed silvery light, and an almost-full moon hid behind a sheath of clouds. There was enough light to see the outline of new buds on the trees and tiny haphazard flowers at their feet.

At the swing set, Katrina handed her a towel. "I come here a lot a night," Katrina said, "to swing." She took her own swing without drying it, held its chain-link ropes in her fists, pumped her legs with unexpected urgency and athleticism, grunting happily, until she got quite high in the air. The chains rattled.

Maeve dried her own swing and settled into it, but swinging made her queasy. Her inner ear no longer tolerated it. After a few minutes, Katrina returned to her side.

The air was loaded with water, heavier suddenly, the wind picking up.

"Maeve, I did something stupid."

Maeve watched the breeze touch Katrina's bangs, faintly disrupt them.

"We fought."

"You and Willie?"

"Yes."

"About the book?"

Katrina didn't say. Instead she said, "I think Harry's suspicious of me. Like I have the power to pull the plug or something."

Maeve felt uneasy. "He's an anxious person."

"*Harry?* Ha."

"He hides it, but he is. I really think so."

"Some people are so good at being themselves."

Maeve didn't know what that meant. "He wants you to like him," I know he does. He wants to do right by you and Willie."

"I know," Katrina said, tersely.

It was going to rain again. Any moment. Maeve had the instinct to hold her breath.

Maeve's heart could not take it. She wanted to cry out. Once her girl had been a monkey on these bars, a swinger on these swings. Maeve wanted that lost time back again. She wanted *herself* back.

"Paige went here," she said.

"Of course. I know that."

"She's not coming home this summer."

"Oh Maeve. I'm sorry."

"Everything's gone at once."

She wanted to be new again, shelving at the library, just hired, signing the paperwork with her mother's old fountain pen—

She began to explain this, was trying, but Katrina cut her off: "There are other great libraries."

"Yes," Maeve said, embarrassed, misunderstood. "I know."

The rain fell harder, so they walked back to the parking lot. They got in Maeve's car, sat listening to it beat the roof.

"Kimberly, my old therapist, said I'm an empath. Says Willie found me for this reason. My new therapist would never ever say something like that. Janet would never say something so self-serving."

"What does Janet say?"

"Loosen the tether. You know, give him space. Healthy boundaries. You can't do his suffering for him. Deal with yourself. I like her better, for now."

"That does sound better," Maeve agreed.

"Willie doesn't go to therapy. I'm always trying to get him to go to therapy. It may be a Western idea, but it's in my blood. Listen to the rain. God. Wait, is it *hail*?"

Hail, yes. A rattling upon them, white beads pinging off the windshield. It only lasted a minute, and soon the beads melted, vanished, as if it had never happened, and regular rain fell again.

Katrina finally admitted what she and Willie had argued about. Her voice was low, as if they might be overheard, at the same frequency as the rain, so that a canceling effect occurred. Maeve struggled to hear, though Katrina's face was quite close, her breath warm and minty. It was not her intention, not at all.

"Not your intention to what?"

"To kiss Harrison."

"*What?*"

No, Maeve had misheard. "To read his email again," Katrina had said. It had not been her intention to read his email again. The email was open, she explained. Willie's email. Or: not logged out.

"Oh dear," Maeve said.

"A message to a woman. It said Willie would have money for her soon. It caught my eye."

"Oh dear."

"I told him that I looked. I did, right away. The next day."

"That's good."

"He was angry, but he didn't yell. Willie never yells. He forgave me. I took responsibility. I apologized profusely, and he said he forgave me. But I wanted to know what was happening. Who is this? He said there was a person he has an obligation to. A woman. She's dead now. He was writing to her cousin. That's all he'd tell me."

"What kind of an obligation?"

"He didn't say! He was quite—private. And that's his prerogative. I don't get to decide what he tells me. But is he telling Harry? I think I was jealous of that. He said no. He doesn't want to bring it up with Harry either, he says. But he wants *half* the money to go to this cousin in Kenya. Half! It's quite a lot. I said he could do whatever he wanted with his money. I want him to tell me, though. I was confused that he didn't tell me. He usually tells me things, give or take."

"Oh Katrina."

"The worst things. My mind goes there. I know I'd love him anyway. Lots of people had to do terrible things. He might have been forced to do something really bad, something he doesn't think I can handle knowing. I can take it. He thinks I can't but I can."

Maeve said, gently, "You're both doing your best."

Suddenly her face turned hard. "It's a terrible breach of privacy, Maeve. You shouldn't let me off the hook. That was his private writing. It wasn't for me. You're too nice."

Maeve shrugged. "Be kind, for everyone—"

"Fighting a hard battle. I know. I know how you roll. You like to give people the benefit of the doubt."

As if it was an endearing quirk Maeve would one day grow out of. "Is that so bad?"

The rain grew sharper, more dramatic.

"Of course not," Katrina said. "It's wonderful." She sighed sadly. "But some people aren't fighting hard battles, they're just assholes. Also, it isn't Plato. Harrison told me and Willie that it's popularly assumed to be Plato, but it's some Scottish guy who said it. 'Be *pitiful*, for everyone is fighting a hard battle.' That what this Scot said, originally. Not *kind*. But it was a long time ago . . . maybe *pitiful* meant *kind*?"

"Everything is changing . . ." Maeve heard herself say.

Katrina was going to get out of Maeve's car in a moment. Her hand was on the door handle.

"Stay strong, Maeve. I have a good feeling for you. A new adventure."

Before she got out she admitted that she'd smoked a really intense joint before she called Maeve.

"I didn't know how intense. I'd been saving it forever. My friend Pina gave it to me. Does that bother you?"

Maeve wanted to be cool, to say no, but it did bother her, a little.

"It's just a thing that grows in the earth."

"I know," said Maeve. "You're right."

Then she said, "Maybe I just wish I'd been offered some!" and Katrina laughed and said, "Next time, Mommy. Maybe it's just what you need."

"Mommy?"

"What?"

"You said Mommy."

"Ha-ha, no I didn't."

Katrina pulled the door handle, blew a kiss.

29

AT THE BEGINNING, before it got corrupted, she enjoyed thinking about them in the stall, pressing their bodies together; it was like having an experience for herself—out of time and chronology, but hers somehow. Like returning to a seminal moment, or a moment that should have been, when she had missed something, had a lapse in bravery or attention and forgone some opportunity, but now coming back and making it right. The pleasure of secreting yourself away to kiss your beloved, of being manhandled. Held, kneaded. She had missed out on a certain kind of desperation. She had been too nervous back then. Kept herself in the basement.

In her imagination, she was not a human presence in the scene, not an "I" in the next stall but an eye above, omniscient. Maeve, then, had never considered the crack, the place where the metal meets the wall, until the day in the middle of February when she happened to be peeing there and Libby and the boy came in. Only then did she even realize there was a crack.

The word *crack* is problematic. The gap. Call it a gap. Libby, using the word *crack* in her letter, made it subversive, dark.

Libby saw Maeve go in; Libby followed her. Maeve was absolutely sure of that now. If Maeve had reported it right away, there would have been no problem, but Libby knew she wouldn't report it. She knew Maeve wouldn't and Maeve didn't and then Maeve couldn't explain herself when Libby made the accusation.

You betrayed me, she wants to say to Libby. I thought I was giving you space. You set me up!

She knows that when you say these words to a minor, to a child, you are very likely yourself a problematic person. You are very likely hiding something. Did you betray me, or did I betray you? Who betrayed whom? She didn't say these things aloud. The only person who could make her a criminal was herself.

She needed to talk to someone. Jack was right. Someone objective. Whose name she didn't even know.

She liked that the life coach was not geographically situated. She was nowhere, a blank screen, a woman deliberately without a country. The same generic mountain behind her. Once they faced each other, Maeve was so glad she called again. Glad she'd decided it didn't matter what Jack thought—it was her decision who she turned to for support.

The coach had a serious, focused, nonjudgmental expression. Remarkable, how seen Maeve felt in the beam of her attention. And yet, too, how protected, for she could turn the monitor off at any moment.

How will our session show up on the credit card? Maeve asked, and the coach said: "Well & Good LLC." Maeve decided to tell Jack it was a charge for vitamins. He'd believe that. And if he didn't, oh well. This filled her with a sense of possibility. She said with more surety now, "My husband wants me to be happy."

The coach seemed pleased to hear this—she lifted her hand and made the A-OK sign.

"What is happening in Maeve's world?" the coach asked.

Maeve started at the beginning: She had invented a library program. She had written several letters to a well-known writer, inviting him. He called, asked for her. Had been moved by her letters, and wanted to come, but Maeve had been laid off by then.

"He's doing my program."

"This man is a special man, I take it. A man of value."

"He's a brilliant writer."

She wanted to say his name but did not.

"Yet something is bothering you about him."

"Not about him."

"About what, then?"

"About the fact that I've been fired—"

"Laid off, no?"

"Right."

"I must insist on precision of language. You yourself have said: *laid off.*"

"Laid off. Yes."

"What else?"

"I'm adrift. That's precise."

"Is it?"

"Approximately."

"Hmm."

"Betrayed."

"Who betrayed you?" the coach asked, leaning in.

Maeve couldn't say. She wanted to bring up Libby, yet even here, which felt like nowhere, a room in the ether, that was dangerous.

"Betrayed by my boss," she decided to say. "I put in all those years. And now this writer, one of my favorite writers, he's doing this event. *My* event. The program *I* created. And I just found out he's writing a book about my friend's boyfriend, a refugee. I'm not there anymore. And I hate it. And my daughter's not coming home this summer. I just learned that too. Jack's begging me to go to Tampa, where his mother is recovering. And I feel—"

The life coach gazed at the camera in that exceptionally seeing way. Such a knowing way that Maeve stopped searching for the word, because this woman knew.

"Yes?"

"You understand how I feel," she said to the coach.

"But you must say it."

Maeve's mouth felt thick with the wrong words.

"Do not struggle. Just tell me."

She couldn't.

Finally the coach said, "Let me ask this instead. Go back. What were you like, Maeve, as a young person? What is one word you would choose to describe yourself as a child, if you only had only one word."

"Shy!"

"You didn't take long to come up with that." The coach turned her head, rotated it, like a bird. "*Shy* is what other people say about you. I am nearly certain. I have a different word."

"What's that?"

"*Hungry*," the coach said. She lifted her hand before Maeve could speak. "Wait. The right word is sustenance. Let it digest."

After a silence she said, "Maeve, I am no Freudian, but we must discuss your mother."

Hefting sadness, obliterating sadness.

"Do you record these sessions?" A prick of fear at the thought.

"Absolutely not," the coach replied, as if offended by the suggestion. "And I take no notes." She pointed to her head. "It's all here. A steel trap."

"Good."

"Not a trap. Trap is wrong. A box. Up here. That's the only place. In your own box. With your name on it. Only yours."

"Thank you," Maeve said, meaning it, feeling reassured, and then said, "My mother . . ."

"Yes?"

Annoying, voluble. Who got crazy in bad weather. Who had old-fashioned ideas about how a girl should manage her body. Once she got married, Maeve could do whatever she wanted, her mother promised. Until then, she had to shave her legs every other day.

"Every day. She checked my legs. Isn't that sexist? She was homophobic too."

"And your brother is gay. I remember that."

"Correct."

"How did it demonstrate itself, the homophobia?"

That was hard to say. The casual use of slurs, yes. But more than that, it had been demonstrated by never being demonstrated. A long denial on all their parts, like a lake frozen through. Only after the stroke, in the hospital, did her mother tell Maeve the truth. It was so sad, saving this for the last days. What would have happened if she'd said it the first time she had the thought? Only as the lights flickered did Molly admit it, "I *made* him that way."

"That's a very old-fashioned idea," Maeve told her mother. "That it's the mother's fault. We've moved beyond it as a society."

"He was my helper. My sweet boy. He carried my problems. A bucket of blueberries."

"He loves you. He's on his way."

"Sour blueberries."

"He lands at the Jetport at three."

She was weeping again. She had poisoned her sensitive son, ruined her beautiful openhearted boy, would never get the grand-children she wished for, never, and finally Maeve had said, "Well, *I'll* have children."

Her mother stopped crying and looked her straight in the eye and said, "That might be true."

Maeve didn't understand. Did her mother doubt her capacity? Or would Maeve's children be less valuable?

"If you do," her mother said, "keep your thoughts to yourself."

Then she grew calm again—her giant mother on whose once-slender lap she'd sat. Who would die waiting for Lucinda the dental hygienist to die so that their father would return.

The life coach listened with bright, neutral attention, rewarding Maeve with soft sounds of understanding.

"You were second fiddle," the coach said when she was done. Not a question.

"But she did her best," Maeve told her. "She yelled a lot but never hit. Bad things happened to her. Her dad died when she was young, and her own mother was messed up."

"Hurt people hurt people," her coach said, gently. "As the saying goes."

"I never heard that before."

"It's a good one for the pocket. A reminder."

She felt brave, saying the next thing. "Libby's a hurt person too."

"Libby? Who is this?"

"A troubled kid."

The coach lifted an eyebrow.

"A girl in foster care. She used to come to the library. She made up a story about me."

Maeve gave the briefest outline of the events. She said "baseless" several times.

"Every single person told me not to take it personally."

The coach sat unblinking for such a long time Maeve feared the computer had frozen. Finally she said, "Let me make a guess. You're taking it personally."

"I'm trying not to. But I think she's why I got fired."

"Laid off."

"Correlation is not causation, Jack says."

"It most decidedly is not."

"But I can't help feeling she played a part. It's on my mind," she admitted, "but I don't *want* it to be. That's why I'm telling you."

"What resists, persists. A banished thought flies over any fence you erect. What is the worst thought you've ever thought? Whatever it is, it's harmless." She clapped her hands. "Harmless as a clap. You can say it or not say it. It makes no difference, except in the relationship you have to the thought."

"OK," Maeve said.

"Clap," the coach said, and Maeve did.

"You believe me?"

"You're the expert."

"I never made that claim."

"I believe you."

"Would you like some advice, Maeve?"

Quite badly, yes. Please could they get around to the advice, but she nodded politely.

"I sense you're a person who has always followed the rules. Why not try breaking one, right about now?"

"Breaking a rule?"

Her coach nodded.

"Which rule?"

"It won't work if I tell you."

"OK," said Maeve. "I'll think about that."

The coach said, "Is your friend's boyfriend interesting enough to be the subject of a book?"

"He's a refugee from Sudan."

The coach said, "A Lost Boy."

"He doesn't like that term."

"And the writer is—*paying* the boy?"

"Not a boy anymore, he's grown now. Yes, paying him."

"I see."

"The writer says money is the ultimate respect."

For a moment her coach looked stern. Then her face relaxed and she said, a little playfully, "Perhaps you are in love with one of these men?"

"Me?" Maeve felt something lift in her. "No."

"You might be drawn to them both, for different reasons." Then she smiled and said, "This is what we call in the field 'a provocation.'"

"What are you trying to provoke?"

"Get going, Maeve. You have work to do," and the hour was up.

30

THE NEXT DAY there were three mice in a little pile next to the plant in cultivar #3, cuddled in a collection of grass, a nest, bits of the plant scattered around them, soil. She took a picture with her phone.

She sent it to Paige: I think the mice are eating the plants.

Things were worse in Florida. The operation revealed a complicated fracture. Poor Teenie! Teenie was what everyone called Jack's mother, whose given name was Tina. Kelly-Anne, fatuous and hysterical, demanded Jack stay there, for he kept their mother calm. Kelly-Anne insisted his presence would speed the healing.

"You want to fly down, Maeve? You ready for a trip? You can read by the pool. It's a hotel pool. No different from a hotel pool in any city. You won't even know it's Tampa."

But Maeve found herself happy to have these days to herself. The pleasure of her situation had occurred to her at last: To come and go as she pleased. To be alone, to consider her next steps without interference. Or not to consider the future, not yet. Just to be in a story, a present, to nurture a crush. She began to enjoy the openness of the bed, the scissoring of her legs it afforded.

By crush she doesn't mean Harrison per se, or she does, but bigger—his life, the feeling of him, the whole mood. Dora. Willie and Katrina. An amalgam, a collective. She hadn't known that could happen.

"I'm having fun here. It's good being around the book project."

"I'm glad. I really am."

"You're not. If you were, you wouldn't ask me to leave."

"Don't pick a fight, Maeve."

"*Me?*"

"I'm sorry about Paige." He knew she'd gotten the email. "I know it's hard."

Maeve swallowed.

"I expected it. She's got to live her life."

"Lots of mothers go through this."

"Mothers?"

"Parents. I'm sad too, honey."

"I had a career," she told him. "Maybe I'm mourning that?"

"Of course you are."

"Don't make me go to Florida, Jack."

"Make you! I can't make you do anything. I wouldn't if I could. I give you the respect to make your own decisions."

"It's not like last summer. This time I never expected Paige to come home. I won't fall apart."

She heard water running on his end. Then it stopped.

"I want to keep an eye on you," he said.

"I'm keeping an eye on myself, I promise."

Her mother used to tell her, "Never marry a man with more charisma than you have."

But then, after Molly met Jack, she said, "*That* piece of dough?"

Impossible to win: that was the lesson.

"Tune her out," said Deacon. "Change the station. She's only jealous."

"What about that Jewish boy? What was his name?"

"Shut up, Mom," Deacon said.

"Rich," Maeve said. Her college boyfriend, the only one before Jack. "He's not Jewish. He was in a play about the Holocaust."

"She knows perfectly well," said Deacon.

Their mother smiled apologetically. Only Deacon could tame her.

"I like Jack better," was Maeve's last word on the subject.

The day after she met Jack in the bar, she brought him home to her mother. What happens if you do the worst part first? An outrageous idea, but it turned out to be her best act of bravery. Jack Cosgrove had been perfect with Molly. He saw the cluttered, sour home, the mom, the basement, saw Maeve's life in its fullness, and later he said, "Oh Maeve. Your mom's kind of scary, isn't she? Must be hard, a mom like that," and this was the right thing to say, the right kind of open sorrow, no pity. How did he know? Milquetoast Jack, how did he know what she'd been waiting twenty-one years for someone to say? He had a mom like that too, that's how, but at the time it felt like he'd read her mind.

That night, she was in bed in her underwear and had just begun reading a book when Harrison called. In her head he has to be *Harrison*. It excites her, the name on the cover.

"Am I waking you?"

"I'm reading. How did it go today? Did the interview go well?"

First he wanted to know what she was reading. The book was splayed on her chest, a thin paperback. An elderly patron recommended it. *So Long, See You Tomorrow.*

"Oh fuck," Harrison said. "Do you love it? Are you haunted? Do you want to kill yourself when you read a book that good?"

"I only just started it. I'm still waiting for the suicidal ideation."

He gave a deep, rushing sigh. "My book is writing itself," he said. "Though I'm terrified to say that aloud."

She heard a knocking on his end. He instructed her to knock on wood as well, and she did, on the nightstand, loud enough for him to hear.

He talked for a while about the contours and dimensions of the first-person perspective, the requirements of the narrator, or the author performing as the narrator, to account for the space between the "I" telling the story and the "I" experiencing it. An "I" is always a radical thing. A lie fueled by truth. Everyone thinks it's easier, since it's how we speak. But it's not. It's not. It's not! He was practically shouting. It was half playful. He'd been drinking scotch, he told her, but not a lot. "I'm genuinely drunk on work."

Then he said, "Listen. Can I tell you something? It's pretty rotten."

"Alright."

"The truth? Even if it might not make me look so good?"

"Please," she said. Added: "Always."

"*I* wanted to start it. Now. On Willie's spring break. I didn't want to wait until summer. I pushed, just a bit. I was afraid if we didn't start now he'd change his mind. Isn't that indecent?"

He didn't let her answer, which was good, for she needed to think about it.

"I corrected for my rottenness in the contract, as best I could. He has six months to pull out. He keeps the advance, even if he pulls out."

"That seems ethical."

"My lawyer agrees, though that's not saying much."

Harrison explained the ways in which he had—not pushed, not even pushed, but tried to instill in Willie a certain urgency. Because he wanted to start now. *He* needed to write this book, and he really liked Willie, felt sure Willie was the one he was looking for, and he wanted to do it now.

"You were looking for someone?"

"Without knowing. Now I see I was waiting for him. The moment we met, I knew it. I'd had an idea for a while, a vague sense of what my next book could be, but I didn't know its subject."

Maeve said, "I think you're being quite hard on yourself, to be honest."

"Stop. I don't want to be forgiven. That's not what this is. If we're going to be friends, I want you to know who I am."

"OK," she told him. "I know it now."

She felt tenderness between them, a charge on the line.

Then he said, "How close to the bathroom door did you get, Maeve?"

She couldn't believe it.

"I didn't," she said after catching her breath.

"But you knew?"

"I didn't know anything."

"You can tell me. I told you how rotten I am."

His voice was so close to her now. She said, quietly, "I might have wondered."

"We're all free to wonder."

"I didn't get close."

She listened to him breathing. She needed him to say something forgiving, as he'd done before, sweeping his hand across the table. Acquit me. She waited for it.

He said, "Wondering is always permitted."

"Is it?"

"Of course," he said. "Imagination is never against the law."

He dropped something, a clattering—"Oh shit"—and put the phone down. When he came back he said, "I feel the need to confess things to you. You're so warm. So open. Your big eyes. I'll repress it, don't worry."

"I'd rather you didn't repress anything."

She could feel him smiling on the other end.

"It's my Catholic upbringing. I make a confession booth of every quiet woman. That's what Dora says."

"That's funny."

"She'd tell you that if she were here right now. Don't be his confession booth, she'd say to you. I'm saying it on her behalf. Tell me to shut up anytime. Promise?"

Promise.

Then he was talking about the book again, talked for ten minutes straight about the great mystery of it, the detective novel of a life. Willie was going to give him scenes, memories, in the order in which he thinks they occurred, and Harry, after taking down the narrative, would research, correlate points, gather data, clarify, substantiate. In the course of his work Harrison would travel back to Willie's home country, meet the people who'd known him, those who had survived the war and the refugee camps. Then he'd tell it back to Willie, and to everyone else in the world, organized and cohesive, to the very best of his ability. And maybe the book would be a warning. Maybe it would make it a hair less likely for another genocide to take place. At the very least, a record. A story for posterity.

Maeve listened to him talk. Her favorite thing was opening a book of his and seeing the title page. Putting in her earplugs. Taking a breath, going in. She never read the promotional materials or reviews or even the flap before the book itself. It struck her now that *Willie* was the book.

Harry kept talking. About the closeness he felt to Willie, already.

"It's painful, hearing his story, but I'm taking it in, piece by piece. Looking at him, I can practically see the waves coming off his brain."

She had been thinking of a question but was afraid to ask. Finally she said, "How did you know to ask me that?"

"Ask you what?"

"About the bathroom door."

A silence on the line.

"Look, you're not as crazy as you think, Maeve. Kids communicate in weird ways. We're all godforsaken creatures. Did you forget that?" He said, gently, "Where's your husband again? Ohio?"

"Now he's in Tampa."

"Oh right. His mother's hip."

Another silence. She swallowed.

"It's worse than they thought. A more complicated break. He's staying there next week."

"Dora's staying away too. The play she's writing? It's about a grasshopper who can't hop. His name is Sir Wilfred Sugarsack."

A grasshopper. Another bug. Later it would come out that there was a literary agent at this event, that the staging Maeve had imagined was happening in Penelope's living room with cardboard props was in fact taking place at a respectable regional theater.

Harrison was saying, "Listen, I gotta go make some calls while it's morning in Europe."

"Are you calling the queen?"

"You're funny."

"Am I?"

"You're weird, too," he said. "That's a little-known fact."

A pause.

"Please don't tell anyone."

"That you *wondered*?" He laughed heartily, which was the acquittal she'd been waiting for.

That night she had the genital dreams Deacon warned her about—fiddlehead dreams, a day late, pulsing green stalks.

31

THERE WOULD BE no aligning of calendars, no practiced excuses or secret messages. Maeve had to do nothing. Their spouses away, herself laid off, Harrison permitted any activity that was in service to his book—it was as if it could not have been helped. Her life had been thrown so fully off course she came to feel that no transgression would count. I can break a rule. She conjured her life coach's face.

She drove to his house in the late afternoon the next day feeling out of time, righteous. Feeling allowed. She sensed that something was going to happen. Perhaps for this reason she wore a deliberately unflattering thing. A giant sweatshirt. She had no style and she didn't pretend to have any, and it felt good, to not pretend. She wore her regular bra underneath. Be honest, she told herself, waiting to be let into the house. Don't be shy. *Life is bearable for the honest*—a fortune-cookie slip she'd kept in her change purse until it disintegrated returned to her with prickling clarity.

Harrison wasn't meeting Willie that day but he had invited Maeve for a late lunch. He would get up at dawn, he told her, and work like a fiend. He'd work harder knowing he'd have company later. It'll be my reward, he said. Meaning she would be. Then he'd get back to writing, an evening session beginning at five. Maeve would give him energy to continue. Maeve was the fuel. Perhaps the time being so delineated, announced in advance, gave her a sense of permission. In a certain way it was not unlike going to work.

He opened the door.

"Hi," he said.

"Hello."

He asked right away if he could work on her shoulders.

She was not as punched by his handsomeness now. He was becoming familiar. It was exciting in a new way. She said he could, yes. She said she would never refuse a back rub. She carried all her tension there, always had.

He had showered, shaved—the lovely sourness was gone. Now he was piney. His hands were heavy and larger than Jack's. Rougher, as though he were a construction worker or fisherman, not a person who wrote books on a legal pad.

He spent half an hour massaging her shoulders. She sat on the ottoman, he on the chair behind her. While he massaged her, he talked. It was very intimate, the way he spoke to her. "I am a collector of people," he said at one point. She would always remember that, even when she forgot other things.

"Like a serial killer," she said. He liked being teased, she had learned.

"I do actually have several heads in the basement. They belong to cats. It's a long story."

A veterinarian friend had collected skulls of all kinds and bequeathed some to Harrison in his will. He told her about his funny first encounter with the veterinarian, his voice assuming a breathy quality that intensified the pleasure of his hands on her shoulders. He told stories so well. Maeve noticed that in most of his anecdotes, better, more interesting people gave him things. He made himself seem dumb and brave and lucky. Infinitely likable.

"Brilliant guy."

"He collected *cat heads*?"

"There's a museum in Germany with some of them. Of freak things. Those were the deformed cats."

She said normal cats freaked her out, and he didn't take offense. He told her they had a cat in New York City named Norman, a glum calico whom the neighbors took care of when they were away. The neighbors could keep him, for all he cared. Soon they were getting a dog. A rescue. When Imogen and Cy were old enough to walk it on their own.

She confessed to having no pets, now or ever. "It's a moral failing, I know," she said. "I don't like dogs. I'm sure there's something wrong with me. I'm ashamed of myself, but oh well."

His hands stopped moving on her shoulders. He came to her other side. Kneeled so they were at face level. He looked at her quizzically. He said, "I like that you hold yourself to high standards."

There was no fanfare. No equivocation. Only a shy pause, and then he said, "Can I kiss you?"

She nodded.

He began to kiss her, murmuring, "This OK?" and she said yes but then pulled away. She was shaking. Only the speed of it had startled her. Only that. She wanted to tell him so.

He showed her his palms.

"No pressure. We're open, me and Dora. But you have to be comfortable."

"Oh," she said. "'Open'?" It embarrassed her to be shaking. He seemed to sense this, got up, walked to the window, pulled the shade to the side and squinted at the drizzle.

He was wearing jeans again. A denim shirt, untucked.

"Jack and I aren't open."

"Roger that."

"Or—" She didn't know how to say it. "It's never been on the table."

"Different tribes, different vibes. It's probably not a good idea anyway," he told her. "For several reasons."

But she wanted to be in his tribe. She did. She stood up. Took three quick steps, until he was not half a foot away. Saw her hands rise before her.

His face in her hands was bigger than Jack's face, hotter. She closed her eyes and put her mouth into that muzzle. She tasted coffee. They kept kissing, not the way she had ever kissed Jack or her college boyfriend, but she followed his lead, found she liked it. She heard a low, rolling growl, pulled her hips back instinctively. She was overcaffeinated, hyperalert, felt the way she had in college when she took caffeine pills . . . so she could finish *Bleak House* in time,

Middlemarch . . . trembling, alive with sensation, she could kiss him for hours and never get to the end.

Her phone buzzed while they were kissing; she heard it in her bag and thought *Jack!*

She ignored the ringing. Then the ping that indicated someone had left a voicemail.

Would she tell Deacon? Katrina? Jack? No, no, no.

No one, ever. That was how she allowed herself to do it—convincing herself no one would ever know.

"Wow," he said, pulling away, smiling, wide-eyed. She hadn't seen this face. She looked at each feature. His nose was so nicely misaligned. Later he'd tell her he broke it as a teenager, in a skiing accident.

They held hands at a distance, blushing.

"Goddamn." He shook his head. "I can't speak."

She liked that.

It hadn't been Jack who'd called during the kissing, but Katrina.

"Come play Clue with us," Katrina said on the voicemail. "Tomorrow night? Wine and takeout and Clue? Please?"

This was a high point, this moment. Hold here. Harrison Riddles had become a man she kissed. He was in the kitchen making them coffee and turkey sandwiches while she waited by the fire, listening to an invitation to play board games, to go to Katrina and Willie's place. "Just the three of us," Katrina was clear to say on the voicemail. "Tomorrow night. Seven. So we can talk. Catch up."

Nothing had fallen apart yet. She felt wanted in every direction.

32

IT TURNED OUT that Willie and Katrina lived in a faded triple-decker on a busy street, a short walk to a dollar store and a gas station. In their kitchen at the back of the house, an apple tree, a sapling, waited in a plastic container by the sliding glass door. Once it was big enough, Willie said, they would plant it on the south side of the house. The landlord had given them permission. Beyond the slider was a wooden deck—high up, for they lived on the second story—piled with plastic crates and stacked lawn furniture. A staircase off the deck led down to the yard, half of which had gone to seed. In the other half were raised beds, large wooden flats containing dark soil. Katrina and Willie had built these.

"Of course we realize we won't live here forever," Katrina said.

Willie said, "Eventually we'll want to buy a place."

They had money now, or money coming, the feeling of it was vivid and palpable, like a spice in the air before a meal.

Maeve said, "It's wonderful owning your first home."

She remembered their first house, a Cape on an acre in a town abutting Portland. Then Jack got a promotion and they moved to a bigger house, two acres, a short drive to a marsh, then another promotion a few years later and not a bigger but a better house, with the yard for a greenhouse, a patio, a fire pit, state-of-the-art ways to cook meat.

"Sooner rather than later," Katrina added. "With a little yard."

"It hurts us, we decided," Willie said. "Not to feel the earth. We must grow things, even as renters. The apples will be for the next people who live here. Even if we don't eat them ourselves."

"It's practice. Looking forward."

"I love that," Maeve said. "That's a nice way to see it."

Willie was still wearing the UNC sweatshirt. Easter blue. Dora's. Maeve's heart sputtered when he answered the door. I kissed the husband of the owner of that sweatshirt! But she said nothing of the sort.

She had dressed more carefully for the occasion than was her custom, had chosen a red shirt that showed her clavicle, and her favorite jeans, and the black boots from T.J.Maxx that Katrina had several years ago called "bitching." She'd trimmed her bangs the tiniest bit, plucked her eyebrows. Even wore mascara and silver hoops in her ears.

Katrina's eye makeup and lipstick were impeccable, but a nickel-sized Band-Aid had been affixed to the center of her chin. She'd woken up that morning with a nasty pimple, she said, a cystic ruin.

She gave Maeve a long look, as if she sensed something different about her.

"Did you trim your bangs?"

Oh, that was all. She had.

"With my nail scissors."

Katrina nodding approvingly. She said, "You know, you could go even shorter."

They showed her around. Maeve liked their things. White couch. White armchair. White marble-topped coffee table with wrought-iron legs, which Katrina said she'd found at a yard sale for ten bucks. A giant white paper lantern floated over the kitchen table, and on the wall an oil painting of a pair of boots done by Katrina's aunt who showed her work in Boston. Maeve got a glimpse into their bedroom, saw an Indian-looking bedspread in red and orange. There was a cactus on the windowsill, a fern in a macramé hanger. The second bedroom was Willie's office, where he studied and wrote his papers, but that door was closed. Katrina had made curtains for the living room on her sewing machine, cherry blossoms, white and red, Japanese, and had covered the tan industrial carpeting with bamboo mats and throw rugs.

In Maeve's imagination Katrina and Willie had lived in that freestanding cottage at the end of a dead end. She could see it clearly, this place that didn't exist. It had wooden blinds that opened and closed accordion-style. It abutted the woods, as in a fairy tale. Why had she created his place? She was embarrassed by the inaccuracy of her imagination, its lazy contours.

Now they sat together on their white Ikea couch. Maeve took the chair. On the coffee table sat a wooden cutting board, brown crackers, a knife stabbed into a brick of orange cheese. The lighting was dim, accent lamps only, and the mellow electronic music kept a slow beat. They gave her wine, which she drank quickly. Naturally the conversation turned to Harrison.

"I have to say, I had my doubts at first," Katrina said. "A guy like that."

"He is powerful," Willie said. "He is very—certain."

"But not bullish."

"No."

"He does listen."

"He does."

"I worried Willie wasn't ready. I was quite anxious at first."

"I appreciate that she worries," Willie said to Maeve.

"But I don't need to worry," Katrina told her. "It's not my job."

"Right, she does not."

"I have my mind, he has his."

"Correct."

They were rehashing a discussion, or an argument—testing out a resolution. She poured herself more wine. She said, "All this seems very mature."

"I feel better now, Maeve," Katrina said. "Now that his spring break is over. The first round is over. They're going to resume later."

"It was like pulling off a bandage."

"It was an important test for us, I think."

They glanced at each other; there was a charge in the look, a warmth, a postcoital feeling.

I kissed Harrison Riddles!

She wanted to be part of their charge, she *was*, but they didn't know. It was too amazing not to share, but she never would.

Katrina said, "What do you think of the first person, Maeve? Harry told Willie he talked to you about it."

He looked good wearing her sweatshirt. Somehow it was like having Dora in the room.

"I thought it might feel—" She remembered Harrison's words. "Ventriloquizing. Or invasive."

"You understand," Willie said.

"Of course she does," Katrina said sharply.

Maeve blinked.

Willie said, "But then I read the pages. Or heard them. He read them to me."

"He did?"

"Yesterday," Willie said, nodding.

"I heard them too," Katrina said.

"I asked him if I could record it on my phone. So that Katrina could hear."

"It's really fucking good, Maeve. It's crazy good."

"We decided the pages are the answer."

"That it's fundamentally the decision of the pages. *They* get to decide."

"They are too moving to erase."

After Harry read him the pages—that is, read back to Willie in the first person the same story he'd told Harrison the day before, but in a different first person, a new person—Willie knew he would not intervene in the book. Even if it felt weird, like being robbed just a tiny bit.

"No, no, not robbed. Not anymore. It's first person but not my own first person."

"It's no different than if an actor played him," Katrina said. "An actor is another kind of artist. Riddles uses words on the page."

"I thought it might feel like a robbery, but it's not. It's a sharing. There are two people. I understand it, now that I've heard it. And the contract is generous. But the pages are more important than me. I'll approve of them."

Maeve felt uneasy at that. "No, a book is not more important than you are."

"I am just a person. The pages are art. People die. Art lives. Sometimes it does."

"Harry's will live," Katrina said.

Maeve said, "Can I hear the recording?"

"Harry made me delete it in front of him."

"He writes it all on that yellow pad, did you know that?"

"Yes. I know that."

"The whole thing, freehand, until the end. Then he types it up."

"All the old ones are at a library," said Willie. "The yellow notebooks of his old books. The first drafts."

"An archive," Katrina clarified. "At Yale."

"I know," Maeve said again.

"It was super weird, The voice was so strong. So believable and real and intense. But it wasn't Willie. 'My name is William—but everyone calls me Willie.' That was the first line. That was the only thing I could imagine Willie saying, so it didn't feel gross."

"It is another mind," Willie said. "But over my mind. A better mind."

"Maybe that's not the best way to put it." Katrina threw him a cautious look. "Not 'better.' His mind, but more . . ."

"More . . ."

"More . . ."

They looked to Maeve for the word, but she hadn't heard the pages, didn't know the word.

Artful? Lucid? Clear? Brilliant? White?

"I don't know," she said.

Her head swam with wine; she took a handful of crackers.

"I wish I'd heard it," she said, chewing.

"Ask him to read it to you. He trusts you."

Katrina raised an eyebrow. "You've become quite close, huh?"

"I don't know about that."

We kissed. I felt his mouth with my mouth.

"He's working you hard, Willie tells me. Really making use of you."

"I didn't say that," Willie said.

"You implied it. You're like—what, Maeve? His assistant?"

It startled her, this turn in her tone. Was there a sneer in that, in "assistant"?

Maeve said, "Are you upset with me?"

Katrina stopped squinting, frowned. "I'm just jealous."

"Of *me*?"

She took a long sip of wine. Then said, "I know it's a hard time for you. I can see why you'd hang out over there. Why Harry would be a nice change of pace."

But you asked me to be there! Both of you. All of you.

She didn't say this.

Katrina's brutal assessment, the wine, dislodged something, and she said, "I've lost everything I care about. If Harrison—if Harry— wants to spend time with me, why not?" She added, darkly: "I'm not coming out of it with anything."

Instantly wished she had not said it.

Katrina looked at her carefully.

"You're right," she said. "I'm sorry. I'm jealous. It's my worst trait. I don't like being excluded."

"I'm the excluded one. You still have the library! You're Willie's wife! Don't you see?"

The mood shifted the moment she said *wife*. She spoke it acciden- tally, as a point of clarification, rather than *girlfriend* or *partner*, only to indicate the category of relationship. But they looked at each other meaningfully, then back at her, as if she'd performed the ceremony.

"Yes," Willie said to Katrina. "My wife."

"My husband."

Maeve turned away, unnerved.

A few seconds later Katrina said, "You know we love you, Maeve. Don't take my bitchiness personally."

"Bitch," Willie said, pressing his finger into her side. "You really are. A moody bitch. Give Maeve a break."

Katrina shrieked in delight, arched her body against his tickling finger.

I've kissed Harrison Riddles, she could have screamed.

The doorbell screamed instead. A deliveryman, Thai food, which they ate under the glowing white lantern, more wine, and then they all shared a Parliament, tapped the ash into another yard sale discovery, a white woman's ashtray buttocks. All their mouths on the same cigarette. She didn't inhale but put her mouth where theirs had been, pulled in, let it fill her mouth.

Katrina smoked like a movie star, long painted fingernails, and said, exhaling, "You'll land on your feet, Maeve. If only you could see yourself from the outside."

"What do you mean?"

Katrina said to Willie, "It's why she got so spooked by Libby."

Libby!

Willie said, "She's like Clarence, the angel in that movie."

"Too sweet for the world."

"Libby is not sweet," Maeve said.

Katrina laughed. "*You*, Maeve."

You're mean, she wanted to say to Katrina.

Then she said, "You told Willie about Libby?"

"Only Willie."

Willie said, "It's outrageous. No doubt."

Maeve closed her eyes. She felt her face flush. "I'm so embarrassed. I didn't want anyone to know."

"You take things so personally, Maeve," Katrina said. "Too personally."

"I understand why Maeve is embarrassed. When I arrived here, people said things. Someone said I ate a baby in order to survive. I never ate a baby."

Maeve opened her eyes.

"No one believed that," Katrina said, quietly.

"But people thought it. They thought about it. I remember how it felt to think about being thought about like that."

"It's terrible," said Maeve. "It's awful."

"I didn't tell anyone else, Maeve. Only Willie. Only because it reminded me of my cousin, of Mandy. I felt bad for you."

Maeve had the urge to say that Libby was not unlike Willie, a child without a home, cast out. The world had been cruel to her too. Katrina was adding to that cruelty. Reducing her to a bitch. Libby was fucked up, but what had happened to her to make her that way? What mistreatment had she been subjected to, and by whom, and for how long, and who was writing *her* book? Why such disdain for a child, a victim of the system? EMPATHY! she wanted to scream.

But then Willie put Clue before them and opened the box. Oh, the gothic manor. She had forgotten the orderly, elegant board, the secret passageways. It had been years since she'd played. Now she held all the weapons in her palm. They weighed so little, this savage, funny collection. The noose was missing (this Clue came from Goodwill), but Willie had fashioned one out of Katrina's hair elastics.

"Madeline Kahn is brilliant in the movie," Katrina said, pouring more wine into each of their glasses.

Once, playing this game as a child, Paige had said, The judge did it. Judge? Oh no, Maeve had to explain, that was not a judge's collar on Mrs. White, like Ruth Bader Ginsburg's. That was a *maid's* uniform.

Katrina said, "Paige is the answer to the world's problems. We're all cavemen next to that kid."

Willie won. He made the accusation early—Professor Plum, in the library, with the wrench.

"You guessed! What the actual fuck?" Now Katrina was smoking another cigarette, which she didn't offer either of them. She had become louder as the night went on. "How did you know? You couldn't have."

Willie admitted that he'd guessed on Plum, but got everything else. Maeve knew none of it: not victim or location or weapon.

"Lucky fucker," Katrina said. Willie laughed and took the cigarette from her and put it in his own mouth, and said through his clamped jaw, with the sexy clip of an old movie star, "Luckiest man in the world."

33

AGAIN SHE WENT to the library. Libby was not in the Pen. Not in the mezzanine. Not in the room off fiction where Marilyn Monroe read *Ulysses*. Which was good. Maeve feared every variety of encounter, had no idea what sort they would have, could not begin to imagine what Libby would say to her. But—in a strange way— she felt disappointed too, wanted the question forced, to know what would happen. Wanted to take the girl by the bony shoulders and say: Why would you do that? What happened to you? How will you make it better? What can I give to you? How can I help?

Gloria, coming down the stairs in her gray jumper, cable-knit tights—"Maeve! Oh! Oh! Hooray!"

"I came to check out a book," Maeve said tightly, and Gloria beamed, as a person beams at a child when one is proud of their achievement, and that's when Maeve's rage flew to Gloria, who had fired her. Who had sat at her desk and said those hollow corporate things and now smiled at her as if she were a child who'd just learned to sign her name, who'd earned her first library card. Then Nina and Dee Dee came down the stairs too and cheered—"What a treat!"—and asked her to stay for tea, but she couldn't bear to see the staff room, the mailboxes, the cubby without her name, said she had to run.

She did have to run. She had somewhere to be.

"Are you coming for the Harrison Riddles event next week?" one of them said.

She sucked in a breath.

"You know about that, right?"

"He's doing a program for the kids."

"You should come meet him."

"I invited him," Maeve said, sharply. "That's my program."

They all looked at her.

She repeated herself.

"Oh right," said Dee Dee.

"Of course it is," said Nina.

Then Maeve said, "I've already met him. Many times. I'm going to his house right now, in fact. He is a friend of mine."

"He *is*?"

She didn't say *I kissed him* but tried to make her face say it. They looked at her. No one spoke. Then she turned on her heel.

Rage at all of them, who got to keep their jobs, who had never been tested.

Again she had not checked out a book.

Stop going there, she heard Jack say, the Jack whose finger wagged in her head. The one she'd married. They're going to think you're crazy.

I don't care, she told his finger. I'm too mad to stop.

She drove up the coast with her heart beating in her pelvis.

Harrison greeted her. Kissed her cheek so gently she hardly felt it. The rain had stopped. The sun wasn't out, but the white sky pulsed with the possibility for the first time in years. He wore a plain white T-shirt. Gray sweatpants. The most pajama-like of all the clothes she'd seen him in.

"May."

That was her now. May: a month. An expression of possibility, of permission: May I? You May.

He kissed her again, harder, no hesitation.

He said, "Why don't I worry in your radius?"

"I didn't do well in geometry."

"I stop worrying."

"Is that so?"

"You restore me to my factory settings."

Jazz playing, Mingus, he told her, the angry man of jazz. A curl of smoke rose from the incense dish. Half a cantaloupe on a white plate on the coffee table, cleaned of seeds. Two spoons. She had tomatoes for him in a brown paper bag. On the way there she'd stopped at the general store. Jeannie had said, "These are for him?" He didn't need a name. Jeannie had looked at Maeve carefully, so carefully, and Maeve realized: She's jealous. She wishes she could be me.

Jeannie said, "I have something for him, if you hold on a second—a red pepper he'll lose his mind over, you can tell him it's from me," but Maeve left while she was rummaging around in the back.

Today the gifts will only be from Maeve.

Only Maeve will make him lose his mind today.

And now he took the tomatoes, brought one to his nose, inhaled longingly.

Beer, how about it? An allowable time of day for beer, he decided. Also they'd reached that point in their friendship, a level of openness that deserves a beer. Getting to that level was an accomplishment worthy of commemoration.

She told him about dinner last night with Willie and Katrina. What they said about the book. The astonishing voice, the voice that made the first person feel inevitable and true . . .

"Thank you for advocating for me, Maeve."

"Oh no, I didn't do anything. I didn't have to. Stop giving me credit for things I didn't do."

"These arrangements are delicate."

"They said it was the pages that convinced them."

He blushed, truly, which made her blush too.

"Can you read me some of it?"

She hated being the only one not to have heard them.

"It's rough."

"I don't care."

"Alright," he said shyly, hunching his shoulders together, becoming actually smaller. She already knew the first line: "My name is William—but everyone calls me Willie."

She listened as carefully as she was able. Closed her eyes to take it in. Then opened them because she wanted to see his mouth. Willie speaking through his mouth.

He's funny, this version of Willie—observant, sly. Funny and also familiar, ordinary in a way that's pleasing. He wants a certain kind of chocolate treat. He sees a pretty girl and is instantly, immensely awkward. Harrison read her the first page, the second, then flipped forward several pages, toward the middle of the pad, and read a passage from later on, where Willie comes upon an old woman dying in a young woman's arms. Before the war. It's his first time seeing death up close. Only a few paragraphs but the image will stay with Maeve, the young woman like a crocodile, holding a dying woman in her arms the way a crocodile holds a monkey in its jaw. A weird metaphor. It made the comfort of the helper menacing, the young eating the old. It wasn't in the book he published. This would not make what he told Terry Gross he called "the God cut." But it was the part that seared her. That crocodile convinced her to say what she wanted. Allowed her to think: You'd pretty much be a fool not to do this, Maeve. Life offers so few surprises, so few genuinely extraordinary turns. Don't die before trying this.

"No one can know," she began.

"I understand."

She told him what she wanted: no one to know. No one. Not Dora, or Katrina or Willie. Naturally, he said. He crossed his heart with an X.

Her body had its own say. A tiny, honest thumping made itself known. She honored it. Which is not something she had ever done, not this way, honoring that thumping. The sheets were linen, disablingly soft, the color of terra-cotta, and had a smell that went beyond him, which was Dora, her perfume, her shampoo and soap and skin and hair; whatever wasn't him was her. Or were the children, but Maeve didn't think of them until later. The children were not palpable on those sheets, only their parents, their mother whose perfume was herbal rather than floral, had an element of—rosemary? Soon she'd find a bottle on the bathroom shelf and confirm it. Oh it was good. The whole smell of the bed disabled the part of her brain that does words. His pits and creases and densities and hollows.

"What's this called again?"

"Elbow."

"What about this?"

"Navel. I like to gaze at it, the critics say."

"They do not."

His chest was bulkier, more barreled than Jack's. But beyond that she found she didn't feel the need to make comparisons. Their stomachs touched each other. Why did that feel normal?

"Is this a go?"

He was holding a small red thing in his hand. She saw it and thought: STOP. But this was four-sided, a square. He ripped it open. Yes, go.

After, on their backs, watching dark clouds drift across the skylight, she found the courage to ask: "Does this happen a lot?"

"I wouldn't say so. No, it doesn't." Then: "*This*, what just happened between us, does decidedly not happen a lot."

"Does Dora also do this? With other people?"

"Now and then."

"She tells you?"

He said only, "I don't concern myself with it."

"Do you have, like, a policy?"

"We do," he said, but didn't elaborate.

She wanted to ask if Dora saw men or women. Felt nervous to ask.

"Does it make you jealous, when she's with other people? Wait—don't leave."

He didn't, came back.

"You're very soft," he said, pulling her close. "I wasn't really getting up. That was a feint. Are you really interested in knowing this?"

"Kind of." And more definitely, "Yes, I am."

He fell into serious thought.

"Sometimes," he said. "I'm jealous sometimes. But not too often. Our life is sweet. It works."

What she'd seen was real—the easy affection, the comradeship, between him and his wife. The lovely family. Sex with Maeve would not puncture that.

Her lips were tired from kissing.

"I'll never tell Jack. For the record."

"Your call. Up to you."

"I'm sure of it. Never."

"I just don't want a screaming husband at my door. That's all I don't want."

"He wouldn't do that."

"No?"

"It's not his style. But I won't tell him." She sighed. "It'll be a secret. It won't change anything between me and Jack."

She meant it. Believed it, dumbly.

The rectangle of sky above them grew dark. Pattering rain. No hurry.

"What a spell you've put me under, May."

She laughed.

"Yesterday?" he said. "I couldn't stop thinking about that kiss. I haven't been kissed that way in many years."

"You kissed *me* like that."

"No need to get defensive." He put his hand on her ass. "I like how aggressive you are."

"Are you making fun of me?"

"I'm serious," he said, and she realized he was.

"I'm aggressive?"

"Didn't you know?"

Later on, it pleased her to see among Dora's fancy lotions a tube of the same eye cream Maeve used. A drugstore brand, highly regarded by dermatologists, no-nonsense.

———

When she got home that afternoon, there was a raccoon sitting quietly next to Paige's plants. Docile. It was the size of a throw pillow. It only looked at her. She backed away. Perhaps it was rabid? She had the wits to take a picture. It blinked, sleepily.

She wrote to Paige: Look at this. In the subject of the email she wrote: sleepy animals?!

She thought: I'll never tell. Never.

When Jack called that evening, she let it go to voicemail. She wasn't prepared yet. She had the feeling of reading a book, being lost in a book, the way in an absorbing novel you see your own world differently, your own imagination torqued, prodded. The tree out the window has a newly beseeching branch. The sky is a sieve through which rain falls. Life is better, more intense, time stretchier. Coming out of a book can do this, or a movie, or a good dream, and it was how she felt coming out of bed with Harry. It had to be killed before she made the call to her husband, but she wasn't ready to kill it.

Jack left her a voicemail.

"It's balmy here in Tampon. I miss you, honey."

She took out the notebook. Her own yellow legal pad. She wrote in her beautiful cursive along the first line: *My name is Elizabeth but everyone calls me Libby*. Then she tore it up and poured herself a drink. Then she started again. Tore it up. She did this a few more times.

Later on, to feel close to him, she read the novel that made Harrison want to die by his own hand. William Maxwell. The start of chapter 2: "I very much doubt I would have remembered for more than fifty years the murder of a tenant farmer I never laid eyes on if (1) the murderer hadn't been the father of somebody I knew, and (2) I hadn't later done something I was ashamed of afterward. This memoir—if that's the right name for it—is a roundabout, futile way of making amends."

She read the book until her eyes grew heavy. It did not make her feel like dying. It turned her on, knowing it was his favorite, even though it was possibly the saddest thing she'd ever read.

She could never write a memoir. Never. But what about a memoir that pretends to be fiction? That tries, as Maxwell says, to make amends? The urge to write, to be naked with Harrison, to be loved by her husband . . . three urges, twisted together, like a braid in her hair she can't stop stroking.

34

SHE ANTICIPATED DIFFICULTY talking to Jack that night. Would he be able to tell from her voice that she had slept with another man? She kept reminding herself that the Bible is full of what she'd done. Anything that archetypal can't be that wrong. This was a part of humanity, part of the human condition. She could be afforded an allowance, surely. Jack would forgive her, she was sure—and also sure she'd never ever tell him, so it was easy to be sure. She didn't let herself think about what happens to the adulterers in the Maxwell novel.

Anyway, Jack wasn't suspicious in the slightest on the phone.

"Branson confided the surgery didn't go as well as he hoped. A dozen kinds of fuckery."

"Poor Teenie!"

"They're getting it under control. He's not too worried. Can we video chat later, honey? I need to see your face," and of course she agreed.

A relief when she logged on a few hours later. She expected Jack in his hotel room, computer propped on his knees, just the two of them, a bed chat. And how much would he see in her then? But he appeared in the hospital room, Teenie asleep in the bed and Jack in the chair next to her, wearing a cantaloupe-colored polo shirt, his elbow on the armrest, head resting in his palm.

"Hi honey," he said scratchily. "She's too drugged to say hi. She woke up a few minutes ago to ask if Christopher fed the dog."

"Christopher?"

He shrugged. There was no dog either. Maeve saw the sad scene, the misery she was forcing him to contend with alone. The delicate IV into her bloated arm, electronic signals connoting her existence.

"I'm sorry I'm not there," she told him, feeling it, meaning it.

"Meanwhile Riddles is taking you to Asagios."

"I didn't go to Asagios! That was Katrina and Willie."

"I'm joking."

"Did my flowers arrive?"

"They're here. Behind the computer. You can't see them."

"Are they pretty? I told them no carnations."

He said, "I got a copy of *The Palest Winter*. I went to the Barnes & Noble."

Jack was not a reader. This was significant. She'd been encouraging him to read it forever.

"I'm not sure I can focus on it. My concentration's shot. I got to page three before I fell into a coma last night. But I want to know the guy who's writing about Willie."

She said, "You'll love it." Then: "It's Teddy's favorite."

He smiled in a sad way. Her throat narrowed.

"It's been a nice interlude," she told him.

"I'm glad, honey."

"I'm sorry I'm not there, but I'm learning things about writing. And I've gotten to know Willie better. That's been nice." She said something she hadn't planned to say: "I bet I'll get a thank-you in the acknowledgments."

His mother kicked the sheet and, in her sleep, said, "Electricity?"

She told him about Katrina and Willie's apartment, the apple tree, and he smiled in a far-off way.

At the end of the call Maeve said, "Teenie, I know you're sleeping, but if you can hear me, it's me, Maeve, and I'm sending big love from Maine."

"Good night, honey," Jack said with a yawn.

"Good night, Jack."

"Think about coming here, huh?" A sad smile—finally, a guilt-inducing smile. "If there's a lull in the action?"

———

The hospital room in Florida looked exactly like the hospital room in Maine, back at the end of Maeve's mother's life. Those days after her mother's stroke so long ago, Jack had wanted to come to the hospital, offered to sit with Maeve by the bedside, but she'd said no, no thank you. She didn't want her new husband there. She needed to be alone with her mother. She had been protecting Jack and their young relationship, did not want him part of a final triangle, ensnared in one last situation. And surely protecting Molly too, granting her privacy. Because if someone else had been there, it seems unlikely Molly would have said some of the things she said, which Maeve ended up thinking about for a long time.

"I was rooting for you to leave," Molly had said. A tube in her nose, puffy eyes, a croaking voice Maeve didn't recognize. "I always hoped you'd go to New York with your brother. I hope you didn't stay for me."

And Maeve, startled by this disclosure, said, "I met Jack," meaning he was why she stayed, her husband, not Molly, but suddenly she wasn't sure.

Her mom. Her loud, ding-y, angry, only mom. Stomping on the floorboards. Wailing, laughing, being a being. Maeve did not want her to go. It scared her, surprised her, how much she didn't want her mother to leave. She was glad Jack was not there to see her cry.

Now Jack's mother treaded the dark waters down in Florida, or was wading in, but Jack and Kelly-Anne needed to do their own reconciling, to say whatever they needed to say at the bedside. Maeve would only stifle them, interfere with their exchanges of forgiveness.

Though all that was beside the point, or premature, because Teenie wasn't dying yet. Jack and his sister were right there to care for her. It was only a hip.

The next morning, she woke to find the rain had stopped. The strange weather, days of tension, such a zany confluence of fronts, had nearly cleared out, and now the stability in the atmosphere felt unnatural.

The phone rang while Maeve was drinking her coffee on the patio. She had been watching the greenhouse changing color, gray to green to pink, clouds shape-shifting on its panes. A 212 number, New York City, so her first thought was Harry. He'd called before from a local number, his house's landline. This must be his cell. But it was his wife's cell. Dora on the line, husky, drinking her coffee, she said, on a porch in North Carolina, looking at the clouds.

"I'm doing that too," Maeve told her. "Both of those things."

"Cheers," they said.

Why didn't she feel more nervous? She didn't, at first.

"I only wanted to say hello," Dora said, warmly. "And to thank you. I hear you're keeping my husband alive."

"Surely that's an overstatement."

"He wouldn't feed himself."

"I know about husbands."

Dora chuckled; Maeve exhaled.

I am sleeping with your husband. You have a policy that says I can. These were the unfathomable thoughts. Harrison had promised he would not tell Dora, but what did Maeve know of their marriage? Or how they navigated their openness? What did a promise mean from him? She understood he had no allegiance to Maeve.

"Does he say he's a beast?"

"He says that."

"He'd like a name tag. Really he's fine. It's learned helplessness. Plus a God complex."

Maeve's impulse was to keep the conversation on the book, and found herself telling Dora how good it was already—how vivid this new voice, this new Willie. "He read it to us," Maeve said. "It'll mean so much to the world, this book—" But of course Dora knew what her husband was capable of, and she cut Maeve off—

"It'll be wonderful, yes. It will surely win awards. I am confident that Willie is in good hands."

She gave a long sigh.

"How's your play coming?"

Dora inhaled sharply. "It's more moving than I ever antic-ipated, to see something of mine brought to life. Thank you for asking, Maeve." Then she said, "I heard your husband wants you in Florida."

They had talked about her. That Dora said it that way—"wants you." Bewildering, beguiling, and then Maeve felt a kick of dread. How much had Harrison shared?

She heard Dora's breath.

"I try to avoid Florida at all costs."

"Naturally." Dora added: "Though I love Miami."

"This is Tampa. Jack's mother had hip surgery. His sister's there. He has plenty of help."

"Jack, yes. I'd forgotten his name."

She heard a child shout in a room beyond Dora.

"I want you to know that I understand," Dora said. "I completely do. I don't need details, but I understand. I appreciate it, even, in a way; that's the truth. He needs this, every time. Every time he finds it. Every book. I think you should be aware."

Maeve heard the child shout again.

"I'm not sure I understand what you mean."

Dora spoke with clarity and gentleness, a fatigued wisdom: "I'm fond of you. I understand why he is too."

"I'm fond of you too," Maeve began. "Meeting you both—"

Her mouth went dry. Her heart scrambled.

"I am always rooting for him, Maeve. Understand that. Always. There's never a moment when I'm not rooting for him." She sighed. She had to go now. The children were destroying her sister's house. "Be well, I hope."

Something final in it, and sad, and now Maeve didn't want to hang up, felt a ballooning in her belly—

"Don't hang up, Dora."

A silence.

"Yes?"

"He should be there, to see your play."

"He should be. You're right."

"I'll tell him."

"Oh. Oh my. Such a little duck." She said this affectionately, gave a purring laugh. "You tell him. Go ahead."

"I don't mean to interfere."

"I know you don't, believe me. I know you mean well."

"I like you both so much," Maeve heard herself say. The pressure to speak was like a cough she couldn't repress. "It's been such a difficult time for me. Such a hard time. Everything has changed so suddenly."

She thought about her hands on his thighs the day before. Her hands on either side of his pelvis. She couldn't stop herself from putting them wherever they went.

Dora said, "He's surely not the most selfish man in the universe, but he might be in the top ten. Top five even? Is your husband like that?"

"I don't think so."

"Well, I know who I married. Enjoy it, that's really my only advice." Her voice grew tighter now, strained. "Have at it. I mean that, sincerely. I can imagine how good it feels—of course I don't need to imagine. I live it. It's my life. But, Maeve. If you think you have any power to make him *do* anything, you're in for a world of hurt. I offer that in a spirit of actual care. You should also be aware that it will vaporize. So fast you'll think you imagined it. I feel compelled to tell you that . . . Maeve? Are you there?"

"I am," Maeve whispered.

"If you sense that I might take a little pleasure from your hurt, you won't be entirely wrong, but mostly you'll be wrong. Mostly."

Then she hung up.

Dora Dora Dora.

Witchy bitch, Deacon will say, but that's later. Dora's not a bitch, she'll cry, even after her life has resumed. I love her, she won't say—to Deacon, to anyone—yet there it is, inside her, like a tune in a music box waiting for a hand.

Her coffee was cold. She looked out at her yard. The greenhouse.

The fire pit. The scrappy acre of woods that separated their property from the neighbors', shivering pines, a perennial shade. For the life of her, she wasn't sure what was going to happen next. She remembered Libby, back at the library: "Don't tell me. I want to be surprised."

35

FINALLY PAIGE REPLIED to her email. Subject heading: sleepy animals?!

Exceptionally interesting. A compound in this plant may cause unusual behavior. Continue to document. Approach with care. Will confer with Joe this evening. He's in NYC with donor trying to get us dough. (Fingers crossed, please.) In the meantime, I'm putting a net in the mail, to be placed over that section. Make sure door/windows latched at night.

What is this plant? Maeve wrote.

Half an hour later, when Maeve saw a raccoon in the hammock, curled up, paws under its head, she did what Paige said and took a picture.

Harrison sent her a message over email:

What a day. I have filled another notebook. My eyes are burning. I had a nosebleed. A good sign. Blood means good pages. Thank you for your company, dear May.

There was no invitation to return. That was OK. *Dear May*. That was good. That was enough. And she needed a break anyway. She needed to think about what Dora had said. To be alone with Dora, in this way.

She checked the greenhouse, made sure it was latched properly. Then she pulled off one of the leaves. Broke the leaf in two. It was a whim. Then in half again, so what she put her on her tongue— bitter, pleasant, like a tonic—was only a quarter of a leaf. A quarter of a whim.

36

JESSICA FLETCHER WOULD indulge her curiosity.

Wouldn't she?

Half an hour after Maeve ate the leaf, her limbs grew light. She felt more capable. Openhearted. It's only something that grows in the ground, she told herself.

Maeve drove a few laps around the library.

The blond girl with good skin, the white jacket studded with pins, smoked a cigarette by the bike rack. White jacket, white jeans, white skin.

If there had not been a spot, Maeve wouldn't have stopped. She circled the block three times. On the third lap, last chance—a car was pulling out, and she pulled in.

She needed to be quick, didn't want to be seen by her former colleagues. It was afternoon, but the heads of the old people floated in the front window. No, those were teenagers. It was hard to tell. The light hit the glass in such a way.

The nature of this particular whim was to break the ice. No more pussyfooting. To be unruffable, like Jack. Like Libby. Maybe it was the plant acting on her, or maybe she just wanted to do this.

"Excuse me, aren't you a friend of Libby Leanham?"

This girl wore a flat expression, a face for watching television. Her pins said *Peace* and *Free the Uterus* and things that Maeve didn't understand.

"Friend? I mean, I know her. Are you her social worker?"

"No, I'm not. I'm Ms. Cosgrove."

"You look familiar."

"I'm the librarian." She pointed at the building. "Maeve Cosgrove."

"Oh right." She banged the side of her head. Now she smiled, crookedly, looking suddenly sweet. "I recognize you. Sorry. I have really bad cramps. I can't see straight."

What had at first seemed a provocative pose, a sultry sideways arching, now read as pain.

"Yeah, now I recognize you," the girl said. "I know Libby, sure. We're not friends, but I respect her. She's got chutzpah."

"Chutzpah?"

"Maybe I'm not pronouncing that right."

"What's your name, honey?"

"I don't want to say. I'll get in trouble."

She looked at her hand, where a long, light brown cigarette smoked between her fingers.

"I won't report you. I don't even work at the library anymore."

"You don't?"

"I quit," she said.

The girl nodded, as if she approved.

"Vale is my name. Not a bride's veil. V-A-L-E."

"That's a pretty name."

The girl shrugged. "It's a pain. I always have to spell it."

"How does Libby have chutzpah?"

The girl straightened up.

"I just learned that word from my dentist. Maybe I'm not using it right. He said I had *chutzpah* when I told him I didn't trust him to give me gas. I just mean Libby's kind of bold. She's quiet but then she says these intense things."

"Like what?"

"I can't remember, exactly. She just tells intense stories."

"Intense how?"

"Just weird stuff."

"Is she around, do you know? Have you seen her lately?"

"She's been gone for a while. Peg thought she might go to the West Coast. She had some idea about going west."

Could Vale be more specific?

Vale shrugged.

"I heard something," Maeve said. "About a teacher . . ."

At *teacher*, Vale blinked.

Maeve said, "I only want to help her."

Maeve's curiosity, or the word *teacher*, seemed to take Vale aback; she looked up and down the street. Her wincing grew more pronounced.

"I really need some Advil. These cramps are nuclear. And some, you know, women things. If you give me ten bucks for that stuff, it would help a lot."

Poor thing! Cramps! Maeve said she remembered the agony of cramps, teenage cramps being as bad as childbirth, truly. She kept a bottle of Advil in her glove compartment. She gave it to the girl, plus the money.

Money. She gave her money. She could have told her to go to the bathroom in the library, the lower-level women's room. A machine there gave out free pads. Instead, Maeve put a ten-dollar bill in her hand.

You mean you bribed her, Deacon will say later. That's hilarious.

"Don't buy cigarettes," Maeve told Vale.

"I totally won't."

"Or drugs."

"I'm buying pads, I promise." Then: "You could ask the social worker for the actual story."

"I've spoken to the social worker. Frankly—can I be frank?"

Vale nodded.

"The system labels and stigmatizes girls. Girls are more likely to be locked up, medicated. Sometimes the system is a hindrance."

Vale nodded, smiled. As if conceding to Maeve's coolness, she offered her a cigarette.

"Oh no. No. I can't condone smoking. It's bad enough watching you."

"These are mostly herbal."

"Herbal?"

"Not pot. Totally legal herbs. Rose petals and stuff. Light on the tobacco. My cousin gets them for me from New York. You can't get them in Maine."

Maeve sniffed at the smoke, which seemed in no way particular.

Maeve said, "Do you know the teacher's name?"

"He's dead," Vale said, shaking her head, looking disgusted. "He killed himself when she tried to end it. That's what I heard. Not from Libby but from someone who heard it from her."

At her old school, in the central part of the state. Vale wasn't sure what the deal was. Libby threatened to tell, wanted to end it. Or something. Rather than go to jail, or lose her, the guy drove his car into a tree. Supposedly Libby blamed herself.

"She told someone she murdered a guy she loved. It really fucked her up, people say. She might have lit a fire. I heard different things." She rocked on her heels. "It's weird to gossip with the librarian."

"Not gossip," Maeve said, firmly. "I'm trying to help her."

Vale said that was cool. She repeated that she had heard all this secondhand, didn't have more details than that. But the main thing, really, was that she had no idea what was true, and no one did because it was understood the girl was a person who lied. Like, a lot.

"It can be a reaction to trauma—lying. It might not be her fault."

"Huh," Vale said.

Back at home Maeve did her internet sleuthing. She googled: dead teacher, central Maine. Right away: Glenn Scales. He taught physics at a regional high school up there. An article described the crash. Cause unknown. A clear day, speed assumed a factor. *Thank the Lord,* his wife was quoted in the paper, *our baby girl wasn't in the car.* The teacher was called *beloved.* There was nothing in the news about him being a predator, or involved with a minor, or under investigation. No suggestion of impropriety.

Maeve looked for a long time at his face. He had a long nose, a thin mouth, a floppy hairstyle that seemed at once indifferent and vain. He looked sad. She browsed the comments section, under the article.

Brilliant teacher, RIP

You made physics come alive!

My terrific teacher and friend. A soul taken too soon. May the lord bless his soul and the souls of his wife and daughter.

And this one, between the grieving adoration: *he jizzed in my hair.*

But a moment later that comment was gone. She refreshed her screen. Gone. Had Maeve imagined it? That's when she saw faint movement in the wall, beneath the paint, under the surface of the paint, like a school of fish rippling, making all variety of triangles, and she decided it was the bitter leaf letting her see this way, something Paige had engineered in a lab roving in her bloodstream.

Now all she wanted to do was sleep. Pleasant prickling on her skin, and she settled on the floor, curled up on the rug under the window, in a beam of sunlight, thinking Oh, Oh! Now I know what it feels like to be a cat. She had forgotten to be curious.

37

IN THE MORNING she felt perfect. She'd wondered if she'd be hung-over, if the plant would linger, but she felt clear and well rested. He called at seven-thirty, with the brusqueness of a man busy at important work, above the management of logistics. He got to the point. Proposed two hours. He said a word she liked: *assignation*. A delineated time frame.

"Are you in, May? No pressure. Today, this is what I have to offer. If what I have to offer and what you have to offer match—fantastic. If not, no worries."

He spoke quickly, busily, a new voice.

"They match," she said, mirroring his tone.

"Perfect. I'm pleased."

"Me too."

"See you then, my friend."

He hung up.

It's a choice but doesn't feel like one.

On the drive there she listened to NPR. She tried to focus on a story about the prison industrial complex, but her thoughts kept float-ing off. Disabling excitement. The highway became back roads, the oldest bridge in the county. Budding trees made a canopy over the driveway. The loud crunch of gravel, chipmunks darting to avoid her tires.

No more brusqueness. He answered the door in a robe. A robe! The color of cream, soft cotton, with a terry cloth lining. It signaled a new intimacy. He wore pajama pants underneath, soft and blue, like a patient in a hospital.

"I heard Dora called you."

She was relieved that she wouldn't have to decide whether to tell him.

He was drinking herbal tea instead of coffee today, on account of his stomach. He made her a cup too. It was German, he said, not unpleasant once you got used to it, but the first sip tasted like attic.

"Dora has her charms, as you know. But she's goddamn nosy. She can't admit she's jealous, so she befriends."

"She's jealous? Does she know?"

"I'm talking as a personality trait."

"What did she tell you?"

"Only that you had a nice call, but I know Dora."

Her throat beat roughly.

"It was a strange call," she admitted. "Is that it? Is she trying to befriend me?"

He didn't answer.

"Did you tell her about us?"

"I promised I wouldn't and I didn't. But she's psychic. I told you, she intuits." Then he said, "That can't surprise you. Can it really surprise you?"

Everything was surprising her. But also—he was right. Part of the pleasure, she was coming to see, was that Dora knew, or could know, or might suspect.

After a moment she said, "I like her."

"Naturally you do. Everyone does."

Another startling transition, for now he was close to her, his eyes warm again, saying, "But what do *you* want, Maeve? Why are we talking about Dora and not you?"

"Me?"

"You want something. Be honest. Can you be honest about it?"

"I can be."

"*Will* you be?"

He acted as if she were holding something back, restraining herself. But this wasn't true. She had to decide what to say. How to say it. She was slower than he was.

"I'm thinking."

"It's not a thinking matter."

She said, "It is for me."

He nodded. Gave her a moment. Then he said, plainly, steadily, eyes locked on hers: "I want to know what gets you wet. Can you tell me? Can you be honest?"

No one had spoken to her that way before. He knew what to say, knew the tone that would puncture her, a hard factuality. Well alright then. His office—she'd admit it.

"Your office," she said. "Your desk."

She wanted it there, in the big room at the top of the house. Up the twisting stairs they went. They began on top of the desk, which he cleared off with a sweeping arm, like a lusting man in a sitcom, the exact right slapstick note. They were laughing at the beginning. Later they moved onto the wooden floor. Next to the gorgeous cabinet—the antique card catalog. It thrilled her, to be on the hard floor underneath him. To touch the slender leg of the card catalog, to reach back and hold it while he thrust into her. He breathed like a man attuned to his exertion, as if counting push-ups in his head. Afterward he collapsed on her and she gasped, lost her breath. He mistook the gasp for pleasure. She gasped again, pretending, until it became real pleasure, nervous pleasure, grinding under his heavy body, wriggling, frank with need, and then he said, "There's a certain thing I want to do to you. Can I do it?"

He meant with his mouth. A kind of bravado in his execution, exactitude, as if he were making an instructional video, demonstrating all the angles, the methods.

"You have a timeless face," he whispered.

This was later, when the shaking had subsided. He was stroking her cheek. Then her brow. They were still on the floor.

"You don't belong to any era." He blinked a few times. He looked at her so lovingly, as if she were more than a fling, and said: "Shakespeare would have had a girlfriend like you."

Oh! That lit her up.

Deacon would ask, later: Who was that compliment really for? But it felt so good, to be in a sentence with Shakespeare, to be made worthy of the Bard. It was the best thing anyone had ever said to her.

While she put her clothes back on, he went down to use the bathroom. He turned on the stereo downstairs. Orchestral music rose up. Quickly, with her phone, she snapped pictures of a few things. The desk. The mess of desk objects on the floor, Mickey Mouse on his side. The mini trampoline. The card catalog.

Why did she want pictures? To send to Deacon? To have proof? Only to remember? She wasn't stupid. It would end. Only to remember. It was slipping away even as it happened, and having pictures would give her something to hold on to. That was how simple it was. She opened a drawer of that wonderful card catalog, excitement growing—found it empty. Another one—found only a rubber ball, the kind in a vending machine, the color of marmalade. Another—a bundle of incense tied with a red string. Another—a baby's pastel pacifier.

In every drawer, a secret.

Music playing, so she didn't hear him return.

"That came from India."

She swung around. "I'm sorry for poking around! I love this." She touched the cabinet's face. "God, it's beautiful. It's perfect."

"British Colonial. I bought it at auction."

She caressed the wood, fingered its knobs.

"They do their libraries well, the British," she said, Katrina's line.

He was looking at her strangely. Her face grew warmer.

He sat in a chair, the chair Willie had been sitting in when she'd seen them talking that first day. He wore the robe, belted, without the pants now. His legs, muscular, hairy, in a wide V. But not too wide. She knew about his balls now, which were fundamentally regular. She hated that Jezebel piece. Disdained its millennial author.

He asked her to sit across from him. She did.

"I'm private. I don't want to let it pass."

He made his hands a camera.

"Oh no."

"Private," he repeated. "My openness with you notwithstanding. I don't want pictures of this place out there. I don't want to be treated like"—he swallowed—"a novelty. A bit of trivia."

Her face burned. "No! That's not how it is."

"I've been hurt before."

"I wouldn't do that. They're just for me. So after you vanish, I'll remember what this room was like."

He softened at that, it seemed, but did not take issue with *vanish*, as she wished he would.

"Only to remember," she said.

He squinted. "Everything has to be memorialized?"

"Not everything."

"I want to be here with you, in the present tense."

"I'm sorry. I really am. I'm so embarrassed."

But then he went to her, took her in his arms. Gathered her up. They stood together, hugging.

"You're not a creep, Maeve. Don't worry."

"Was it creepy to take pictures?"

He pulled away, looked at her. "I feel like a specimen. I get anxious. Can you imagine it?"

She tried. She said yes. He sat again, and she took the other chair.

She said, "But couldn't you imagine taking a picture of my house? If you went. If you were in my room. To remember it?"

He didn't speak.

She said, shyly, "I hope you could imagine wanting a picture of my house."

"When you put it that way, it's not so bad."

"I'll delete them all."

"I overreacted."

He looked, actually, like he might cry.

"I'm sorry, Harry."

"That's enough apologizing. We're on the same team, you and me."

"I'll delete them," and she did, right then, while he watched.

"I'm just a raw nerve."

"I know."

"You do, don't you? Why do I feel like you know? It's your eyes. You look at me so intently. God, I'm always this way when I start a book. I'm not decent. Now Willie's spring break is over and I'm worried I don't have enough. I feel Dora's anger about the cricket play rising from down south."

"Grasshopper," she said.

"Grasshopper, yes."

Why did she correct him? He bit at his lower lip. Had she annoyed him? Now came her urge to help. To soothe.

"I know something," Maeve said.

She understood what she would do.

A reparation for being too curious, for making him feel like a specimen. He would vanish as Dora had predicted, before Maeve knew what hit her. But not yet. She told him about the conversation yesterday—how Katrina read Willie's email, perceived a mystery, found Willie unexpectedly guarded. A hidden story. A murky layer.

"I thought you should be aware. It's not my business, but I thought it might be, I don't know—helpful? There could be a story there. Something to listen for."

"This is interesting." He drummed his index finger on his lips. "You really are quite observant."

"I didn't observe. Katrina told me."

Immediately she wished she hadn't said it. She felt uncomfortable and transparent. "Maybe I shouldn't have told you. It's not my business. I keep saying things I shouldn't say."

"It's imperative. For me to do a good job, I need to know everything."

"I mean it's Willie's call—whatever he decides, right? But this way, you can be better prepared."

He smiled, said, "Forewarned is forearmed."

Even in the thickness of guilt, even seeing herself, she wanted to give him more.

"Katrina thinks it could be something awful."

"Does she?"

"She says she'll love him anyway."

She didn't want to talk about them anymore and was glad when he said, "Let's take a walk."

They went to the meadow, looked at the trees. Their burls and mushroom ledges. Then took the path to the water, the ocean, rocks, the overcast sky, newsprint gray. A bird roared over them. Jurassic cawing. He said, "Cabot Cove is the best place on earth. And that was before I knew you." He kissed her under that sky.

Then he had to get back to work. Sweet sorrow. He had a book to write.

"You do too, Maeve."

"I do? No I don't."

He said, "Just don't make it about me."

"You're just trying to flatter me."

"Why would I do that? I've already gotten in your pants."

On the drive home, no other cars on this stretch of road, a hawk swooped down and, for several moments, flew along next to her car. Tan feathers, a yellow beak, reptilian feet. How would Harrison describe it? She grew excited, for it stayed close to her for quite some time. It seemed attuned to her Volvo, flew along for several miles, until suddenly it shot across the highway and into the woods.

Why would it do that?

She could not describe the bird well. She felt unequipped to say why any animal did anything.

Back in town, she passed the library. No one at the bike rack. No spots available. That was good. That was better. She was not to be trusted. She felt dangerously magnanimous. Last time she had given away money and her Advil. What next?

38

IN THE MIDDLE OF THE NIGHT, the rumble of the garage door. She sat up, her bedroom swaying. Who was opening the garage? Who knew the code? Only Jack, Paige, but in her sleepiness, in the sway-ing, in the midst of whatever dream (her mind bloomed with green), she felt sure it was Harrison, that he who had so many things would naturally have her garage code too. She got up and rushed to the stairs, not alarmed at all.

In the doorway to the kitchen, suitcase at his feet, stood Jack. Of course Jack, who belonged here, in jeans and a navy sweatshirt and his battered loafers. She descended the stairs, with every step grow-ing more awake.

"I stink," he said amiably, sniffed a pit. "Beware."

"Am I dreaming? Jack?"

"Hi honey."

"You're supposed to be in Tampa."

"This *is* Tampa."

She shook her head.

"Don't confuse me!"

"It's Maine," he said, "decisively." He smiled, put a hand on each shoulder. "It's me. Your only husband." He pulled her into him.

"You smell like airplane."

Riddles. The skylight over his bed. The shaking. What had been occluded by sleep appeared to her vividly, and she pulled back, said, "Why didn't you tell me you were coming?"

"Last minute. Got a late flight. I left you a message?"

"Oh. I haven't played it."

He smiled. He did not seem in any way suspicious. "There's a meeting tomorrow. Burt's in town." Burt Gale was the big boss. "They're doing the quarterly. Figured I should show my face. That's what I said on the message. And that I wanted to see you."

"I fell asleep before I heard it. I'm glad you're not a murderer."

"Me too!"

It was half past one. He hung up his things in the nook between the garage and the kitchen, and then came in and sat at the table and said, "You should have heard Kelly-Anne. She didn't want me to leave. She's terrified Mom will die on her watch. Only one night away, I promised her."

Maeve said, "But the doctor specifically said she was *not* going to die."

"Kelly-Anne's developed a preoccupation."

"You're too pale to have been in Florida," she told him.

"Maybe you'll come back with me? You can drag me to the pool."

She didn't respond. She could not go to Florida. He had come to get her, she understood.

She asked him if he wanted tea before bed. Toast?

"Yes, please."

Their house had felt different since he left—hers but aslant, altered, the way a room can look imperceptibly different in a photograph, through a certain lens. Jack being there made it the old house again, but the new one remained present in her mind, so there were two kitchens.

He untied his shoes. He talked about Kelly-Anne's behavior, the crying. A fight with the manager of the hospital gift shop, who admittedly was an asshole. Maeve listened, feeling—it surprised her—a new protectiveness toward his sister.

"Poor Kelly-Anne," Maeve sighed. "She and Teenie really are attached at the hip. What does Branson say about the infection?"

"Improving."

He'd lost a little weight, even in a week. He needed to shave. She put a cup of tea before him in a plain white mug. Steam in his face.

"Kelly-Anne needs help," Jack said. "Not a Christian therapist, a real one. A proper therapist."

"Huh," said Maeve, and though his sister was annoying, she felt herself bristle. Always therapy. Every difficult woman needed a professional . . . to sweep the crazy from the corners, to clear the gutters of her mind. She could hardly blame Jack for his fear—it ran in both of their families, gutters that needed regular attention. She knew this, and yet she wanted to be angry at him. She heard the life coach say: Easier to be angry than guilty.

She said, "It is a hard thing to come to terms with, a mother's decline. Mine went so fast."

"Poor Molly."

"Two weeks!"

"I remember."

"She's a grown woman, Jack. Kelly-Anne needs to cope. Let the Bible group look after her."

"The Bible group!" He shook his head. "They rile her up. Mom's the one who keeps her calm."

The toaster chimed. She buttered his bread. He took large, neat bites. He spoke about the nature of his mother's bones, her pelvis, sounding dutiful and well informed, doctorly.

"Will you come back with me?" he asked again, when he was done eating.

She knew by now what she was going to say. She spoke in her library voice, tried to expel any defensiveness, did her best. She told him that working on this book, supporting the project, and getting to know Willie and Harrison and Dora—that all this was meaningful to her, and a quirk of fate, and not something she could just fly away from.

"I've lost my job. Paige is gone. I've been invited to work on a project with one of my favorite writers in the whole world. Isn't that reasonable? You see that nothing like this will ever happen again?"

"I miss you." He looked down at his lap. "Forgive me. I'm being selfish."

"No, no."

"I am."

He wiped his mouth of crumbs with the back on his hand.

"Teenie's not dying. And what I'm doing here with the book is time-sensitive. You must understand that. I'll visit afterward."

"After . . . ?"

"The library event. *My* event."

"The library," he said with a long sigh. "Those fuckers."

He looked at her tenderly. "I'm jealous, alright? It's not unheard of. You've never heard of the jealous husband?"

She pretended to be confused, flabbergasted. Which wasn't a lie— astonishment was her primary state right now. She just leaned into it, did the adulterer's lines, ready-made, floating in the cosmos to be plucked by a person in need: "Jealous! Of who? Of what?"

"This Svengali."

"Please."

"Your new friends. This house of his. This wife. All of it."

Her crush, an amalgam—his jealousy too. Oh Jack.

She took his hands. "There's nothing to be jealous of."

It's a worse crime than the sex, this pretending. She wanted to be honest about the heart of it, at least. To be candid within a lie, help him understand, so she said, "It's a transitional period. A bridge to a new place. After losing my job. Being around that kind of creative energy is good for me. It's different." She swallowed. "I'll figure out what to do next."

"I don't want to hold you back," he said. His face was serious. "I understand. I'm not an asshole."

"I'll come after the event. I'll fly down soon."

He nodded stoically, biting at his bottom lip.

"Don't be jealous, Jack."

"I'll try not to be."

"Don't stew," she said.

"Me?"

He smiled, such a good sport.

Upstairs, he turned on CNN and got into the shower. Footage of a rally. People holding signs: *Send Obama Back to Kenya. Impeach President Food Stamps.*

Some newspaper editorials said the nation had healed its racial wounds, but then you turned on the TV and saw signs like that. All the birth certificate nonsense! She felt protective of Obama in the same way she felt protective of Harrison when people griped about the way he sat, the overspreading bullshit.

While Jack was in the bathroom, she ran back downstairs, sent an email: Jack came back for one night. A meeting. He's going to make partner soon. —M

Don't call tonight, she didn't have to write. Don't wake me up.

Upstairs again. Talking heads on the TV, one Black woman, one white man, and she pressed mute.

It is weird and awful and exciting how totally a person can become a new thing. One day a person becomes an adulterer. Or a thief. Or a creep. Or worse, of course, much. One has never ever done a thing, and then one has. Sometimes in nightmares Maeve is responsible for a person's death, has killed a stranger, shot a blurry figure in darkness. *Now I am a murderer*, is always the dream-thought. *Now I am a person who has murdered. I will never not be.* The dream-vibe returns to Maeve now, awake, in the middle of the night, Jack in the shower.

Then Jack came out, pink and handsome, with a fluffy white towel around his waist. He'd shaved in there, using his special antifog mirror. She knew how soft his face would feel. She saw his youngest self, the boy in the bar under the Christmas lights, the boy in the brochure selling a certain kind of life. She had seen him and wanted that life, and he'd done nothing but give it to her. She was stabbed with guilt, seeing his body.

He said, "Maybe I just needed some human touch."

His belly button, the dearest crater.

"Of course you did. You do."

"Maybe I just wanted to see you."

He was the equivalent of Deacon in his own family of women. The sane, stable, dependable point in the triangle.

"Oh Jack."

She went to him, took his face in her hands, told him how grateful she was that he'd come home. She'd missed him. She had. She had not seen him since she got laid off. He touched her extra gently, as if she were recovering from a flu. Miraculous. Relief flooded her like gas before a procedure.

Afterward he held her, smoothed her hair, cooed what a poor thing, how unfair, how unfair, the board deluded, plain as day. The fucking board. He tended finally to this new wound. Maeve had not realized how much she needed what he said, how he said it, how he stroked her neck, her ears. Maeve did not deserve what happened to her. Deluded, he kept saying, the word appearing in her head as on one of those Zen writing tablets, evaporating as soon as you put it down. When it disappeared, he said it again.

A relief not to wonder if the phone would ring. Even if she hadn't been sleeping with Harrison, she would not have gone to Florida. It made her feel better to tell herself this. Maybe it was even true.

The skylight, the office, the shaking: they didn't happen.

"Denial is not a river in Egypt," her mother used to say.

In the morning Jack was hurried, nervous about his meeting. He hadn't slept well. He woke her with coffee. His hair was wet from another shower and he wore navy pants and a short-sleeved undershirt, like a police officer.

She sat up in bed.

"I dreamed about some fish in a river," he said in a gravelly voice. He was holding up two ties—one yellow, one green.

"What were they doing?"

"Swimming." He shook his head. "I can't remember any more."

He wiggled both ties, like fish he'd reeled in, tossed the yellow aside.

The meeting at nine would last until two, he told her. He'd go directly to the airport. He lamented his early flight but his mother was doing better, awake more, demanding, and Kelly-Anne had called at 6 a.m. to say she was having a panic attack and needed him back pronto.

"I mean, of course she's having an episode. Does a bear shit in the woods?"

"She really does need a better therapist," Maeve said, despite herself.

He'd put on a white dress shirt and was tying the tie.

"Hey, there's a résumé workshop at the Y. Thursdays at noon. If you're going to stay in town, you might as well."

"Katrina said she'd help me."

"Katrina?"

"The library offers a workshop too. Katrina *teaches* it, Jack."

"Well, good." He looked like he wanted to say something else, but didn't.

"Dreaming about fish is good luck," she said. "I think it means prosperity."

She went downstairs to prepare him eggs. He followed her into the kitchen, pulling his suitcase behind him. She cooked his eggs the way he liked them, over-easy. When he wished aloud for bacon, she reminded him what Paige said: the cruel and unusual suffering of the pig.

"I know, I know. But I'm helpless. My stomach makes the choice."

Eating pig is frankly akin to cannibalism, Paige had told them. You would never ever eat a pig if you could understand how capable they were of higher-order thought, of discerning the dimensions of the horror perpetrated upon them. Octopuses too.

Maybe Paige took it too far sometimes, but Maeve admired her daughter's fervor. For every food she banished she offered a new one in return. It had been such a pleasure to learn about millet and amaranth and spelt—"ancient grains," Paige called them, making them sound mystical.

Today Maeve served Jack eggs with avocado and a slice of ordinary rye, but when his plate was empty she felt that he needed more. The daylight emphasized the thinness of his face. The meagerness of the meal struck her as symbolic.

"You need to trust your stomach. Go to the pancake place near your office. Get a side of bacon."

He told her it was plenty, patted his belly. He had more color in his cheeks now. He was right: he just needed some human touch.

"I'm ready. Got to scoot."

She wished him luck with Burt.

He flashed an insider's smile. "I hear it's looking good. Doug tells me, if I play my cards right . . ." but he didn't say what would happen.

"You always play them right, Jack."

"I don't know about always," but she saw pride in his face, knew he was going to get another promotion soon.

Liebe und Arbeit.

He kissed her. They said goodbye. She heard the car engine, and then the racket of the garage door, up and down, and then it was quiet again and she was alone, fully. She could seek what she wanted. It was only eight-thirty in the morning.

39

SHE HAD A HEADACHE after he left. She felt a little queasy. But the day could be redeemed. She had a sense of how it might be, and went to the greenhouse. A quarter of a leaf—plus a hair more. An experiment. A gradual increase, how a scientist would do it.

Next, she sent Harrison an email saying that Jack left again. He's gone back to Tampa. I hope your progress continues! —M

Half an hour later, she found herself in the hammock in the yard, much restored. A light wind touched her face. There was a greenish sky, a briny breeze. She imagined the molecules of Paige's plant dissolving in her bloodstream. She felt cleansed of Jack. As if at the sound of a bell, she knew it was time to go, knew her mission. She got out of the hammock, put on a coral-colored scarf, sunglasses, and drove.

The universe spoke to her, brazenly. NPR was playing when she started the car, a man's voice: "We need self-control as a society. Rational compassion, not just mushy feelings. We think our irrational hearts are right, but how very often they are wrong, or dangerous, our hearts—how very often they are cruel—"

Oh but it was the end of the hour, Terry Gross said, full of regret. She thanked the author, a sociologist promoting a book called *Dumb at Heart*, about the dangers of valorizing empathy as a special virtue. There was a whoosh of percussion, a commercial.

Talk of empathy everywhere. Obama had said there was "an empathy deficit" in America. Now came the blowback: too much empathy makes us myopic.

Maeve felt airy and bright and open, as if every single thing in the universe was speaking to her.

The trees leaned in the direction where she was going—the wind sped up her car.

No spot in front of the library, but across the street there was, and Maeve parallel parked masterfully, if she did say so.

At the bike rack was a girl with short black hair and light brown skin whom Maeve didn't recognize. She wore a tracksuit in emerald green. Next to her, a familiar white boy in a Red Sox hat was attempting to roll a cigarette. A math textbook balanced on the bike rack was spread with rolling papers and tobacco.

"It's not a joint!" the boy said as Maeve approached. "You can't call the cops on a cigarette. We're not on library property anyway."

"I'm not going to call the cops," Maeve promised.

The girl said, "We don't have any pot, we told you already."

"That was the other lady," the boy said. "This one's the librarian."

"Oh. Sorry. I thought you were someone else."

"I'm Maeve," Maeve said. She remembered a word from high school: "I'm not a narc."

The boy smiled. Freckles ran across his nose in a hard stripe, like a Band-Aid. "Right on," he said, and resumed his work on the cigarette.

"I'm looking for Libby Leanham," Maeve said, no hesitation this time. "Have you seen her around?"

The boy said, "The one who was bleeping her teacher?"

"Shh," the girl said.

"I know about the teacher," Maeve said.

The girl seemed surprised. The boy too.

"He drove into the river," he said, gravely. "I heard."

A tree, Maeve did not say.

"We shouldn't be talking to her." The girl squinted at Maeve. "You're the librarian?"

"I used to be," Maeve said. "I quit."

"Cool," said the boy. He made a fist in solidarity. "I quit the drugstore."

"Have you seen her lately? Libby?"

They had not.

"What else do you know about her?"

"She burned down a gazebo," the boy said.

"A swing set," the girl added.

"A whole playground, I think."

"She told Margot she has no regrets."

"Weird girl."

"Her mom too."

"Bad stock."

"Bad stock?" Maeve said. "That's awful. You shouldn't talk like that."

The girl frowned.

"I'm worried about her," Maeve said.

They looked at her. Blinked. Their indifference blasted her. Their casual disdain. Why, their eyes said, worry about trash like that?

"Imagine what it would be like," Maeve found herself saying, "if people were gossiping about you like this."

"*You* asked," he said, shrugging.

"Be kind," Maeve said. "Everyone—"

"Everyone talks about everyone," the girl said huffily, and they gathered their things, moved off to smoke in the privacy of the bus stop.

This conversation might have disturbed Maeve under ordinary circumstances, but in her new role it was bracing. She felt like a spy, like Harriet from her favorite children's novel, which she read in fourth grade and again every few years, and then aloud to Paige in the brief window when Maeve had been permitted to tuck her in at night. Harriet is a curious girl, an eavesdropper, desperate to see beyond surfaces. She famously puts herself in a dumbwaiter to spy on a woman in her bedroom. She sneaks onto a roof to peer through skylights.

Jack was in the air, officially on the plane back to Florida.

She drove home again. She took a bath. She felt ticklish, and touched herself. Like fireworks that go on longer than you think possible, an infinite grand finale, it didn't stop but slowed, or faded, hung in her body, as smoke hangs in the sky after the show ends. Then she was starving, ruthlessly hungry. Bacon. She wanted salty, unethical meat, so she went to the market and got some, came home, cooked it. The lavish fat. The gristle. The animal satisfaction of tearing it with her teeth.

For company, she turned on the TV. On PBS Bob Ross whispered how easy it really was to capture the weather, a simple flick. On History the secrets of the gulags. On Bravo a real-life family spitting wicked insults, and she decided this family would keep her company, this worse and richer family. She ate and ate. She went back to the computer. Googled the dead teacher again, poked around. All she wanted was to help the girl. The anger had vanished. She felt clarity in her purpose, empathy and decency. To tell Libby: Whatever happened was not your fault.

Whatever happened, none of it was your fault.

You are a child, and it's not your fault!

She had the clear sense that no one had ever said that to the girl. The poor girl! She took her pad and wrote: *The poor girl!*

She wrote a few more things but threw them away.

It was the plant talking. Or the bacon? The plant, she was sure.

She went outside. She saw a porcupine, or a groundhog, something brown and prickly, doing something at the far end of the yard, where the grass met the pines. Somersaults? It appeared in play. Or perhaps it was cleaning its fur. Rolling. Pausing. Rolling. It occurred to her that she should call animal control, but tried Paige instead.

Paige didn't answer the phone. "Darling, I would like to discuss this tray of plants," she said to her voicemail. "The animals are acting strange."

She wanted to call Harrison but didn't dare.

A woman for every book, Dora had insinuated. Well, so what?
Maeve had no illusions. One of a series of lovers wasn't too terrible.
It occurred to her: his life was interesting to other people, therefore
she was interesting to other people. In a biography about him, her
name could appear. Thrilling, dangerous, to be noted in the biography as a lover. As long as someone wrote it after she was dead, and
Jack. As long as there weren't too many. Then she'd cease to be an
individual and become one of a mass, like one of Don Juan's, whom
no one thought about in specifics. How many lovers were there?
How many were too many? Idle thoughts. Not unhappy. Were there
other lovers here in Maine?

The notion of a biography might have alarmed her but, again, she
felt clearheaded and calm. She felt sure that the plant had acted upon
her in some way, and she looked around the yard as if in solidarity
with the wild, rustling things.

She got into the hammock with a book she found herself drawn
to, another she'd had on her shelf for years but never cracked, *The
White Bone*, a novel from the point of view of a herd of African elephants. It had a glossary of invented words, elephant language, slow
at first but she got the hang of it, and after a few chapters it did that
thing, sharpened her vision, so that she was seeing with the elephants. When she looked up, she felt she could see her own backyard
in hyperfocus. Dusk approaching, the earth spangled in shadow.
The worms underfoot, wriggling signals, a city of roots and bugs
and fungi, a language just as real but which no human could speak.

The somersaulting porcupine was gone now. She wanted him
back. She felt watched by the animals. Whatever the plant had done,
combined with whatever the book had done, plus the spring air, the
storm being over, Jack coming and going, Harrison—whatever factors caused it, she felt benevolent and sharp-sighted and *good*. For
the first time since she'd been axed.

Well and good.

Benevolent.

She heard the phone ringing in the kitchen, the landline, and gingerly removed herself from the hammock, moved toward the sound, wanting it to be Harry telling her to get in her car. Now. He needed her again.

"Jack's gone? Come over."

"He's gone. I will."

"However you want it. You must tell me how."

And she would tell him how she wanted it, and where, outside this time, on the flat gray face of an ordinary-seeming rock in the shade of pine boughs. He'd told her it had Indigenous significance, that restless spirits converged there.

But it was not Harrison. It was Willie.

"Maeve? Oh Maeve. I need to talk so badly. I need to see you, please."

40

AT HIS NATURALIZATION CEREMONY, freshman year of high
school, Willie had held a little American flag on a wooden stick,
gazed at it like a sparkler. All the librarians went to these ceremo-
nies to support the New Mainers. Willie had been shy, smaller than
his friends. This changed by the time he and Katrina began seeing
each other. By then he was his full height, broad and gallant when
they walked off together in the evenings. The shyness had trans-
formed into a quiet self-possession.

In all the years Maeve had known him, Willie never appeared
upset. And so it was a great shock to hear him hyperventilating on
the phone. A panic attack, he told her. They happened occasionally.
Moaning, hiccupping, the poor kid.

She was instantly clearheaded.

"Take a breath," she told him. "You're fine. There's no danger
here. None at all." She talked him down.

"Can I come to you?" he asked. "I need a bit of—just some space.
A few minutes."

His breathing collapsed again.

"Just keep breathing. Yes, just like that. Very good. Your only
task is to breathe. I'll come get you."

"Meet me at the dollar store near our place. I'll tell her I'm going
for a walk."

She drove to that dollar store prepared to hold him in her arms,
ready for closeness, but by the time she arrived he was serene

again in that way he had, self-contained. The storm had passed, he told her.

"But can we still go to your house? I need some space."

"Of course we can."

He was sweaty and spent, dazed. In the car there was a sweetish, clammy smell she recognized from the library. He wore his jean jacket. Was shivering, and she turned on the heat. She felt glad he wasn't still in Dora's sweatshirt.

It was dinnertime but he hadn't eaten all day. "You need to eat something," she told him. He conceded. "A cheeseburger and fries." They went through the drive-through, then back to her house, which he'd never been to before. They came in through the garage, into the kitchen. He nodded at the appliances, the granite countertop. From the big window across the back of the house he saw the greenhouse in the yard, the hammock, the flagstone walkway, accent lights on either side, glowing in the dusk.

"Nice place. Real nice."

"Thanks," she said. "Jack does well. This isn't on account of my librarian salary—my former salary, I should say."

"Yes. It's so sad."

"He's an accountant," she offered, though Willie hadn't asked. "A specialized kind of accounting. He came home last night."

"He's here?"

"No, he left again today. You just missed him."

"That's too bad," Willie said. Then, touching the countertop, he said, "Your kid got lucky."

"I did too." She felt the instinct to tell him she had been poor, growing up. But decided not to say it.

"We're all lucky now," Willie said.

"That's a nice way to look at it."

"He's a nice guy, Jack. I remember that fire he put out at the barbecue."

In the living room, he pointed at a photograph on the mantel, Paige in a strawberry field, shielding her face from the sun, tan and lanky, seven years old.

"Pretty," he said in a polite, neutral way. "A biologist?"

"Botanist."

"Ah. Plants, right. I remember from dinner: seeds."

He sat on the floor with his back against the couch and put his cheeseburger on the coffee table.

Maeve said, "She hates being pretty. She says it's a privilege she can't choose not to use, so she resents it."

"That's her greenhouse?"

"She built it with Jack when she was sixteen."

Maeve found it difficult to be precise about scientific things, struggled to recall the exact words. Paige did genetic work with seeds, she said, in a lab in California, was exploring the effects of hybridity.

"She's into ethical ways of growing, food equity."

Willie smiled and said, "Maybe she'll be on the cover of *Time* someday."

He finished the cheeseburger. He drank a glass of water and she got him another, and he drank half of this second glass and then said, "Do you have any beer?"

She didn't. Would he like some wine?

"I am not one to drink, but these days require a little . . ." He searched for the word, one of Katrina's words. "Lubrication."

"I'm not judging you," she assured him.

She poured herself a splash too. A pinot noir called Ethos.

After a few sips he said, "Thank you, Ms. Cosgrove, for your hospitality," and while she didn't want to be *Ms. Cosgrove*, she understood he sought to restore some formality, needed this emotionally, so did not correct him.

She wasn't sure when or if ever they would have time to talk again, to be alone like this. What exactly had triggered the panic attack? She could not ask directly, but she could voice for him the possible sources of his distress.

"I'm here for you, Willie. Please know that. It's all happening so fast, isn't it? You've only just met Harrison. It can't be easy to be interviewed this way by someone you've only just met."

"Oh, I'm not upset about that."

"No?"

"I'm not doing the book for *me*. My feelings are beside the point. It's for my people."

"But you're the person Harrison is interviewing."

"That's true."

"That's a burden *you're* taking on."

He smiled. "I've had harder ones. And never got paid so well." He shrugged, lifted his hand. "Honestly, I get tired when I talk. Katrina's worried I'm going to have a nervous breakdown, but mostly I just get sleepy. I'm reporting a story."

"It might be good to have someone to talk to who's more objective. Who's not writing a book about you."

"A therapist? This has been recommended to me on several occasions." He sniffed suspiciously. "You can say it."

"I meant"—she felt herself warm—"I meant you can always talk to me." He smiled, and she felt stupid, for why would he want to talk to *her*? How could she help him? "I didn't mean a therapist. Jack is always trying to get me to a therapist. I hate it. I really do."

"Jack does that too?" He laughed.

She liked that they had this in common.

"Therapy makes Katrina feel better, so she thinks it will make me feel better too. It makes her feel safe. Me? Not so much. I had a counselor when I first came here. I had groups. I have online friends. But the kind of therapist Katrina has—sitting and talking like that, week by week—does not appeal to me."

"Me neither," Maeve said, feeling close to him. "Not at all. Although—it's weird—I found a coach recently. A life coach. I see her on video chat."

"What's the difference between that and a therapist?"

"I'm not sure, to be honest. She doesn't take insurance. And you can be at home, at any hour. You can request her. It's kind of amazing, actually."

"Where is she? Here in Maine?"

"I don't know where, that's the interesting thing. Isn't that strange? She told me it's preferred. I don't know her name or where she is or anything." And then she said something she hadn't realized until she spoke it: "I always feel much better after I see her."

Willie rubbed his temples. "I talked to Jarvis about the book. I swore him to secrecy."

"The driver?"

"He has a strong viewpoint."

He didn't say what it was.

"Did *you* tell anyone, Maeve?" he said suddenly.

She vowed not to lie to him.

"Jack," she admitted. "Only Jack. I swore him to secrecy."

Of course she had told Deacon too, she realized, but she didn't say it.

Loose-lipped Maeve.

"Did you tell the coach?"

"Well, actually. It did come up with my coach." She pointed to the computer monitor, the screen black, waiting under the staircase. He raised his eyebrows, and she felt her face get warm. "But no details. I said nothing identifying. Just that a writer was writing a book about my friend. That I lost my job. That I've been angry about that. That I was—nothing specific about anyone. It was *me* I spoke about. Not you."

He nodded.

"I didn't tell the coach anything that would identify you. I didn't even say Harrison's name."

"It's your life." He lifted a shoulder. "You're allowed to discuss it."

She did not like feeling sneaky with Willie. Her heart ached with affection. Such affection! Like a son.

He said he would go to the yard to call Katrina. She saw through the window that he got in the hammock, saw him swing gently, one foot on the ground. He took a long time on the phone.

She needed to think. While he was outside, Maeve put her hands under cold running water. She thought about the CD player by the Riddleses' bed, scattered CDs on the floor. That first time, Harrison put on *Graceland*, Paul Simon, his old favorite. Miracle and wonder. She wanted to close her eyes and be in the bed, those clay-colored sheets, wanted to be at the beginning of the affair and not—she sensed—its end. Or was it? Could this thing go on, secretly, sweetly, bothering no one? For how long? How long could she keep a secret like that from Jack? How long until Jack looked at Maeve and knew?

Did Willie suspect what had happened between Maeve and Harrison? It seemed impossible to her that anyone would think she was capable of an affair. Not Maeve Cosgrove. Yet under the floorboards of every conversation beat the fact of their fucking. She felt sick with secrets, glutted, thrilled. Her palms were damp as soon as she dried her hands, so she washed them again.

When Willie came inside he seemed happier. Everything's better, he said. They'd argued earlier but he felt much better now. He admitted that Katrina had read his email—that's what set him off.

Again? But Maeve didn't ask, not wanting to betray Katrina's confidence. Maeve would get the same story from another POV.

"An email? She shouldn't have done that."

Willie was at the kitchen table now, steam from tea in his face. She sat with him. She said, "Listen, it doesn't matter what the email was about. She must respect your space. That's a terrible violation."

"It wasn't the first time."

"It wasn't? Oh dear."

He shook his head, looking sad.

"She wants to make sure she knows everything first, doesn't she, Willie?"

He was quiet for a moment and then said, "She wants to know everything. No secrets. No privacy."

She thought about Katrina, smoking bitchily while they'd played Clue.

Again she used her firmest voice, drew the librarian up from her soul. "I can't blame her for being concerned. To an extent. But I sense there are pieces of your story you don't want to share. *You* get to decide how much or little. Remember that. Not Katrina. Not Harrison. Only you, Willie. It's perfectly reasonable for there to be things even your spouse doesn't know. There are things I have chosen not to tell Jack, for instance."

She said it before she realized what she meant. Then she felt Willie listening with harder attention, and said, "You're allowed to have privacy. No matter how much you're being compensated. No one owns your mind or your body. Katrina needs to respect your boundaries. And Harry too. No amount of money requires you to—surrender yourself."

He smiled. "You're a mind reader, Maeve."

"I'm most certainly not."

"I had a friend," he told her. "Someone I don't feel the need to tell Katrina about."

"You don't have to tell me, either."

He spoke stoically: "She was my best friend. Not officially my wife, but in our hearts."

"Willie, really."

The girl was a neighborhood friend since childhood. They grew up together, fell in love. In retrospect, from adulthood, he can see how rare it was, their bond. They would surely have married, and their families would have been pleased—this wasn't some Romeo and Juliet situation—but the war came. She saved his life, he said. He did not tell Maeve how except in the broadest strokes, which will not be repeated here. He wanted half of everything from Harry's book to go to her family, a cousin.

"We were children. But we were not. It's a private story. The most important story is private, so I can tell the other things. Please keep this to yourself, Maeve."

"I will," she said, meaning it fiercely.

She wanted to put her hand on top of his, as Dora had, but couldn't find the courage. Then she realized he might not want her to touch him. Perhaps he had not wanted Dora to touch him. It was a possibility she hadn't considered.

Yet she felt sick, for she had already sold Willie out. Already planted a seed for Harrison. Two-faced Maeve!

"In my heart Katrina is my second wife. Katrina will ask: Do you love me best?"

"No she won't. Katrina is a mature woman. She had lovers before you."

"She'll need to know that I love her best." He spoke strenuously, as if it pained him. "I am sure of this. I love her, but a flaw of hers is that she'll ask."

"What is her name?" she asked, gently. "Your first wife's name."

He shook his head, drew a line.

"It would be easier for Katrina to think I raped or killed. I swear it would be easier."

"Than *love*? That can't be true."

"Some things happened to Katrina. It makes her—" He shook his head. As though there was a word he wanted to say but would not. "I don't want my first wife to be part of a situation in her mind."

"Oh," said Maeve.

"You must know what I mean?"

She did and she didn't. Then she had an idea.

"Willie, do you want to talk my coach? A session. On me."

"Now?"

"If she's free. You just click on a button. We can see if she answers. On me."

"Why would I want to talk to her?"

"She is a wise woman," Maeve told him. "And she's Black."

"Black?"

"A Black woman with red glasses. She just appears, when you call on her. Right here."

She pointed to the computer monitor, tucked in the alcove.

He rubbed his chin. "What kind of Black?"

Maeve didn't know, said she wasn't supposed to know, that this was the method. "She won't tell me where she's from. Not even her name."

Willie took a breath. He looked confused, wary, tired. Tired. More than anything, tired. He said yes, alright then, he'd give it a shot.

41

A YEAR AGO, when Paige came home with Joe Hess and announced she was traveling to Uganda, Maeve had grown frantic. She ran to the internet. Where in Africa was Uganda? And how stable was the government? What languages did they speak? American arrogance, cluelessness, to see the continent as a monolith, a conceptual blur. She knew that, and yet what *was* Africa? It was where the McKendricks and the Baylors went on safari. A place from which the New Mainers fled. She knew apartheid. Ebola. Colonization, decolonization. She knew profoundly little. She wanted the best for Africa, she did, but she also wanted her daughter here for the summer, in Maine, with her.

At dinner last May, Paige had sat at the head of the table, where she didn't usually sit, beautiful, austere, like a queen unafraid of being hated. She wore a gray sweatshirt she'd had since middle school, the fabric thin from so many washings you could see the shape of her clavicle. Her braid came over her left shoulder, draped like a fine tassel or a lion's tail.

Everyone was saying so many things.

Maeve kept drinking wine, couldn't follow the conversation. Was too upset. A strangeness pulsed in the background. A kind of death, losing these months with her daughter. Why did none of them see that? Feel that?

"Homo sapiens are unreasonable. Consciousness is only something like sixty thousand years old," Paige was saying. "The brain can't keep up with our technology. Like a hardware and a software thing."

Jack pursed his mouth like a scholar. "Huh."

"Can you pass the wine, honey?" Maeve asked him.

"If a culture becomes habituated to violence, it's too late."

Joe Hess said, "It's controversial, of course. But nature, nudged in a certain direction, provides the answer . . ."

"The wine?"

"Nudged how?"

"The *wine*?" Maeve tapped Jack and he reached for the bottle, poured her some, absently.

Joe was talking about slight modifications to the grain. What happens, theoretically, is that it can be grown and harvested for pennies, extracted without difficulty, can be added to nearly everything, and is known to make people who eat it feel—

Paige said, "Be careful. You don't want to give the wrong idea."

"Cooperative, is all I was going to say."

"Certainly."

"More able to let go of old grievances. To see the other side."

Paige said, "That's exactly right."

"Of course what's required in the Global South are stable institutions, not just better oatmeal," Joe said.

"Sure, sure," said Jack.

"But resentments must be softened too."

"It's a chicken-and-egg thing," Paige added.

"Every human being on earth deserves a healthy breakfast."

"To even think straight."

And then Paige and Joe were talking of a terrorist group who'd kidnapped some kids, a whole school of girls, captured and put into trucks—

"No!" Maeve sat upright. Banged her hands on the table. "You can't go. I can't let you!"

Everyone jumped. "Jesus, Mom," Paige said. "That was nowhere near Uganda!"

Maeve began to laugh, then everyone did, and she said, feebly, pulling on the ends of her hair for comic effect, "I'm such a worrywart."

"You're a mom," said Joe Hess.

"Oh honey." Jack put his arm around her, squeezed her shoulder. "We all understand."

They went on talking about the importing of a genetically modified plant. Carefully, with allies on the ground, stakeholders on the inside.

"A giving back, not another taking."

"Is this what they're teaching you at school?" Maeve said. "Are you getting credit for this?"

"It can be added to any sauce, to any batch of rice, to any curry or stew."

"Repairing society through plant life."

"But *who* needs repairing?" Joe said. "That's where it gets tricky. And how to convince people—"

Paige waved her arm. "It's not tricky," she said.

"Your daughter tends toward the radical side."

"Joe! I do not. Don't get her worked up again."

Maeve gave up trying to understand. She was ashamed of her outburst. Her own mother would have done something like that. Never again, she admonished herself.

Did she think of this conversation now, nibbling on these leaves, almost a year later? Yes, that dinner came to mind. But the memory was drunken. She had been sloshed, grief-blotto. She recalled it vaguely. Seeds in Africa? Plants in the sauce?

The leaves relaxed her. The mind didn't linger on little hurts. That was the magic of it, maybe most of all, how it made you feel OK to let go.

It backfired, logging on to the computer, introducing Willie and the coach.

She left them together in the living room. Upstairs in her bedroom, she returned to *The White Bone.* Barbara Gowdy spoke for the elephants. *Longbody* meant cheetah. A *honker* was a goose and a *hump* a termite mound, and the sun was *she-eye* and an insect a *speck. Hindleggers* were humans. But Maeve struggled to concentrate. She thought lasciviously about the plant. She went to the window, looked out. A shadow moved across the greenhouse, something small with a long, thin, segmented tail. An opossum. What words might it have in its head? For love? For sex? For their brethren crushed on the side of the road?

She wanted Harrison to call. For him to say, I know it's late. Are you too tired to drive?

I am not too tired.

She wanted to be underneath his body. Her shoulders grew tight. She put these words in his head. She put her hands on her hipbones. Then she heard noise downstairs, a shout, and sped to the top of the stairs. Willie and the coach were talking briskly, arguing, it seemed, in a language she did not recognize.

What could account for such intensity? She had never heard this barking, self-sure voice coming from Willie, nor the coach's punching syllables. Both so definite, as if picking up a discussion they'd been having for a long time.

After the hour was up, she found Willie sitting on the couch, looking pissed off, leaning forward, elbows on his knees. The computer monitor was black.

"There's no such thing as objective," he said.

He looked at her with welling eyes.

"Willie, I'm so—sorry. So very very sorry."

"There is nothing to be sorry for. Thank you for the gift."

Oh Maeve, Deacon will say when she finally tells him. He'll laugh and laugh. Connecting the two Black people you know, expecting them to be grateful. Eventually she'll have to laugh too, at how badly it had gone, at her witlessness. I was trying to help, only help, she'll say, and Deacon will remind her that altruism hasn't been a valid excuse for quite some time.

Willie said he would call Katrina to get a ride home, but Maeve insisted on driving him. The Volvo still smelled like cheeseburger. The silence felt heavy. She sensed some reprised frustration in him and regretted her failure as a friend. They didn't say anything until they stopped at a red light at the intersection of Main and Founders, and abruptly he said, "Don't worry, Maeve. I don't want you to feel bad."

She was glad she was Maeve again.

"You've had a hard day," she said. "That must have been a bad way to end. I had no idea."

He said, "No harm, no foul."

Three miles from his house now. She wanted to slow down. Rooted for red lights.

"You were speaking a different language."

"Arabic. Don't worry—I'm not mad. I had a question and she gave me an answer. I got that."

"What kind of question?"

"She thinks it's a racket. She thinks I'm being played. She calls it 'sentimental racism.' Not that it matters. I will incur anger. I know that. If I wanted to look good, to stay free of conflict, I would never have gotten involved."

"She disapproves?"

He faced the window, away from her. "Jarvis said he wished it were him. He said I should take every penny I can get. Help your people. Amplify the cause. But your coach says write your own book. She says if my letters impressed him so much, why can't I write my own book?"

"Your letters?"

He took a breath and said, "I wrote to him too."

"You did? I didn't know that."

"How would you? I didn't tell anyone."

She understood in waves. Maeve had not connected Willie and Harrison. Willie had done that himself. Of course. *Willie* had.

The arrogance, to think it had been her.

"When did you write?"

"I wrote for a long time," he said.

"Did he write back?"

He didn't answer. He said, quietly, looking out the window, "I saw your yellow notebook. Are you at it too, Maeve?"

"No."

"It's not a crime."

"I know that."

"He said your letters had real style." Then: "Forget about the coach. You had no idea she would push my buttons. I know you were being my friend."

A red light. But she looked straight ahead. She was glad it was dark so he couldn't see her flush. A desire to confess, to connect, a surge of—empathy? love?

"I really like you, Willie. I respect you. I like you so much that I wish I didn't. So I could say 'I *don't* like you.' How no one says? I wish I could say that so you know that I'm honest. But I really do like you. I like you even more than I like Katrina. Maybe that's my secret. Maybe I wish you were marrying Paige and not Katrina. Maybe I wish you loved Paige and she was here. Maybe that's my other secret."

It amazed her, that she'd said such a thing, but she didn't retract it. Her throat pulsed. It was true.

He didn't say anything. But he took his own hand and put it over hers on the steering wheel. He left it there, on top of her knuckles, when the light turned green, as she took the turn, changed lanes, so that for a few moments they were driving the car together. Then he put it back on his lap and looked out the window.

They passed the dollar store where she'd picked him up.

"She's in Minneapolis, your life coach."

"Oh."

"Before that Ethiopia. Before that—I'll spare you. Her sister is dead. Two brothers are dead. She said nothing about you."

He didn't say any of this meanly, but in a soft, musing manner.

"I trusted her," Maeve said, her voice tight.

"She revealed nothing about you. She was not unkind. Certain people believe in the healing powers of Black people. Certain people gain comfort there, your coach said. They grow up guilty and don't know why. She says it's plantational. Magical Negro stuff. She uses what she knows. She has a whole philosophy about helping. You can ask her about it. She said nothing about you, Maeve. The person she was critical of is me."

"You? But she has no business being critical of you."

"I asked a question. She answered it honesty. That's all we can do."

"But what have you done wrong?"

"I am contributing to the literary oppression of my people. Complicit in the imperial project. She's a hard-liner, your coach."

"I don't understand—"

"Right," he said. "You do not."

The spell with the coach was broken—he made sure. This was her punishment, and she accepted it, nodded her head, and said nothing more. Then they arrived at the triple-decker, Katrina sitting on the stoop in glowing tangerine pajamas. She rushed to the curb, wrapped her arms around Willie as he emerged from the Volvo. "Baby, I'm sorry," she cooed. "My love. My love. My only heart." Katrina didn't seem to notice Maeve, just raised a hand in generic thanks, as if he'd gotten out of a taxi.

Back at home she burned with shame. Did not have the courage to call up the life coach again. She paced the living room. So much she didn't understand.

She heard Jack say, You got what you deserved.

She heard Deacon say, Poor dumb Bug.

She felt small as an earthworm.

42

IN HIS FAMOUS SHORT STORY "The Library of Babel," Jorge Luis
Borges invents a library containing every book that could theoretically exist, every story, every plot, every character, every possible
combination of letters and words, an infinite library organized in
ingenious hexagonal stacks. Impossibly, cosmically vast, so that
explorers are fated to find only gibberish, volumes of nonsense,
will die or go crazy before locating the book they seek. Consider
that. Every possible book. The one that says everything you need
or want, that will answer every question, solve any riddle: it's there
but can't be located. The book that you yourself wrote. That your
lover wrote. That Maeve Cosgrove wrote. The one that explains
why Molly yelled so much, and the one in which she is freed from
her suffering, the one in which Willie's village is not decimated,
and in which Willie's wife survives, and the life coach's siblings,
and all the children washed away in Fukushima, and on and on,
all the small people everywhere who did not deserve to go so soon.
The one in which Libby has a happy home, a mother who does not
pawn her off. In which the physics teacher doesn't off himself. In
which Cedric stays alive and Maeve's own father, why not, gets
treatment, comes home, returns from his hero's journey a func-
tional man. The one in which everything goes back to the way it
was, Maeve at the library.

She used to like spooky, mind-bending things before bed, the
magic realists of the Southern Hemisphere and their clever shape-
shifting, but her dreams got too strange. Lately she found it was
better to fall asleep to J. B. Fletcher. Her decency, wit, her beauti-

ful way of managing bullies and brutes. Jessica was a moral center unlike any on TV, certainly back then and maybe still, and naturally this had everything to do with Angela Lansbury's moral center, the actress herself. It was her dignity on display, her gutsy resolve. Brilliant performer, star of the stage, she carried a network television show for twelve seasons. Harrison had met her in London but couldn't remember what she said. Couldn't recall their conversation. If Maeve ever met Angela Lansbury, she would listen to what she had to say.

Or maybe Harrison was only starstruck. Maybe he was too nervous to remember. She was flirting with anger at him. It was tentative, easily reined in. So many ways the story could still go.

Harrison called her in the morning, early. Woke her. It was the day of the library event.

"Are you alone?"

"I am."

"Good. I'm nervous. Really nervous." She could tell he was drinking coffee from the way he sighed after he swallowed. "Kids are the hardest audience. I gave a talk last month at Yale, no problem. I read at the fucking White House. But a roomful of kids? I near collapse."

"You're going to be great."

"Two kinds of people in this world. Those who defer to the intelligence of children, and idiots."

"I'd lose my head over you if I were seven."

He told her he was sorry for waking her. He told her she should feel no pressure to attend the event. He could understand how she might not want to be back there, given the circumstances. But maybe he could come over beforehand?

"I'd like to see your house. To see where May lives."

"I won't take any pictures," he said, a joke. And then, "Or maybe I will, with your permission."

She wasn't sure she wanted him there, at her house. Everything felt permitted at his. But at her own? The chairs would gasp. The

cabinets. The bed would not understand. She felt actual pain, thinking of the bed's confusion.

"You can calm me down before the kids tear me up. One last hug
before I'm thrown to the lions?"

"Such hyperbole," she said, the way Dora would say it.

It wasn't a choice—she could have him at her house, or not at
all. The tiny throbbing, yes, but also—closeness to him. She did not
know how to turn it down. She gave him the address. Then said, "Of
course I'm going to the library event."

He said he liked the sound of her voice in the morning. He had
been wondering what she sounded like in the morning.

The trespass was much bigger, him coming here. Once she woke
up more fully, drank her own coffee, she realized how big. A part of
her absolutely did not want to have sex with Harrison in her own
house, but his presence would disable that part. Once he stepped
inside, stood in her living room, it was as good as done.

He would arrive in a little over an hour. She had the impulse to
desensitize herself, as she'd done with the airplane phobia. She had
watched planes take off, allowed her body to adapt to the noise, so
the stimuli no longer induced such flagrant arousal of the senses.
You can teach the irrational signals to behave. Now she put Harrison Riddles in an image search, got rows and rows of him, his
same warm eyes. A belt she knew. Hair she'd touched. There with
the president. There with Bruce Springsteen. With Dora. With his
children. In a tuxedo. In a wetsuit. Soon he'd be there with Willie,
never her. But she only got more turned on, and so left the computer
and went to the mantel and there, that's what she was looking for.
Jack and Maeve and Molly and Deacon on their wedding day at the
Holiday Inn.

Her mother assumed Maeve was pregnant, as Deacon had, couldn't
understand the rush. Maeve found it hard to explain. She had wanted
the question resolved. She wanted to know: Here or there? In or
out? She would decide rather than wait to find out. But she told her

mother, "I'll never love anyone more than him," because her mother could relate to that. Oh boy could she, Molly.

To everyone's surprise, Molly had very much enjoyed Maeve and Jack's wedding. She came on her new electric scooter. Moved along the buffet, back and forth, eating shrimp puffs, chatting merrily with the guests, who were nearly all from the groom's side. At one point she found Maeve catching her breath in the hall near the bathrooms.

"Are you having fun, Mom?"

Her mother took her hand tenderly.

"Don't worry," Molly said, looking up into her daughter's eyes from her scooter. "I'm not going to give you any advice. Not today. Not a single bit."

Maeve was supposed to feel remorse looking at her wedding picture, but she did not. Nor did desire for Harry abate. Everything would end soon. Dora would come back. Jack would come back. Then the Riddleses would return to New York City and Maeve would have nothing to do. Maeve would be left with the classifieds. What harm did a tryst do? No harm.

It would vaporize.

The doorbell rang louder than before.

It rang in her clit, God help her.

He looked like a person going on TV. Black loafers, crisp charcoal pants. A white button-down with a polka-dotted tie, coral with large cream spots.

"Does the tie pander?" This was how he addressed her.

"It's great. Come in."

He stood before the gilt-framed mirror that hung in the entry-way, appraised himself, then unknotted and removed the tie. Next to him in the mirror she appeared slight, not as pretty as Dora but not un-pretty. Having him in the mirror with her made her look different to herself. She looked sexier, rosier, like a woman having an affair.

"Much better without the tie," he said. He mussed his hair. "I thought a tie might show respect. Like: You kids matter as much as those Yale assholes. I was going for that. But the polka dots force the matter."

He was different out of his house. More nervous, jumpy. She liked that. She felt calmer here, in control. He rolled the tie and put it on the table in the entryway. Opened the buttons of his shirt so she could see his collarbone.

"Good call," she told him. "Though I didn't feel pandered to."

He turned to face her. Put his hands on her shoulders. Seemed to relax.

"Is that so, Ms. May?"

Oh she liked that. She leaned in. Kissed him, but chastely. See? I can be like this too. I am not so aggressive. I am hungry. These are different things.

"Nice house," he said, but did not take his eyes from hers. Then the kissing became harder, wetter, both of them responsible, moving in tandem. She perceived a new synchronization. There will be many things she regrets about her interlude with Harrison Riddles, but the way they kissed that day in her foyer won't be one of them.

He left his briefcase and his clothes in the foyer. The guest room. She didn't give him a choice. The last person who'd slept there was Joe Hess, nearly a year ago. As they got deeper into it, ground their bodies into the bed, she recognized the presence of—how to describe it? Spicy, deep . . . old smoke, smoke from Amazonian campfires rising from the foam in the mattress, restored by friction and heat. The smell had disturbed her last summer. Now it was like a gift from the Southern Hemisphere: like magic, but real, in the actual air they breathed. Like a detail from García Márquez, she told him afterward, explaining it, their bodies wound together in the sheets. The scent of Macondo.

"Ha! That's wonderful. I don't smell it, I have to admit." He sniffed the air. "Maybe. It's faint."

"I love García Márquez," she said, dreamily.

"'The problem with marriage is that it ends every night after making love, and it must be rebuilt every morning before breakfast.' That's García Márquez."

"Hmm."

"'Necessity has the face of a dog.' That's him too. I love that."

"What does that mean, 'a dog'?"

He didn't answer, mounted her again, this time more urgently, as if it would be the last, and kissed her face and neck a hundred times.

For some reason her mind tipped toward Mr. Scales. She thought about his floppy hair. About Libby's body in his hands. How utterly wrong to be fucked by your teacher. How dangerous and wrong and illegal. But how nice it might feel to be wanted by someone who has that power, who has everything to lose, has given you a kind of power in return, is trusting you with this helpless part.

"Oh my God," she heard him say.

If she had known it would be the last time, she would not have allowed herself to imagine Mr. Scales, not even for a moment. She had lost touch with reality—was thinking with her senses, the way an octopus is said to think with its tentacles.

After sex was coffee, of course. A full pot.

"I've been doing nothing but working, May. I have three notebooks. It's like the first time. I'm never not shocked. When I find my way in again, it's always a miracle. I found it. Praise Jesus."

He added his cream. Picked up a spoon, stirred.

She could feel, in the next moment of quiet, that he was preparing to say something she would not like. The two kitchens appeared in her mind, as when Jack was here, a new and old place overlapping.

He frowned and said, "I might go down to see Dora's play after all. Tomorrow, once the library thing is over."

She felt it right then, a pulling away. It was strange, almost physical, like an actual pulling out.

"I talked to her last night. She's not holding back. She put Cy on to ask for me. 'Daddy, where are you?' His itty-bitty voice. I'm sorry, Maeve. I wish I didn't have to go."

Maeve said, "Dora told me—"

Don't vaporize. Tell me you won't.

"—that she's fond of me."

Please don't vaporize! She could not say it.

"'Fond,'" he said. He bit at his bottom lip. "That's a lot, coming from her. She can be rough in these situations. She likes you."

"And she said that—"

It will vaporize. That's what she can't say. Will you leave my life as quickly as you came?

Her phone rang; she ignored it.

"Go ahead," Harry said, gesturing to it buzzing on the counter. "I have to piss anyway."

"No," she said. "No, there's no one else I want to talk to."

"I have to piss anyway, May." He smiled. "Mayday."

He pissed. She sat at the table and listened to a hard, long stream of urine hitting toilet water. She remembered that phrase: *pissed like a racehorse*. And another: *hung like a horse*.

He was perfectly hung, not like a horse but like a human.

Mayday, mayday. Her heart was breaking. She felt it happening, how quickly all this was going to end, how very little she would have to show for it.

The water in the bathroom ran for a while. She checked her phone, saw that Katrina had left a message, but didn't listen because she just then saw his briefcase, on its side in the foyer, the notebooks edging out of it. One day they'd be in an archive at Yale for scholars to examine, but now they were on the floor of her foyer. She stopped and looked at them and her heart beat fast, and then she snapped a picture, for this was her own house, she was allowed, and a moment later Harrison emerged from the bathroom, his hair neatened, damp at the front, like a boy's before church. This boyishness gave her the nerve to say it:

"Dora told me it would vaporize. Is that what I should be expecting?"

His face hardened.

"No," he said after a moment. "No that's not what you should expect."

"I don't want you to vaporize."

"She can be a real bitch. I'm really sorry. Sometimes I think—" He winced, his color got high, he said, "Maeve, my nerves, and the coffee. I wonder if— It's embarrassing, but is there a bathroom that's a little more private?"

———

It wasn't really IBS. He knew it wasn't. He was just drinking so much coffee. He was the one making the bowels irritable. He didn't care at this point in his life—shitting was how he stayed thin, alert, close to home. It was a kind of penance. And he needed coffee to read and write. He'd write about this years later, in the enlightened future, an essay called "Deferred Pain." He wasn't tending to the right thing. In the essay he cleverly likened the condition to geopolitics, to the situation in a certain African nation. He wove a compelling narrative, moved from his own gut to the world stage in just a few sentences, with such ease, such a sense that of course these things were connected, his intestines, the complexities of masculinity, the plight of a village wracked by typhoid.

When he came back from the bathroom, he sat down again at the table. He pushed the mug away.

He said, "Can I be honest? It might make me nervous to have you at the library."

"Really?"

"I'll be worried about you. You won't enjoy it."

"Why do you say that? I want to be there!"

"You get upset when you talk about Gloria. I see it upsets you."

The same paternalism she heard in Jack. The desire to settle her down.

"So? I mean, a little upset. I can handle it."

She tried to explain. She was Harry's friend now. And she had been the one to extend the original invitation. The program was hers. Now it will disturb her? Could he understand how offensive that was to her? How diminishing? The library had been her home. Her circle. Her pride. These were her family members—

"Yes," he said. "I see. I'm sorry."

Then he said, "Maeve, my assistant in New York got the mail from my P.O. I got that last letter. The letter you wrote. The petulant one."

"You got it?"

"My assistant read it to me."

"Your assistant? Who's that?"

"Xander reads everything first. I didn't tell you about Xander? Look, Maeve. I felt your rage in that letter."

"I told you about that letter. I warned you. I told you I was upset when I wrote it."

"Let it go," he said. "You can let it go now. You're allowed to. You know that, right?"

"Xander reads everything first?"

"You don't need to prove anything to that gaggle of librarians. They don't deserve so much attention. That's all I'm saying. You have so much more to give the world."

Then it was her own stomach, a cramp like a knife being turned, and she didn't want to use the bathroom nearby where she could be heard and so raced to the next one, but of course it had just been used by him, the air full, and so she went upstairs, threw herself on the toilet upstairs, let herself explode in private, like a woman in a padded room.

It took more time than she wanted. She came back down shaky.

"You feel OK?" he asked, shyly.

"Yeah. You?"

"Yeah."

It had gotten late so fast. He had to go. They wanted him there in advance to sign some books. He stood up and took her hands and said, quietly, "I'm sorry, Maeve. I hit a nerve. I don't want you to misunderstand. Come if you want. Just don't feel pressure to come. Gloria pisses you off. And if that borderline girl's there."

She nodded. Felt very strange. The lower half of her body was numb, exhausted, as though she'd run a long way. He gathered his things. He almost forgot the tie but spotted it, picked it up, seeming to reconsider. He flipped it over his shoulders, looked at himself one last time in the mirror.

"This might be the winner. I'll wear it like a scarf."

He opened the front door. She saw his car in the driveway, a dark blue Audi SUV. Orange New York plates. The sky was blue, nearly blinding, cloudless.

She felt immensely sad.

"I don't know if this will make you feel any better, but Dora is fond of very few people. You should know that. We both think you're wonderful. But, look—" He shook his head. "I do have some bad habits. I won't lie about it, out of respect for you. Whatever happens, know that this has been meaningful to me. Please know that."

"'Whatever happens'? What do you mean?"

"I mean exactly that." He took her hand. He said, "Isn't that a nice thing to know? Can't you see how nice it is? If you look at it that way?"

"I can," she tried. "I'll try." She did try. She would. She said, feeling helpless, "Will you help me get my job back?"

"I told you. I meant it. I'll absolutely do what I can."

"I didn't deserve to be fired."

"You should be running that place!" Then: "You're a love. You don't know how much you've done already. I'll do anything I can for you."

He hugged her. Pulled her in, avuncular. Then closer.

"Take care, May," he said as he got into the car.

He was freshly laid and television-handsome and ready to inspire the young people of her town. She watched him drive off. What had happened? What was happening? She was shaking and furious and full of dread. A tightening in her shoulders. Her neck. Her jaw. She should call Paige. Paige would restore her to her factory settings. Only Paige could do it. And just then, wonder of wonder, miracle of miracles, Paige called her.

43

THE BEST THING was listening to Paige talk about plants. The girl spoke with such precision and authority, without pause, so there was no way to interrupt:

"We got your messages. We saw the pictures. We didn't know how intense this reaction would be. Joe says it's a bigger deal than I realized."

"That's great, sweetheart—"

"I planted it before Uganda, on a hunch. And then you followed my directions so perfectly. Thank you, Mom. We didn't expect it to do so well, especially given these conditions. Which brings us to this situation. Joe happens to be in New York right now to meet the donor, and we've made a plan, which is he'll rent a car first thing tomorrow and drive up to Maine and grab them, and since there are restrictions on transporting plants and the project is technically off-the-record, he can't fly commercial, so he's going to take my old car. Is that alright? I said he could. It was my idea. He's going to drive the plants back to Palo Alto. That's OK, right? In the Toyota? No one's using it now, right?"

She stopped. Took a breath.

The car sat in the garage, a secondhand sedan they'd gotten her the fall of her senior year so she could drive to high school and to her research sites. She had been doing an independent project with a professor at USM. A gold Corolla.

"I'll drive it home after we're done with this project, when I have time. What do you think? Good? Joe's waiting to pull the trigger."

"You should come here to get the plants. Not Joe. *You* should."

"I thought about it. But he's so close already. And do you really want me driving cross-country alone?"

"With Joe," Maeve said, though she didn't like that either. Or with me? Could she do it? She badly wanted to see her girl. It would do her a world of good right now. But before she could make a suggestion, Paige said, "Well, Joe and I aren't both going. That's just inefficient. And honestly—I can't leave the lab right now. I just can't. It's truly the most exciting thing that's ever happened to me—"

She began to talk about a certain kind of vine, how scrappy and improbable and merciless this vine was, biologically speaking, how it fought to get the most light at all costs. A lesson in that vine, a message she was taking to heart. But she'd come for a weekend. Next month.

"I'm not inhuman, Mom. I miss you guys too. You and Dad will take care of Joe?"

"Dad's with Teenie in Florida. Didn't he tell you?"

"He left a message. I forgot." She moaned. "Poor thing. I should call."

"When I saw her on the video she looked pretty haggard. She was out of it. Don't be alarmed."

"So you'll deal with Joe? He won't even stay overnight. He'll grab the plants and go and camp on the highway. I told him he could take my camping stuff too."

Everything was already decided.

Maeve would not tell her that she'd tasted the leaf.

After Maeve hung up, she saw the notification on her phone. Katrina, from earlier. That had been the call when Harrison used the bathroom. Maeve listened. She listened again. It was not right or fair, what Maeve heard. Plain deranged, what Katrina said in the message.

"You really disturbed him, Maeve. Putting him on with that bitch. She called him an Uncle Tom. Not cool, Maeve. Not cool."

She dialed Katrina's cell. Before Maeve even spoke, Katrina said,

"I'm over it. Willie told me to give you a break. I've calmed down. I was overreacting. Forgive me, can you? My hormones are out of whack."

Maeve had never heard Katrina say such a thing before, about hormones. Never had she blamed a mood on PMS. She wasn't a sharer of that sort of information. Pregnant, Maeve thought.

"I felt like you were hitting him," Katrina said. "Hitting Willie when he was already down. But I know that wasn't your intention."

" 'Hitting him'! I was only trying to help. You yourself told me you wished he had a therapist."

"I didn't say that. I said the opposite. I said it *wasn't* my job to take care of him. I said I am trying *not* to manage his emotional life. And in any case I wouldn't have assumed my own therapist would be the best fit."

"A life coach," she said, helplessly, feeling so stupid.

"But hey, Maeve? Really, we know you were trying to help. Please delete that message. I'm not rational right now! I better go. It's all-hands-on-deck over here. We're bringing up all the folding chairs from the basement."

"There are more chairs in the gallery storage room."

"Hey—oh, Harry just arrived . . . he looks great. Cool tie. I've got to run now. I love you, Maeve."

She hung up.

A vast, culminating rage, at all of them, at every single one.

A glorious day. Spring like an epiphany. She went outside. She separated one plant from the rest of them, a careful handful of dirt in a mug, a precious bundle. Put it in her bedroom, in a ray of sunshine on her dresser top. One for herself. Joe Hess could take the rest. And then she placed a quarter of a leaf on her tongue, and then another quarter—a half total—let these leaf pieces sit there, let the enzymes in her saliva work on them, releasing whatever they had in store.

Then she went to the library.

Libby was not in attendance.

Libby, Libby, Libby.

But Maeve channeled her. Maeve put her there, imagined her. Saw as if through her. It only took guts, she discovered. Not more than guts. Guts and a little whatever it was, botanical magic, plant wisdom. Harry had said a voice was not something you could un-hear once it made itself known, and he was right, she discovered. Once Maeve began to hear it, she agreed in full, and was too excited to sleep that night, stayed awake with the yellow pad, nibbling on plant leaves and inventing.

44

USUALLY ON SATURDAYS I go to the farmers' market. Alone we're ignorable, but a bunch of us together freak out the farmers. They're wise to be wary. We skulk around until they put out plates of food, fifty yards away, like dog bowls. They feed us to keep us from bothering their booths. Radishes and tomatoes and bad bruised fruit. We howl demands for organic. That's our joke. Only organic, bitch. Today is blisteringly nice and I need the nutrients, but I'm going to the library instead of the farmers' market. Will have cookies and a juice box for breakfast because I want to lay eyes on this asshole, Riddles.

The librarian is gone. Nervous as a mouse, Maeve. Little and furtive like a Borrower. Her practical tennis shoes. Her nylon purse.

She was interesting, but she's gone now. Fired.

Budget cuts, someone said.

The death of civilization, someone said.

I am guilty of the prank but also refuse to accept responsibility for what I didn't do. I learned that in Al-Anon. That's all I will say on the matter.

Honestly I don't think Riddles is such hot shit, even though there's a collective jizzing when he puts out a book. He isn't a total con. I recognize it's hard not to be a con at least some of the time. His record is better than most. Chapters of that Afghan novel deserve the praise, but *The Palest Winter* is a slog. Lesser Rushdie is right.

I see Maeve now. She comes in late, slips in the back of the reading room, which has been emptied of its furniture for the event. It's weird how different it feels in here. I see her notice how weird. The shelves, the furniture, the glass partitions of the Pen: gone. I watch her see how strange it is. People and chairs, nothing else. Harrison Riddles on the makeshift stage.

I can tell she is distressed.

He says, Hello, everyone! Hello!

Much applause.

He reads the kids' book he wrote. I'm half listening. I'm interested in other things. How certain people devastate you with their face. How it hurts to see them. A certain kind of face does it—a different kind for all of us. My foster mother Mina was obsessed with the man who ended up killing her, Phil, and his slummy face had done it to her, because it doesn't have to be attractive or even remotely decent. It's only happened to me once so far, and it was my physics teacher, who told me my face had done that to him. When your faces do it to each other, that's sublime.

Riddles's face turns Maeve on, I see that. I watch her, watching him. He stands next to a podium, rests an arm on it.

I was fifteen when I saw my teacher's face. He killed himself when I told him we had to stop. I didn't murder him. I only told him no, which I'll regret forever, and he did the murdering. I myself feel no face-love for Harrison Riddles. To be clear. I find him—not smarmy, but in that territory. Not a man I'd trust. There's a mic clipped to his shirt, like a fly that's landed there. He is wearing a clown tie and tight pants and has the crazed eyes of Tom Cruise in love.

Surrounding him on the floor are cross-legged children. Then teenagers in folding chairs in a semicircle around the children, and beyond them the adults, packed in. Three video cameras. A person from the newspaper with a camera.

Thank you for having me, Harrison Riddles says. What a beautiful library on such a beautiful day. Thank you to Gloria and Katrina and Dee Dee and Nina and everyone here at the library, you've been amazing. What a beautiful invitation. This program, storytelling for everyone, reminds us that we can all be writers. Reading and writing are how we understand and shape the world.

I watch Maeve watching him, lovesick.

My physics teacher had a dent in his chin and unusually bright blue eyes. He wore a tiny pouch of leather on a rawhide string around his neck. The pouch hung to his belly button. In this pouch was a stone I gave him. Just a pebble, just something that had been in my shoe one day while we were walking, which I stopped to remove, but he asked for it and held it to his heart. I still wear his socks in the winter. Wool and very heavy. I stole them from his dresser and his wife doesn't know. I stole a few other things. She cremated him and put the ashes in the lake where he learned to swim, and I have an AriZona iced tea bottle of that lake water in my metal trunk.

I don't know who I'm telling this to. Whoever is reading, I guess: You.

I have no idea how to tell a story. I don't understand how to order it—I have to say it as it comes into my mind or I'll forget. The interesting part is coming so I hope you are still reading.

After the recitation of his book, Harrison Riddles calls up his helpers, Katrina and Nina, who pass out notebooks for each of the kids, black-and-white composition books like Harriet the Spy's. They pass out pens with a transparent part where you can watch a ship move toward a shore and away again. The pen says: JOURNEY ON.

Can we keep this? a small child wonders, and he says, These tools are yours to have! and there's a great gasp of joy.

Riddles announces: I have a challenge for the community, young and old alike. It takes a while to shush the children. He wants everyone to tell a story of a journey, any kind of journey, using this paper and these pens and these markers—now packs of washable markers are being distributed (ah! oh!). He says, You can tell it any way you like. In pictures, or in words, in some other way. A true story or a fiction, made up. Only two rules: A problem is solved, and love prevails. A problem of any variety. A love of any variety.

Love is not always tidy, he reminds us.

For the little ones—A rabbit is on his way to school one day . . .

For the older—The strangest day of my life was . . .

These are our only tools, my friends, he says. Right here in our hands.

He talks about the things wrong with our world—global warming, rising tides, fundamentalist forces of every sort, racism and poverty. I wish I could say technology will save us. You know what I think? These technologies here—pen, paper. They will save us. Write to remind us of our better selves. Write to each other. Say what you know. Admit what you don't know. Read. Read your weight in books. Get to know what it feels like to *be someone else*. In this way and only in this way can we generate enough empathy to save the world. Paper and pen. These tools, my friends, are as much yours as they are mine.

The young ones are already busy with their notebooks, which gives him time to say things to the older ones, like: You can imagine anyone's life! He brings up Aina from *The School for Seeing*. Isn't it kind of fucked up, though, the way he talks about hearing her, owning her? So what, that he can make you feel something for Aina? What good does that do her?

Imagine your way into *any life*, he tells the children. Then he sets everyone to writing for twenty minutes. A big yellow clock on the podium counts down. Young and old. Everyone. And a peculiar hush comes over the library, which amplifies the sound of scribbling. It's a churchy feeling. He's like a preacher. It has a Christian edge. Borrows from the born-again. Write and ye shall set yourself free.

The world has its sufferers and its recorders of suffering. The nonsufferers get to read books and feel sad for the sufferers. To feel better about not having to suffer, to feel good about recognizing another's suffering, having had the experience. The nonsufferers get to feel cleansed, awakened. Then they go on benefiting from the status quo.

Fuck this fucker.

I look around and everyone is writing, everyone deep in concentration, it seems, except for Maeve, who is looking right at me. At me! I see her eyes, moving between mine and the briefcase resting next to the podium. It's clear right away that she's giving me an assignment.

Look, I am not sharing my "journey-in-progress" in a small group of people my age. My journey is none of their business or yours. You could not withstand my journey, just like you could not withstand Aina's, or Willie's. You can barely stand your own, right?

During that portion of the event, I go up to the bathroom, the one in the mezzanine. I just sit in the stall. In the dark. Someone slips in too. My secret sharer. We sit in our respective stalls, not looking. We don't have to say a word. We don't need to look at the crack. No words but it's a conference. It's as good as done, what we are going to do.

Someone knocks on the door, people are waiting. Someone flips on the light.

She leaves, and then I do.

Downstairs, Harrison Riddles is waving his hands and everyone is laughing.

I don't like what he says next, either. About Goodwill. During the Q&A someone asks, Where do you get your story ideas, Mr. Riddles?

Be a scavenger! That's my advice, he says. Look for interesting objects. Goodwill, Salvation Army. Any old junk store. Imagine the histories of objects you find. Make it up. Who owned it? What did it mean to them? Stuff and things. Stuff and things. Those are my four words of advice: Stuff and things. Pen and paper.

Someone says, That's six words.

Stuff. Things. Pen. Paper. And people, he adds.

Five words!

He concedes, five.

Like a koan.

It's almost over. The smallest children at his feet are getting restless. What is the sound of paper crinkling?

The library director swoops in with a surprise gift for him, bookends of marble from a nearby quarry. They once belonged to the great Maine writer Sarah Orne Jewett! He seems genuinely touched. Everyone is released then. A success. There is applause, general clamoring. I strain to hear. I get closer. He is saying to the director, Wow. Great bookends. Wow. These are just—very cool.

I think: Why should he get those bookends?

I read *The Country of the Pointed Firs* when I was eleven. I remember where I was: on the soggy green carpet of a group home. That the country of the firs was my home blew my mind.

Gloria says, You were great, Harry. What a thrill. They'll remember it forever. We all will.

Maeve is watching. I see her watching. Her face is alarmed. Her shoulders are like a bent hanger.

He says, My pleasure. Let's keep it up. I want to make a donation. I have a check, so you can keep doing this for the kids. He actually pulls out a pale blue check, right then and there. The kids are pushing at him, want to show him their drawings, their pages, the beginnings of their own important journeys.

Goodwill is where I get my clothes. It's where I got this shitty backpack I had to repair with the fabric from my old backpack. It's where I got my mittens and my cup and my spoon. Asshole. Asshole. I do the most right thing. Which is still a wrong thing. While the kids are pushing for him, while the briefcase is just for a moment out of his sight. Even if Maeve hadn't wanted me to, I would have done it. Because you know what I love? I love a donation dumpster with a big mouth, like a mailbox. I used to put in the shoes I outgrew. The coats. Otherwise I took, but not from the bin. Once you put something in the donation bin, you can't get it back again. Like a mailbox, its latch only goes one way.

It would be especially sick to put a fine leather briefcase in a receptacle like that. Don't you think? Especially wrong to watch a fine briefcase slide into a big metal box of castoffs in a parking lot, in the sun, in the rain, moldering, filled with lice and dandruff. Who knows when it will be emptied, onto what truck it will be dumped, what warehouse in what backwater. Lots of that stuff gets shipped overseas, I heard, American excess to kids in need, kids even worse off than me. As far away as Africa, this stuff gets sent! Which is why you might see a child in Kenya wearing a Power 92 FM T-shirt from a radio station in Phoenix. Or a Topeka Little League hat. No saying where the contents of those bins will go. A donation bin between a Kohl's and a Lowe's, a Home Depot and a Walmart, I honestly can't remember which one.

45

ON THE RADIO, years ahead, Harrison will call it "the God cut." Meaning it was an act of God, to lose the manuscript. But it was neither God nor, despite her confession, Libby who did it. It was Maeve. She needs to be honest. Did it *as* Libby maybe, channeling Libby's audacity, but that's not the same as Libby. The guilty party, no matter how she spins it, is Maeve. Maeve is the agent of the action. Maeve, with her guts, in the library.

She saw it there, leaning against the base of the podium. She had worked in this space for so many years, moved with invisible authority. When the crowd descended, she was the one who slipped in, tossed the briefcase into an open box of supplies—blank notebooks, name tags, pens, markers—a box that had been sitting beyond the podium—and put the cardboard lid on, and walked out just as she had done on so many days. She slipped the box into her Volvo's trunk and returned to the event, where he was signing autographs and admiring the work of children. It had been easier than she imagined it could be. There was no telltale anything.

The next day, in the privacy of her own home, the curtains closed, Maeve held his yellow notebooks and felt their power. They felt warm to the touch. She read some but not all. She could not burn a book, never, but she could hide it out of sight. For how long out of sight, only time would tell. The donation box slot felt like a fitting punishment. The whole point of the slot was not to dispose or destroy, not to lose—it was to get more life out of the thing.

Maeve, too, had worn clothes from Goodwill. She, too, had

searched for shoes to fit her feet among those stinking pairs. When Cedric was in town, he felt her toes through her shoes. Do these hurt? They did. He brought her to Goodwill and helped her find her size.

She can't imagine the pain of Harrison's loss, losing your own book-in-progress. Except she can. That's why she did it. He'd start again in any case. She was only slowing down the process. She was only saying: Be more careful with this boy. It's not OK, your rottenness. There has to be some accounting.

Maeve had gone back inside. When Harrison couldn't find his briefcase, his face grew red, and a vein Maeve hadn't seen before pulsed in his temple. I have made that vein pulse, Maeve thought.

"Oh my God. No. No. Check the cameras!"

By this time the crowd was gone. The librarians had cleared the place. He made the sounds one makes when a small helpless thing is about to be pummeled, when a truck barrels down a highway and one duckling hasn't quite made it across. He was nearly weeping, and then he was. He had brought the notebooks because he could not let them out of his sight. He couldn't be apart from a book in that state. "It's umbilical," he kept saying. Joan Didion said the same—she sleeps in the same room with her book. He kept muttering about Didion, the cameras.

"Oh my God. The cameras!"

The cameras, right. Maeve grew anxious . . . but not for long. A quick investigation followed. Videos and photographs of the event did not show the floor, the base of the podium, did not show the briefcase, nor anyone getting near. Or rather: everyone is near, a huddle of kids, plus the librarians, plus some teenagers, parents. They've crowded around Riddles to show him their stories and drawings, their nascent masterworks, and in this fray someone snatched it. Anyone could have.

"Umbilical," he said, crying actual tears, and most of the librarians cried too.

———

That night, flat on her back in the middle of their bed, it occurred to Maeve quite suddenly that her marriage to Jack was over. Or rather, any marriage they would have from here on out would be a fundamentally different one. He deserved to know that she wasn't the same person anymore. Would she have to tell him? Would he still love her, stay with her, if he knew about her true self? She remembered García Márquez. That marriage must be rebuilt every morning before breakfast.

Harrison called Maeve a few days later, when he got to South Carolina.

Mostly air on the line. Five minutes of strange quiet.

"I'm devastated. Devastated in every direction."

She was too, she said.

"You think that borderline girl did it?"

How could she answer that?

Libby Libby Libby.

"Maybe."

He said, "Well, I asked Gloria. She said she wasn't there."

"You asked Gloria about Libby?

"I forgot her name. I said, What about that crazy kid who tried to get Maeve in trouble? I wanted to leave no stone unturned."

She swallowed.

"What did Gloria say?"

"'Poor Maeve,'" he said. "That's what she said. And that the girl wasn't there. That she hadn't been around in ages."

A long pause.

"I keep thinking someone's taken it hostage. That I'm going to get a phone call. A muffled voice. I'd pay anything. I wish someone would call me. Or send me a note."

She felt a pulsing in her forehead.

"Cut-up letters from a magazine?"

"I'd do anything."

The longest pause.

"I wish I could help you," she finally said.

"What do I do?"

"Start again," she told him. "You must. You owe it to Willie."

She heard a dog barking in the distance, on the line.

"Are you angry with me, Maeve?"

"No."

"I'm sorry if I upset you."

"I'm not angry. But you owe it to Willie to continue."

"If you can help me, please do."

Everything changed, of course. It was going to change anyway. She'd just made it change faster.

He'd had a chance to say something to Gloria, to remind Gloria of Maeve. Of Maeve who made it happen. To say something publicly about Maeve, the one who'd created the program, and he had not. He'd said nothing. He'd come to the podium. He'd looked out at the audience. He'd caught her eye, held her eye. They were lovers, friends. He had sucked her breasts hours before. He had shit in her bathroom. She had written him those letters. But he didn't even include her name among the people he thanked.

Dora called the day after he did.

"He's here now," Dora said.

"I know. He called me."

"Did he?"

"Yesterday."

"It's not been pretty." A long-drawn-out sigh. "He's a beast, it's true."

"I'm so sorry about the manuscript. It sucks," Maeve said, "it really sucks," and Dora made a strangled sound, as if suppressing a cry.

Maeve had not wanted to hurt Dora. Did not want to hurt Dora or Katrina or Willie—only him, Harrison Riddles.

"He's going around saying it's ruined. The whole project, obliterated."

"But he just started."

"Naturally. I keep saying that. But he was in the *flow*, he says. He had a lot. He'd nailed the voice."

"He'll start again. He has to. He'll remember the voice."

"He's in a state," Dora said, gloomily.

"Hyperbole."

A pause.

Dora said, "That's my line."

"I only mean—"

"Of course he'll start again. He only has two settings, and one of them is frantic. He just wants to pull the attention away from my play. It'll pass. I know he'll be fine. It's not the loss he thinks it is."

"He's been working on it for, what, a week?"

Dora took a long breath.

"You don't know how bad it got. He was anxious for a long time. Not in a good place. That whole letter thing—that fishing expedition. You can't imagine what he was like before those letters."

"Fishing?"

"Convinced he was dried up. He never expected so many. He had to hire Xander! I keep telling him, he still has Willie. He can start again. But the way he's going on about it. Moaning in his sleep. I keep saying: It's a book, you motherfucker, it's only a book."

Maeve's heart, pounding.

Dora said, "Part of me thinks he can't handle all this attention on me. He can empower the masses to tell stories, but not so excited when it's his own wife."

"Your play. How was your play?"

"Impressive, evidently. A hoot. But I'm not sure this family can handle two writers. Anyway, take care of yourself. I have to go now. There's an iguana on this countertop staring at me. Penny! *Penny!*" she yelled.

Then, muffled, holding the phone to her chest: "Jesus, Penelope, can you please put Eminem back in his cage?"

A clatter. The murmuring of voices, the twin's voice. The sound of a door closing.

"I have to go," Dora said, softly.

But she didn't hang up.

"I'm impressed," Dora said.

"By what?"

"You're bolder than I gave you credit for."

"I don't know what you mean."

"I tip my hat to you," was all she said. Then, "Goodbye, Maeve. It was nice to know you."

"Goodbye," said Maeve, startled and seen. "It was nice to know you too."

46

JOE HESS WAS COMING AGAIN and Maeve would be sober for it. She had been foolish and addled the last time he'd been here. She'd be a grown-up now. Paige Cosgrove's mother—Maeve Cosgrove. Not some drunken empty-nester clinging to her baby. Not a provincial Yankee frightened by Africa!

The year had been good to him. The scraggly beard was gone. He wore a clean white T-shirt, cargo pants, and heavy work boots. He smelled like her husband, in fact: Neutrogena for Men. He was in a good mood; the money had come through from the eccentric donor.

She had washed the sheets in the guest room and vacuumed the rug with a special powder that smelled of lavender, in case he wanted to stay. She feared he'd say yes, couldn't bear a different man in the room where she and Harrison had been, but she asked out of duty: Would he like to spend the night?

Oh no, no, Joe said. He needed to hit the road. Time was tight . . . she was a taskmaster, Maeve's daughter. He and the plants were on a schedule.

Maeve took him to the greenhouse, expecting something crazy—a groundhog and a possum cuddling, a raccoon blowing dandelion fluff—but saw nothing out of the ordinary. No animals at all. He examined the plants. It was all rather anticlimactic.

She said, "Are the leaves edible?"

"Sure," he told her. "These wouldn't kill you, but they won't taste good."

"If you ate a leaf—what would happen?"

"Nope, it's the root that's got the power."

"What kind of power?"

"I'm not the kind of male scientist who takes credit for what his assistant does. I promise you that. It was her hunch, all hers."

"But what about the leaves?"

"Root's where it's at." He winked: "But don't tell anyone."

You're wrong, she wanted to say. But naturally did not.

In a certain way, Paige had helped her mother through this period, though it would take a while for Maeve to see this. Placebo or not, whatever she'd been eating had changed her. It had.

To prepare for Joe's visit, she had put all the camping gear in the foyer. He carried it out to the car. She had filled the tank with gas and he thanked her. There was another change in him she only noticed then: he'd fixed his teeth. Or was in the process of fixing them. They were straighter. He was wearing invisible braces, a film over the enamel.

She had been hard on him during that first visit, she realized. Too caught off guard. He was not as hideous as she remembered. What else had she exaggerated? In what other ways had she overreacted?

"Take care of her," she said, her hand on the roof of the car. It was sexist but she had to say it. He nodded, his eyes glassy. He loved Paige. He would suffer for a long time over her, just as she would.

"She's going to change the world, your daughter. Whatever you did, raising her"— he lifted his hand, moved it left and right, indicating this—her home, the life Jack and Maeve had created—

"I didn't ruin her. Or I ruined her in the right way."

"The best way," he laughed.

"I worry about her."

"Sure you do." He nodded. "She seems cold, but after a while it falls away."

"It does?"

"Sometimes," he said. Then he said something she'd think about for a long time: "A lot of people get caught up in gray areas. Myself included. We just end up waiting. We think. We never act. Very few people like Paige. It can be hard, though. People will misunderstand. She's going to do some bold things."

What did he mean, that people would "misunderstand"?

He only said, "I have deep respect for her. I want you to know that."

It would take them a while to see their daughter fully, to see her myopia, her willfulness. Eventually trouble would find her—criticism would come. Because really, how much empathy did Paige have? She forged ahead regardless of other people's feelings. She acted without authorization. Maeve and Jack could not deny this once it all came out, once her university pulled her funding under not insignificant pressure from the State Department.

But that hasn't happened yet. Today, standing before Joe, who adored Paige just as she did, who was teaching Maeve how to understand her, Maeve shivered with pride.

Her daughter could see the bigger picture in a way so few could, and might actually effect real change in the world. So she gave less to her family of origin; she gave more to the global family. She could be impulsive, yes, because she prioritized action. For a long time, this would be how Maeve managed her long absences, missed holidays and birthdays—the world was about to be massively improved by something Paige Cosgrove was doing.

Maeve hugged Joe Hess before he left. She was not disgusted any longer and felt sorry for throwing away his sock. He got in the car, turned the ignition. The plants rode in the backseat, bungee-corded to a piece of plywood he'd rigged, like a car seat for an infant. She saw he'd double-checked the straps, as if a baby were riding with him to California, which made her say, "Take good care of my grand-plants."

47

THE NEXT DAY she called Jack and told him she'd like the name of the therapist. "Really? That's great, honey!"

A few days later she had an appointment. The insurance company required a diagnosis. "Borderline?" she asked the new therapist, who looked startled and said, "Let's try depression to begin, shall we?"

This therapist welcomed the patient's participation in making the diagnosis, said it was the more progressive way. Maeve looked at the list of symptoms she was meant to be experiencing. But she wasn't all that tired, or hopeless, or rageful. Her thoughts were like a knot she set out to untie, like a fine-gauge necklace chain, knotted and knotted, knots in the knots. She wanted only to be alone with her mind, to work that chain as with a needle.

Her name was Dr. Harwood, a white woman in her sixties with a diploma from an Ivy on her wall. An actual psychiatrist—which was rare these days, a medical doctor who preferred talk therapy, who still liked to probe the parental corners, poke at the secret history. This one believed shame was the root of trouble. She wore silver clogs, a black turtleneck. Her wide black pants swooshed like a skirt. She had a magnificent dumb dog, a golden retriever, who came and put her head on Maeve's lap as she talked on that first day.

Dr. Harwood said, "Push her away if you want. Some people like dogs and some people don't. Either way is perfectly fine. It's absolutely your choice. I will not take it personally, and neither will she."

Maeve didn't push her away. She was allowed to, but found she didn't want to. The dog was called Jessie. Maeve, for the first time in her life, found herself connecting with a dog. When the doctor suggested an antidepressant, she did so knowing everything, and made such a simple and compassionate case that Maeve wondered why she hadn't tried pills long ago. Those were some things that happened after Harrison Riddles left: She got a therapist. She went on medication. She started petting a dog.

During this period, Maeve relented and went to Tampa. Jack says that's why Teenie made such a remarkable recovery, that it began right when Maeve arrived, but Maeve didn't believe that. She had been recovering all along, and Maeve arrived for the last part. Not worth getting into, those difficult days. Only a week but it felt longer. She held Teenie's hand and brought water to her lips. "Thank you for being a good husband," drugged-up Teenie said to Maeve. "Wife," she corrected, and Teenie laughed spookily. The days passed. The fresh orange juice was plentiful at least. One afternoon at their condo complex she boiled herself in a public hot tub with a man in his sixties who wore a big gold cross on his necklace, nestled in his chest hair. "Cliff is a swinger," her sister-in-law said later. "He has a big crush on you." Maeve was mortified, which Kelly-Anne seemed to enjoy. Borderline! Maeve had not meant to think it but she did. She could not retire the slur. The only good part of Tampa had been the hot tub, but she didn't go in again.

During this same week, Deacon and Teddy got engaged in the Poconos, but they would wait to marry until they had the legal right to fly to Vegas and do it in an Elvis chapel like every idiot straight couple. When that time came, not for a few more years, she'd put the photo next to Maeve and Jack at the Holiday Inn: Deacon and Teddy and the fat Elvis who proclaimed them husbands.

Katrina was pregnant. Maeve had known it! The surprise was that she and Willie were moving to California. To LA.

"Whoa!" Jack said.

"You're leaving?"

It all came out on the patio at Jack and Maeve's house, on an early evening in mid-June. Maeve had invited them over, per Dr. Harwood's suggestion. It was a lovely day, the sky dabbed with wispy clouds, the sunset still far off. She and Katrina drank seltzer, the men beer. Katrina wasn't showing but kept her hand on her belly. Her breasts were already bigger, and she wore a deep-necked blouse with a drawstring top, like a girl selling beer at a Renaissance fair.

Los Angeles had been on their vista for a while, Katrina explained. And now Harry happened to be spending some time out there, working on a script, overseeing production of a TV series based on one of his early stories. Willie would take college classes in LA and resume work with Harry on the book. A new, better book. A book that wasn't rushed, jammed into his spring break.

"He wants to write it more deliberately, he says. With greater transparency."

"What does 'transparency' mean?" Maeve asked.

"He says he was trying too hard before," Katrina explained. "Rushing it. He was ashamed that he pushed it with Willie."

"*I* didn't feel pushed," Willie said. "If I'd felt pushed, I would have stopped."

"Harry doesn't want to do the first person anymore,"

"He doesn't?"

"That's *his* call. For the record," Willie said.

"He says it's thievery."

"I wouldn't go so far," Willie said. He took a long sip of beer. "Saying that means I was stolen. I made a choice." He added wistfully, "It was good, though, wasn't it?"

They agreed.

"But Harry doesn't regret it," Katrina told them. "It primed him for the real book. He said it was the best process he'd ever had, despite everything."

Maeve's heart thumped. She looked at Jack, holding his beer, smiling at the greenhouse, its panes glimmering. He seemed in no way suspicious. How could that be? It distressed her. Why did he not sense what she had done? How had he let go so easily of the jealousy he'd expressed the night he came home? It upset her, not being held to account. She wanted her own punishment—as she had meted it out to Harrison.

"The City of Angels," Jack said, lifting his beer. "You know, we have an office in El Segundo. I'll take you to dinner when I'm out there for work."

Katrina told them she'd always had a secret dream of working at the Los Angeles Public Library, the downtown branch with the pyramid on top, a true city library.

Maeve said, "That's been your secret dream?"

"Yep," Katrina said, smugly, Maeve thought, and what Katrina said next hurt like getting the wind knocked out of her, a foot to her ribs: Harry had put in a good word for her there. He had gotten her a job.

"Congratulations," said Jack. "That's fabulous news."

Later Willie told them he was thinking of writing a screenplay. "I have an idea. My own idea. Pure fiction."

"He's keeping it to himself," Katrina said. "Even I don't know."

"I learned a lot from my book about Aristotle for screenwriters."

"Like what?" Maeve asked.

Willie thought, said, "Errors in judgment power a plot. That's number one."

"Ha!" Katrina cried, her hand on her stomach. "You can say that again."

"And desire," Willie said, smiling at the sky. "A character is their desire."

"I'll buy a ticket," Jack said. "I'll be first in line."

In bed at night, Jack still stroked her hair. Though in her depression she didn't want sex, frankly didn't feel the need, she did it, to prove she could—to prove to herself that the affair hadn't killed her marriage, nor medication killed the sensation, as it was sometimes said to do. But none of the fireworks, none of the sublime detachment from herself she'd experienced that day alone in the bathtub, after eating Paige's leaf, or the trembling on Harrison's floor. Not like that.

She wanted to tell Jack about Harrison, come out with it. But why? Who did that serve? He would be wounded. He would cry. She couldn't bear it. But how could they begin again if he didn't know?

They watched *Columbo* now. Peter Falk, another wonder. His wrinkled coat, his ambling performance of the fool. All these wonders, lost to time. That's part of her sadness, that Peter Falk is dead, that Angela Lansbury will die soon, so she lets herself cry. The nostalgia channel will only feature her pleasures for so long. Only briefly will Maeve and Jack be the market. She wants to enjoy the nostalgia while it lasts but is crying too hard.

Dr. Harwood's third-floor office had tan walls and pale blue seating, which made Maeve think of a robin's nest. A contraption near the door emitted a windy sound, for your privacy. The dog sat with Maeve when she was there, on the love seat. She kept a hand buried in the scruff of her neck.

"This is not neurotic suffering, Maeve," said Dr. Harwood one day. "We need to make that clear. This is legitimate grief."

"How do you know? What's the difference?"

"Your shoulders go down when you cry. Have you noticed?"

"They do?"

"You haven't noticed."

And then she did.

She said, "But I think with my shoulders."

"Can you try thinking another way?"

She remembered the notepads, buried between their winter sweaters in the cedar closet upstairs.

"No," she said. "I can't."

Jessie the dog lifted her head from Maeve's lap, raised her eyes. Even she knew better.

Harrison Riddles had sent one more email, which said only:

Your absence has gone through me
Like thread through a needle.
Everything I do is stitched with its color.

No sign-off, no attribution, nothing. She googled it. Not even his. W. S. Merwin! She wanted Dora to have sent it. If Dora had sent it, Maeve wouldn't have googled it. Would have let Dora author it.

Only once did Maeve get in the car and drive to the town where Libby was from. Which she understood seemed like an obsessive thing to do. (That word, *obsessed*, Jack's word, still bothered her.) But only once, she reminded herself. And after that, never again. It hadn't been difficult to find Glenn Scales's former address, which was his widow's current address, his widow Iris and his daughter, whose name—it was not difficult to find—was Hannah, who was still a baby. Iris was a woman not unlike Maeve, who carried a practical nylon purse, squinted at the prices in the supermarket, handed grapes to the toddler to keep her happy in the cart. Did Iris know about Libby? Did she know what her husband had done? Did she think it was an accident, his car into the tree?

Not Maeve's business, but she wondered anyway. Followed her, Iris. Something in her gait suggested that she knew, a fatigued hitch, and then when Maeve got closer, in the frozen food aisle, and saw her grieving eyes, the darkness beneath them, she knew that she knew. This sad tangle. The poor woman. How did she get by?

Maeve willed love at her, at the baby, as if yelling through a megaphone. But silently. A clenching, her whole self, stem to stern, a pushing outward with her stomach, that meant: Love to you. Love! It made her tired. And then she left and never went back.

Will never. She's done with them.

"Totally done."

"Hmm," said Dr. Harwood, but Maeve had zero doubt.

48

AT THE END OF AUGUST, soon after Willie and Katrina moved to LA, Maeve got a phone call. It was Gloria.

"Can you come to the library, Maeve?"

A chill ran through her. Trouble! Trouble! Someone had found a video. Or unearthed a photograph. There was proof now, that she had taken his briefcase. Or something else? Had the girl come back to tell another story?

"Of course," she said.

Half an hour later she was back in Gloria's office.

Gloria sat at her desk, wearing her amber necklace. The lucky paw, waving. *Reading Is the Bee's Knees.* It was hot now, a shade pulled against the glare. Maeve's heart began chugging.

Gloria said, "I wonder if—well." She paused, seeming uncomfortable. Maeve saw dampness on her upper lip.

"Yes?"

She tried to prepare a denial but her mind was blank, scrubbed by fear.

Gloria said, "You might feel you've been a bit mistreated by us. Not fully appreciated. And to be frank, I can see how you might feel that way."

"Oh," Maeve said. "No. No ill will." Then she said, "I've accepted it."

Gloria smiled. "Good," she said, and put her hands down on the desk, letting out a sigh, as though laying down her cards. "In that case, I'll just come out and say it. Everything is so much harder without you. 'Where's Maeve?' we all keep moaning . . . Even before Katrina left, we were moaning. I wonder if you'll consider coming back. We have a spot now that Katrina's gone. Would you consider it?"

Maeve had learned something over these last months about keeping herself in order. About holding back. Controlling her face. She said she was interested but would need to think about it. To discuss it with her husband.

Gloria seemed not to have been expecting this. She smiled, as if with new respect. "Of course," Gloria said. "Certainly. And—just so you know, the board has approved you for a raise. Up to Katrina's salary. Even though you don't have a master's degree. You've brought a lot to this place over the years, Maeve. The board agrees your salary should be commensurate with that."

Maeve's neck felt warm, tingly. She said, "I'll be in touch soon."

Downstairs again, the girl was not in the lounge. Not in the Pen, or the room off fiction. On her way out, Maeve stopped at the bulletin board. The newspaper clipping, Harrison in his polka-dotted tie—AUTHOR INSPIRES AT LIBRARY: RIDDLES LEADS JOURNEY FOR YOUTH. The reporters were gone by the time he discovered his briefcase was missing, so there had been no story about that. No pictures of him crying, or Katrina holding him. Losing the book was not part of the story until he decided it would be, or until his publicist did—part of the press package when the actual book was released, a trial that made the book even more of a triumph.

She accepted the job the next day. But I can't start for a month, she said, because that's what Dr. Harwood recommended—Maeve needed to develop some new skills before she went back to work.

All her agonizing, and she hadn't needed Harrison's help after all.

Why didn't she feel better? Shouldn't she have? In these weeks after the job offer but before she returned to work, her unease did not relent. She felt worse as each day passed. A sour, antsy feeling. She felt—busy inside. Hard-bellied. She got her period, wasn't pregnant.

It wasn't that, though it felt like that, a heaviness, a portentousness, a desire to expel the thing, to admit it into their lives. Had she gotten away with everything? Would there be no accountability?

Jack's worried eyes, his generous back rubs, made it worse. The Maeve he had known, his wife, had left. That other Maeve, timid Maeve, had been a false self, a child's construction, a girl in need of protection. Didn't he see this too? Why couldn't he?

It turns out he did. One night as he was rubbing her shoulders he suddenly stopped and said, "You know what? Get a masseuse."

"What?"

"I have feelings too," he snapped.

He apologized, then, for he'd made her cry. But she'd only cried because she was startled. Really she was relieved. He would not pretend she was the same. He could see it. She knew, now, that she would pay in some way, wanted to pay, and had to steel herself for it, or get out ahead of it. She knew she would tell him. The question of how remained, of when.

Nearly three years later, when Harrison's book comes out, Maeve will hear Harrison and Willie on NPR talking about it with Terry Gross, who'll say, Is it true that your manuscript was lost? How on earth did you deal with that? He will tell her that it brought him closer to his subject. Forced him to put every thought on trial. To recalibrate. That it became a more honest book.

Honest, how?

It was almost in first person, Harrison will say, but that narrator died. When that book was lost, it was as if that narrator, too, was dead. And he realized he did not want to speak *as* William. The first person would have been a sort of thievery. He came to feel this powerfully. A form of appropriation. But more than that: soul thievery. It might have been good, but so what? Just because you can do something doesn't make it right.

Harrison tells Terry Gross that every writer should have a book taken away. It was painful, yes, goddamn, but it was the humbling, on-your-knees pain he needed. What the mind doesn't resurrect wasn't meant to be.

Willie, William now, is on the radio too.

"I didn't feel stolen," he says. "For the record."

Terry Gross says, "Let's go back to the beginning. How did you two meet?"

"I wrote to him," William says.

"And I wrote back."

"We began a correspondence."

"What did you say in that first letter?

"It's embarrassing now."

Harrison laughs. "It's not too embarrassing, Willie. It's sweet."

"I had a crush on someone. A singer. I talked about her." The men are laughing and Terry Gross says, "C'mon, spill it!"

Willie says, "Gwen Stefani."

"The letter was a list of things Willie loved. Bullet points. Gwen was first on his list. Things he loved that had nothing to do with being a refugee."

"My English teacher had me do it. Gary Shephard. He was always having me make lists."

"Lists? Of what?"

"Movies. Foods. Inspiring people. Words. Weirdos. Things I missed from home. Things I hate with a passion. This was high school. My teacher liked this list. He said a really good list can be a poem. He encouraged me to send it to Harrison Riddles. Hi Mr. Shep, if you're listening!"

Terry Gross says, "What else was on the list?"

"My girlfriend, Katrina. She worked at the library. She's my wife now. Hi Katrina, my only one. Ms. Stefani, if you're listening, I am no longer single."

He is perfect on the radio. Their patter, Willie and Riddles, fills her with longing and regret.

"The library was on that list too," Harrison Riddles says.

"I was always at the library."

Terry Gross says, "The public library?"

"I grew up there. I didn't have to perform. I love libraries. I love quiet. I love the order and the kindness."

"And Maeve," said Harrison. "She was on that list."

"That was a different list. The next one."

"Who is Maeve?" asks Terry Gross. "What list is that?"

"Maeve Cosgrove," says Willie. "A librarian. She kept an eye on everyone. She started a program, which is how I met my wife. New Mainers! Represent, 207. She helped me and Harry tell this story."

"She sure did," Harrison says.

"Hi Maeve, if you're listening!"

"Hi Maeve," said Riddles, and then Terry said it too, the three of them, all across America.

"Hello," Maeve said back, not believing her ears, speaking from the embankment on the highway where she'd pulled over when the segment began. Then a break for the news, music rising, but they hadn't answered Terry's question. Now she would never know. What list? What list is that?

49

IN THOSE WEEKS between accepting Gloria's offer and starting up again at the library, Maeve wasn't sure what to do with herself. She did her chores in the greenhouse, though now that the important plants were gone, Paige wasn't so concerned. Still Maeve went there, breathed the air, closed her eyes, let the hurt wash over her.

If the leaves were a placebo, what would happen when she tried the roots? There was still that one plant Joe didn't take, the one she'd put in the mug before he'd arrived. After he left, she had replanted it in the greenhouse.

One day, Jack in Phoenix on a quick trip, she thought: Why not? It was two weeks until she returned to the library job. Her days were free. Why not try the roots? That's where the power was, Joe Hess had said.

The plant had grown in the month since Joe had been there, its stalk thicker, more tuberous. Now she pulled it up, all of it, and brought it inside the house. The root was an oblong heart dripping with hairs. She removed as much soil as she could but didn't want to rinse it clear for fear of disturbing the hairs, which were long and pronged, delicate. With a great surge of finality, she chopped it up and dumped it in the blender. It smelled lemony, earthy, wormy. She added lemonade, frozen raspberries, blueberries. It was like drinking hair. Sweet dirt, and hair. She had made her daughter purees like this, as a baby, had spooned concoctions for her health that looked like this.

Maybe the root would help her resolve whatever these last months had done to her. Help her find her way back to her proper life. She drank some more. Half. She took pleasure in pouring the rest of it down the drain. Pleasure in knowing that this part of this story was over. After this, whatever she did would be of her own accord. She'd stop drinking wine, too. Straight-edge, like the skater kids Raul was always chasing off the premises.

Almost immediately Maeve was slammed by a wave of care for Libby unlike any wave of care to date.

Poor Libby! Poor Libby! The fullness of the love she felt, the bigness of her care, was what the roots made different. It was Maeve's best self, enlarged. Her most decent being. Poor Libby, who had been trying to get Maeve's attention. Who Maeve hadn't helped. Who got sent to the hospital instead. Whose foster mother was murdered. Whose physics teacher took her to bed and then killed himself. The pain of children was the worst pain of all. She couldn't stand it. The pain of a child was like the pain of an animal. Unbearable, the suffering of those without language for hurt. She got the notepad out. Turned on the TV, for noise, to keep from spooking herself. "I'm literally obsessed with this bra," said a woman on an infomercial. After this was a documentary about the spice trade, about how the world was upended when people got a taste of plants from far away, but she was only half paying attention, keeping her eyes on her yellow pad. And then it was evening already and she'd done nothing of importance and she thought—Oh well. I had a peaceful day.

New optimism, new hope . . . look at that, Maeve. Maybe the root or maybe her own will, frankly it did not matter. For the first time, she saw a happy ending. If not for herself, then for Libby. For Libby at least.

50

I MISS HIM, that boy in the bathroom. No one gives him a thought. I regret that about this book. These pages may be an act of empowerment or amends, and I don't want to take that away from Maeve. Certain injustices must be corrected, I don't deny that, a boy from Africa who lost everything deserves extra attention. But you can't deny that certain people fall through the cracks. A boy like B. is a different kind of invisible in America. White and dumb and broke, but not so broke or so dumb that he gets actual help.

My name is Libby, for the record. Not Elizabeth. I don't know why a person would be so suckered by the monarchy to think Elizabeth is better. I am a voice to nowhere on a yellow pad.

In the trash.

Not important.

I am the part you don't expect, off-key and out of character.

I did like him, that quiet boy. Very much. I will worry about him forever. Not mute, not technically. He talked. At school, if absolutely essential. Once in a while he talked to me. His mom drank before he came out, but not so much that he couldn't talk. Brace is his name. At least he got an interesting name. A name like a last name, like a family line. My name's a giggle, a sound. My mother had no style. A social worker once promised me: There's something inside her she wishes she could say. There's something inside her, beneath the fucked-upness, a part that very clearly and simply loves her daughter.

That's a nice thought, but I don't believe in ventriloquizing the dead. The most I can believe is that my mother didn't want me to suffer. On good days I believe that. On bad days, I remember how it seemed she did want me to suffer, seemed expressly committed to it, but the social worker promised me that was only her illness.

Anyhow. That's done. I'm leaving now.

I will try not to miss Mr. Scales and his chin. I'll try not to miss those groups I hate so much, my fellow borderlines, the endless reading of the Steps and Traditions. I'll try not to miss Maeve, the librarian I tormented.

I'm moving on, as we speak.

I'm being launched.

I'm going west in a golden car.

I'm going to a library to learn about things. It's important to know things, I believe. Not just to know where to find them. There's a library out there in a great desert city. It has a pyramid on top. I made a list of all the things to learn, all the things I want to know, and all of them are in the library.

Maybe there will be a new librarian to torment?

That's a joke.

God. No one these days can take a joke.

FINALLY MAEVE GOES BACK to the library, resumes her proper employment. By the time she returns, sits again at her desk looking out over the Pen, a process of transformation has been made complete. That it isn't a visible change makes it harder. She has to be alone with it. She almost wants a horn or a tail, a mark of some variety. In a certain kind of story she would wake up with scales, or an udder. But she looks great. Grief staunches the appetite. Restlessness brings high color.

That first day back, everyone says—Wow, Maeve! What have you been doing?

Mrs. Cosgrove, You're lit.

Dr. Harwood thought she should confess. That what goes unsaid corrodes. But the idea of speaking head-on disturbed her. Where would she begin? She could not sit with Jack on the couch, or at the kitchen table, or—worst of all—in bed, and tell him she'd conducted an affair with a famous writer and was half in love with him and half with his wife. She would have to tell him too much first. To set it up. He'd need so much backstory, so much interiority!

A stack of yellow pads. Her atonement and her ambition, fused. Why not? She wanted Paige's plant. She wanted the expansiveness to return, the honesty, the boldness. It would be easier under the influence of Paige's plant to write it all down. But that was gone. She'd have to do it herself, using her wits.

Once, when she'd been close to Harrison, cheek to cheek, stomach to stomach, she'd had a thought. Why you and not me? A brightness popped in her core, like a match to a pilot light. But she'd blown it out. It had been enough then, to know it could be lit.

A fiction is where you can hide your secrets in plain sight. She can't say it straight on. I'm sorry for what I did. But a memoir, disguised as a fiction, a "she" and not an "I," so that Harrison, Dora, Katrina, Willie, Deacon, Jack, Paige—not their real names—will know: Her too. Maeve too, a beast like all of us, in the stacks so it can't be denied.

Just one more thing. One last bit so no one can say she held back.

A few days before she returned to the library, Maeve got in her Volvo to go for a drive. It was the first day in a long time that she'd had an impulse to be outside, to drive without a destination. Jack was away on a business trip, Chicago now, coming home tomorrow. He was still keeping close tabs on her and never left for more than a few days. She knew that the impulse to drive was good, a sign that her inability to experience joy—"anhedonia," the new therapist called it—was fading. This was a *joy*ride, after all. Dr. Harwood would be pleased.

She bought two doughnuts and a coffee at Tony's. Two? One for now, one for the next morning. This, too, seemed a sign that her health was returning. A desire for sugar, for fat. She turned on the radio. Freddie Mercury, a voice calling back through the years. Don't you hear me calling you?

The song moved her, but not so much that she had to pull over or cry, which she took as a sign she was on the mend. Her broken heart made the good song better—a good thing more good. Lovesickness does that, briefly, before it relents but after it's most terrible, a momentary sweet spot.

Driving past the dollar store in Katrina and Willie's old neighborhood, she saw a girl walking in traffic. The girl wore a black beanie, a backpack. The girl ignored the sidewalk, moved along the shoulder, keeping mainly out of the way, but still cars honked. As Maeve's car approached, the girl took a right, turned down a side street. Maeve saw her in profile.

This was the ending she wanted, the final stitch, her world repairing itself fully.

Be honest, Maeve told herself. That's all you have to do. Tell her it wasn't her fault.

All the bad things that happened to you—not your fault. You were a child. You deserved care. I'm sorry I didn't give you that care.

She had new empathy, and would show her.

At the next intersection she pulled off, turned around. By the time she crossed the thoroughfare and returned, Libby was gone. But there was only one way to go, down another side street, and Maeve followed it. The houses were small here, close together, with scrappy, overgrown yards. Another turn and there she was, walking with her head down, still avoiding the sidewalks.

She had a new backpack now, big and black, which seemed to strain her shoulders. A baggy maroon coat with belt loops but no belt, New Balance sneakers in outlet-store beige, socks with pink pom-poms at the heels. Maeve pulled the car to the curb. She pressed the button that lowered the passenger window.

"Hey," Maeve said, calmly, as the car came to a full stop. "Hello, Libby."

Libby stopped. Looked at Maeve. Her eyebrows were darker now, penciled in. She was wearing makeup, but clumsily, funnily, as if for Halloween, gloss on her lips that made her seem ethereal. Blue eyeliner, top and bottom.

"Mrs. Cosgrove," Maeve said. "From the library."

Libby turned slightly, as if to check from her peripheral vision.

"I'm the librarian."

"The librarian?" Libby rubbed her lips together. She appeared uncertain. "You're not the librarian."

"I am," Maeve said, and then: "I'll be back on Wednesday."

The girl took a step back.

"Libby," Maeve said, "what happened was not your fault. I want you to know that."

"What do you mean, 'what happened'? Nothing happened."

Slow down, Maeve told herself. Don't scare her off.

"You're carrying a big load there. If you want a lift, I can drive you wherever you're going."

Libby shook her head.

"I bought two doughnuts." She lifted the bag. "Would you like one?"

Again a head shake. Now Maeve saw she was chewing a big piece of blue gum. Blue gum, blue eyeliner.

Dear God, did I offer her a doughnut?

Libby Libby Libby.

Don't run, Libby.

Say it, Maeve. Say it. Libby may have arranged the scenario, but that didn't make it her fault. Admit your eyes met hers in the crack. Say: I felt something. Saw something. And some sort of pleasure entered me through the navel, because who can control that? We all look, glimpses are unavoidable, we're biologically programmed to feel. Yes, it turned her on. But after that, even more terrible, Maeve had called Libby a liar. Worse than seeing, happening to see, worse than any reflex of her body, was calling a child who had not lied a liar.

A squirrel on a wire overhead, watching them.

Maeve moved to open her door but Libby snapped her gum, said, "Lady, I think you're confusing me with someone else. I don't know you, not even a little."

It's Maeve, Maeve wanted to say.

Maeve, Maeve, Maeve.

But she found she could not.

Libby shrugged. "Not even a little," she said, and did not run but turned on her heel, slipped between two houses, into a flaming orange thicket.

Acknowledgments

FOR THEIR SUPPORT during the writing of this book, my deepest gratitude goes to Bill Clegg and everyone at the Clegg Agency, and Jill Bialosky and the W. W. Norton team. Thank you to the Maine Writers & Publishers Alliance, the T. S. Eliot Foundation, and my colleagues and students at Colby College. Thank you to Adrian Blevins, Debra Spark, Sarah Shun-lien Bynum, Cate Marvin. Michael Barakiva, and Novel Readings. Beloved band: Kate Christensen, Lewis Robinson, Bill Roorbach, Monica Wood. Brian Shuff, for the long haul. My parents, every single one.